APOPHENIA

YANKO TSVETKOV

APOPHENIA

MYTHS, TALES AND LEGENDS FROM AN IMAGINARY WORLD

ALPHADESIGNER
Valencia 2022

APOPHENIA
MYTHS, TALES AND LEGENDS FROM AN IMAGINARY WORLD

Extended omnibus edition

Written by Yanko Tsvetkov
in Valencia, Turin, Munich, Maspalomas, and Granada

Cover, illustrations, design, and print layout by Alphadesigner
Copy editing and typesetting by The Illuminati
Art direction by The Powers That Be
Special agent: Martin Brinkmann

Published on August 31, 2022
in Valencia (Spain) by Alphadesigner

©2022 by Yanko Tsvetkov. All rights reserved.

ISBN (paperback): 978-84-09-43720-7
ISBN (hardcover): 978-84-09-43637-8

ISNI: 0000 0004 0208 7779
VIAF ID: 296971239

Official website: alphadesigner.com
Instagram: alphadesigner
Twitter: @alphadesigner
Email: alphadesigner@gmail.com
Patreon: patreon.com/alphadesigner

To all my lovers: past, present, and future.
And their lovers, too.

To all who have survived being in love.

To those who didn't know how to love
but were brave enough to learn.

To all my Patreon supporters,
and especially to my Super Readers:
Joe Williams, Marco Salinas, and Werner.

"There's nothing new under the Sun.
All new things reside in complete darkness,
waiting for someone to excavate them."
Maurucius 14:6

"There are no known unknowns."
Lucius 10:2

Contents

APOPHENIA WORLD MAP

Hemisphere of Reason x
Hemisphere of Magic xi

I. SEX, DRUGS AND TALES OF WONDER

The Merchant from Abharazarhadarad 3
Original Bliss 21
The Book of Love 29
Sophisticus the Wise and Occam the Barbarian 37
- The Wings of Love 37
- Harbinger of Doom 38
- Róisín and the Shepherd 44
- Interlude: Monsters Are No Laughing Matter 49
- The Greatest King that Ever Lived 51
- Epilogue: In vino veritas 56

The Masks of Beauty 61
Genesis 71
The Seed of Love 73
- Meconopsis violacea 73
- Heaven's High 74

II. CODEX HYPERBOREANUS

Terror Birds and Wanton Hearts 83
- Grandmistress of Fear 83
- Love in Times of Barbarity 84
- Interlude: Harnessed Icebergs 88

- The Enchanted Stew 89
- Interlude: Of Love and Privilege 93
- The Monstrous Bride 93
- Interlude: The Etymology of Love 99
- The Legend of Ana Loveless 100
- Interlude: Pride and Punishment 109
- Esther and the Hyperborean (Take One) 113
- Esther and the Hyperborean (Take Two) 120
- Epilogue: Love Triumphs and Someone Dies 130

THE EBBS AND FLOWS OF THE GREAT HYPERBOREAN EMPIRE 135

- Humble Beginnings 135
- Magnae Matres 137
- The Taming of the Shrew 141
- The Rise of an Empire 144
- The Fall of an Empire 145
- Blood and Decadence 149
- A Flare of Populism 154
- Emancipation 155
- A Matter of Size 158

III. BULLS, OLIVES AND HEARTS ON FIRE

THE DANCING PLAGUE 167
THE OLIVE CHILD 171
THE GREAT CAUDILLIAN SCHISM 173
JUAN MEQUETREFE AND THE BULL THAT LAID GOLDEN EGGS 177
THE ASCENT OF SANTA LUCÍA 181
THE TWO SIDES OF DOLORES URDEMALAS 185
FROG EMPRESS 187
HEAD CRUSHER 191
RUBICÓN'S DAUGHTER 193
THE GRUESOME DEATH OF DIEGO SUÁREZ 195
SUGAR RUSH 199
LET THERE BE LIGHT 201
THE BULL'S BRIDE 203

EXTRAS

A Succinctly Brief Encyclopaedia of Clangorous Hearsay, Curious Factoids, and Occasional Spoilers 207
- Geography 207
- Herbiary 212
- Bestiary 214
- Science and Scripture 217
- Pantheon 221
- Notable Characters 222

Story Notes 229

About the Author 241

A MOST AND ACCURATE

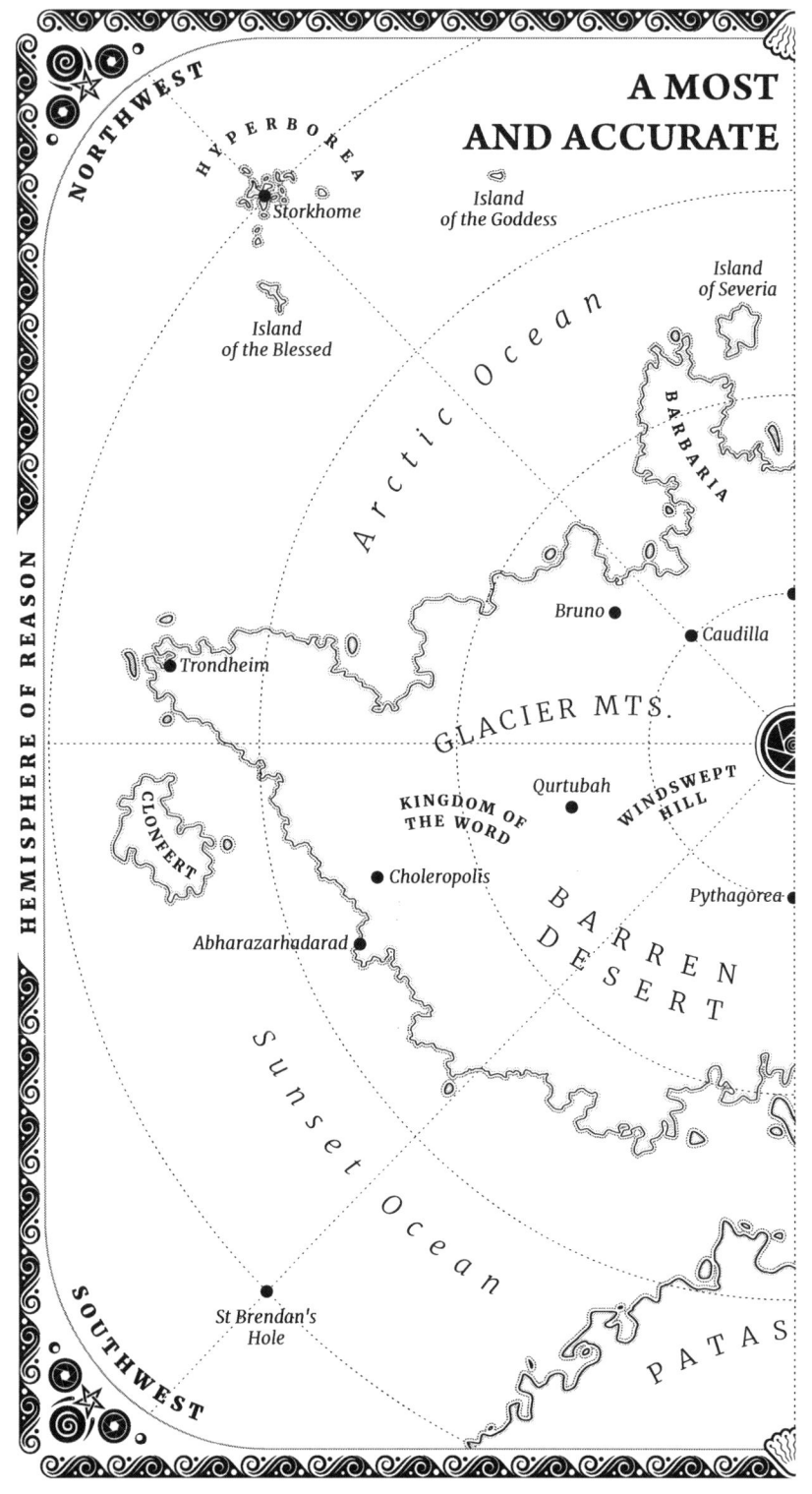

NORTHWEST

HEMISPHERE OF REASON

SOUTHWEST

- HYPERBOREA
  - Storkhome
- Island of the Goddess
- Island of Severia
- Island of the Blessed
- Arctic Ocean
- BARBARIA
- Trondheim
- Bruno
- Caudilla
- GLACIER MTS.
- CLONFERT
- KINGDOM OF THE WORD
- Qurtubah
- WINDSWEPT HILL
- Choleropolis
- Pythagorea
- Abharazarhadarad
- BARREN DESERT
- Sunset Ocean
- St Brendan's Hole
- PATAS

DESIGNED BY ALPHADESIGNER

COMPLETE MAP OF THE WORLD

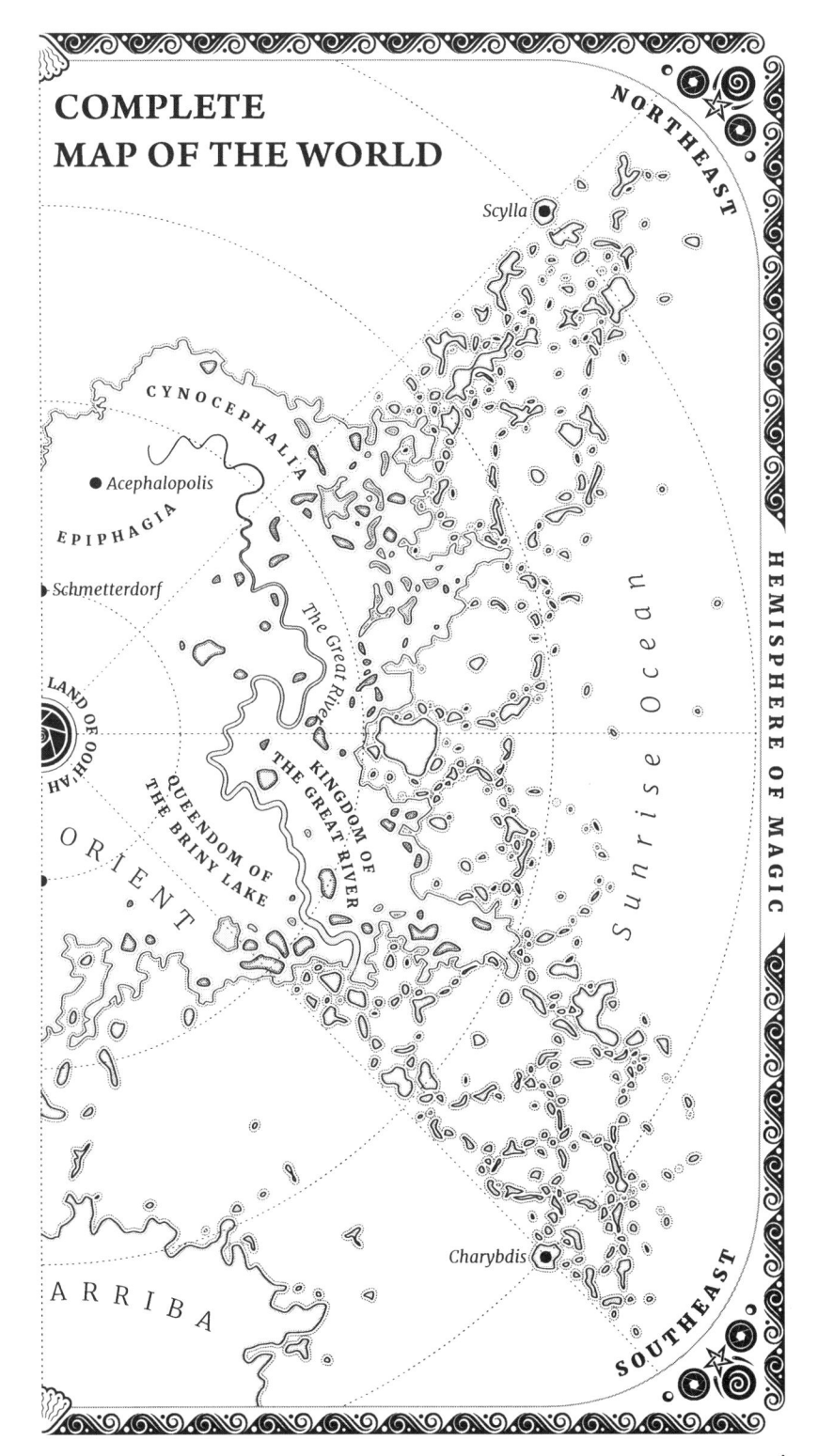

NORTHEAST

Scylla

CYNOCEPHALIA

Acephalopolis

EPIPHAGIA

Schmetterdorf

LAND OF OOH/AH

The Great River

KINGDOM OF THE GREAT RIVER

QUEENDOM OF THE BRINY LAKE

ORIENT

Sunrise Ocean

HEMISPHERE OF MAGIC

ARRIBA

Charybdis

SOUTHEAST

LIBRARY OF SUPERB ENLIGHTENMENT

Part One

SEX, DRUGS AND TALES OF WONDER

"Roots are for trees, not people."
Old Abharazarhadaradian proverb

The Merchant from Abharazarhadarad

FEW PEOPLE DARED TO VENTURE in the Far West, where the Barren Desert met the salty waters of the Sunset Ocean. Those lands were inhospitable and treacherous; they abounded with demons that could seduce even the greatest skeptics and lead them to a path of willful oblivion.

They say exploration is driven by wanderlust, that curiosity inspires brave men and women to fearfully leave their homes and discover exciting new things. A glittering mountain top or a forest full of beasts have an allure that sets the imagination on fire. Unlike them, the lifeless monotony of the desert doesn't tempt the adventurous. Only people who had lost the taste for life sought the company of the sands, and only to them they revealed their secrets.

On the coast of the ocean, where the moist northern winds turned the sandy dunes into fertile mud, there was a great city called Abharazarhadarad. Merchants from all over the world flocked there to trade. Some traveled for years to reach it, overcoming unspeakable perils and adversities. The city was unlike any other. It didn't have a king and was ruled by its own citizens, a way of governing the locals called *republican*. By some miracle, although most of them were politically incompetent, the citizens avoided the anarchy that imperiled other places without a designated sovereign. No king also meant no royal palace, which was unfortunate because instead of being shaped into expensive regalia, all the gold in the city was molded into rectangular cuboids and kept in silos called *banks*. The city had no walls. Throughout its existence, it had never been threatened by an army. Even when the lands around it were engulfed in bloody wars, Abharazarhadarad was quiet and prosperous. Feuding of any kind was frowned upon at its markets, where fierce enemies were expected to treat each other with respect and amicably shake hands as they exchange goods and services. Anybody who disregarded this custom was severely punished since the Abharazarhadaradians considered such behavior nothing short of blasphemy—the markets were their shrines, and trade was their religion. The biggest offenders had their licenses revoked and were obliged to undergo a cleansing therapy—a form of contemplative redemption—performed under the supervision of an experienced businessman. Stories of millionaires who went bankrupt because of bad temper, but later repented to recover their wealth, were a common subject of all kinds of entertainment.

Rules and regulations were observed by the *Supreme Board of Trade Etiquette*, a council of business-savvy clergymen, whose central office was located on the highest floor of the *Cathedral of Our Lady the Shopkeeper*, colloquially known as the *Grand Bazaar*. Every five hours one of them went out on the terrace, turned his back on the sea, and—facing the desert horizon—recited the lines:

There is no goddess but the Goddess! Praised be Her business acumen!

The ritual was as ancient as the world itself. Billions of years ago, when eternal night still reigned over the earth and all words ended on consonants, the Goddess, riding her favorite camel, came out of the Barren Desert and headed to the ocean for a swim. The cold water made her teeth chatter, and she cursed the darkness repeatedly. Her anger subsided when she realized that as a chief demiurgess, she had no one else to blame for her discomfort.

"There's only one way to fix this," she said.

She took a handful of coins out of her handbag and threw them towards the sky. Thus she created the moon and the stars, and although their light was faint, it was enough to warm up the ocean.

When she came out of the water, the Goddess looked at her naked body and said, "I wish there were more light, so I could marvel at my curvaceous beauty."

And so she opened her handbag again, and from it—like a caged bird yearning to be free—sprang up the sun and bathed her in golden light from head to toe.

"I am now content," said the Goddess with blissful relief, "praised be everything that glitters!"

Once upon a time in Abharazarhadarad lived a great merchant whose trading skills were so refined, people claimed he could persuade the vilest demon to kneel at the altar of the Goddess and swear perpetual allegiance in exchange for a single grain of rice. His wealth was so vast, it rivaled that of many kings and queens. Only his accountants knew the exact number of rectangular cuboids he had stored in the banks. Like his fellow citizens, he strove to live a simple life and resisted the distraction of luxury. Every day he recited the commandments of the holy scriptures and praised the Goddess for her unparalleled pragmatism. He ate the best food, but in moderation. He drank the most exquisite wine, but never got drunk. His house was comfortable, but modest, and his clothes were custom-tailored, but humble. He possessed the pristine sobriety of a virtuous man and never let bad thoughts and evil tongues distract him.

"Those who envy me," the merchant used to say, "have no idea about the great responsibility I carry on my shoulders. For it is said in the Great Book that a fortune left on its own will wither like a flower under the desert sun. It has to be tended to, day and night."

His talent for quoting scripture didn't prevent his detractors from spreading malicious rumors. "He is indeed a very skillful businessman," they used to say, "so skillful that he once convinced a mother to sell her newborn baby for a bag of garlic."

One day a big caravan arrived in Abharazarhadarad. It was drawn by seventy two camels and thirty six elephants, guided by people whose smooth skin glittered in the daylight like the finest chocolate, while under the austere glow of the moon it turned black like roasted coffee. They unpacked their load and built a huge tent decorated with the most exquisite textiles. When their camp was ready, they sent a messenger to the Grand Bazaar, carrying a letter to the famous merchant. It said:

Oh, exalted deal-maker, your fame is spreading around the world like sunlight over the horizon. I am the Queen of the Orient and I have come to trade with you my most precious possessions. Should you decide to honor my offer, visit my camp at dusk.

The merchant was intrigued. "It isn't customary to trade in private, much less after sunset," he said to his advisors, "for it is said in the Great Book that people who make deals at night in the confines of privacy offer goods of dubious value."

"It is most certainly so, sire!" agreed the advisors. "Praise be to the One who brought us the light of reason!"

"However," said the merchant, "I know that in this world, of which our city is just a speck, there are people with different customs, to whom our own ones appear illogical and even amoral. So I will give this queen the benefit of the doubt, and I will not reject her offer, unless I am sure it is indeed against our cherished principles."

"Your insight, sire, is unsurpassed, as usual!" agreed the advisors in one voice.

At dusk the merchant headed to the camp. He felt uneasy, yet curious. What kind of goods did this queen have that she was so reluctant to display them on the market? Perhaps her letter was just a facade, and what she really wanted was his advice?

When he arrived at the camp, the first stars were already glittering in the night sky. He handed the invitation letter to the guards. Without saying a word one of them started examining him with his piercing black eyes.

"You are not dressed appropriately," said the guard and clapped his hands. Four women appeared out of thin air: the first carried a golden bucket full of water, the second—a towel, the third—a bag of dried rose petals, and the fourth—a folded robe made of golden silk.

"Please undress!" said the guard.

"Forgive me, but I won't feel comfortable standing naked in front of you," answered the merchant.

The women burst in laughter. The men in the back started giggling along.

"Silence!" scolded them the guard. "Please excuse my people," he said to the merchant, "they know little about your customs."

"No offense taken," replied the merchant, "you probably know more about mine than I know about yours. I hope you could make an exception as a sign of good will."

"That won't be possible. If you wish to see the queen, we have to follow the safety protocols," said the guard.

The merchant took off his shirt, but hesitated when he got to his trousers. Was he ready to give up his dignity just to indulge his curiosity and meet a queen he knew nothing about? He looked around. The cheerfulness of the women was turning to impatience. The merchant reminded himself of a passage from the Great Book:

It is better to waste one's gold than to waste one's time, for gold can be acquired from a mine, sold, gifted, or stored in a bank. Time has no master and no shape. No rock can contain it, and nobody can own it.

Time is the breath of the Goddess, the rhythm of her chest, the pulse of her beating heart.

His job had put him in awkward situations before. Years ago, waiting for an audience with the Sultan of the Dry Sea, he had to spend three days fasting because facing the sovereign of that realm with a full stomach was considered disrespectful. The Abharazarhadaradians didn't have a social stigma on fasting, thus the compromise, although difficult, didn't carry a sense of shame.

"Isn't it ironic," thought the merchant, "that spending three days without food seems easier than a moment of casual nudity."

He swallowed his pride and unbuttoned his trousers. He could feel his pulse on his cheeks, as if his heart was stuck in his mouth. The first woman approached him and started washing his body. When she was done, the second one came and dried him with the towel. Then the third one took a handful of petals, rubbed them with her palms, and blew a cloud of fine dust over his chest. The sweet smell of roses spread in the air. Finally, the fourth woman came and dressed him in the golden robe.

"The queen will see you now," said the guard and clapped his hands. The heavy curtain over the entrance opened, and the merchant stepped in. The tent looked much bigger on the inside. The walls were made from polished marble. The ceiling was adorned with hanging statues of nude adolescent jinns. A sprawling staircase in the center swirled up like the dissected body of a snake wrapped around a giant column. Its top was engulfed in bright light.

"Thank you for accepting my invitation," said a voice from above.

The merchant looked up and squinted against the light. The glittering silhouette of the queen started descending with a steady, elegant pace. The scent of hyacinth and myrrh filled the air.

"Our protocol must have confused you," she said. "According to my grand vizier, your introduction rituals are quite different than ours. He said you extended hands towards each other, grasped them tightly, and then shook them intensely. I started practicing, but I still find it a bit confusing. There is a pause between the grasp and the shake. I can't quite figure out the right timing. Can you teach me how to do it?"

"It will be an honor," said the merchant.

"Then I'm looking forward to it," said the queen, whose descending figure was now obscured from view by the column that supported the spiraling staircase. "Rituals are important, no matter how arbitrary they might seem to foreigners. Who's to say what's the right way to greet a stranger? We could spend years arguing about details, but wise people focus on the common things first. Do you know my subjects believe the world was created by an omnipotent Universal Mother? She lives up in the sky, and nothing can escape her watchful eyes. Yet she reveals her divine face only to those who have drunk too much wine. When sober people look up, they see nothing but clouds and stars. One might argue they don't have to see the goddess to believe in her. But you and me, dear guest, know that if a belief is left without a proof for too long, it fades to fantasy. I've been told that your people also believe the world was created by a goddess."

"That is indeed true," said the merchant.

"Can they see her?"

"It is said in the Great Book that those who happen to see her real face can't remain in this world for long, so there aren't many people who are willing to try."

"And how do the rest of you honor her?" asked the queen.

"We lay wreaths on her statues."

"So you see her after all. If she refuses to reveal her real face, you build an image on your own and worship it," said the queen.

"This is true," replied the merchant, "her divine image, just like her grace, is everywhere."

"In my queendom it is forbidden to depict the Goddess in any way—in stone, on coins, or paintings on the walls of our shrines. My people prefer to worship living flesh," said the queen as she appeared from behind the column. "So here I am, the Universe personified!"

She was still far from him, but for the first time he could see her features unobstructed by the blinding light. Her body was slender, yet curvaceous. Her hair was pitch dark, and her eyebrows arched over her hazel eyes like the crescent of the moon.

"Do I look majestic?" she asked and her plump lips extended in a glittering smile.

"You look beautiful!" said the merchant.

"Your honesty flatters me," said the queen. "There's a difference between *beautiful* and *majestic*, isn't there? My people won't feel comfortable calling me beautiful. That's a word they use for their loved ones. They look at me and see something bigger than life. I am a queen, a mother, a lover, and an executioner, all in one."

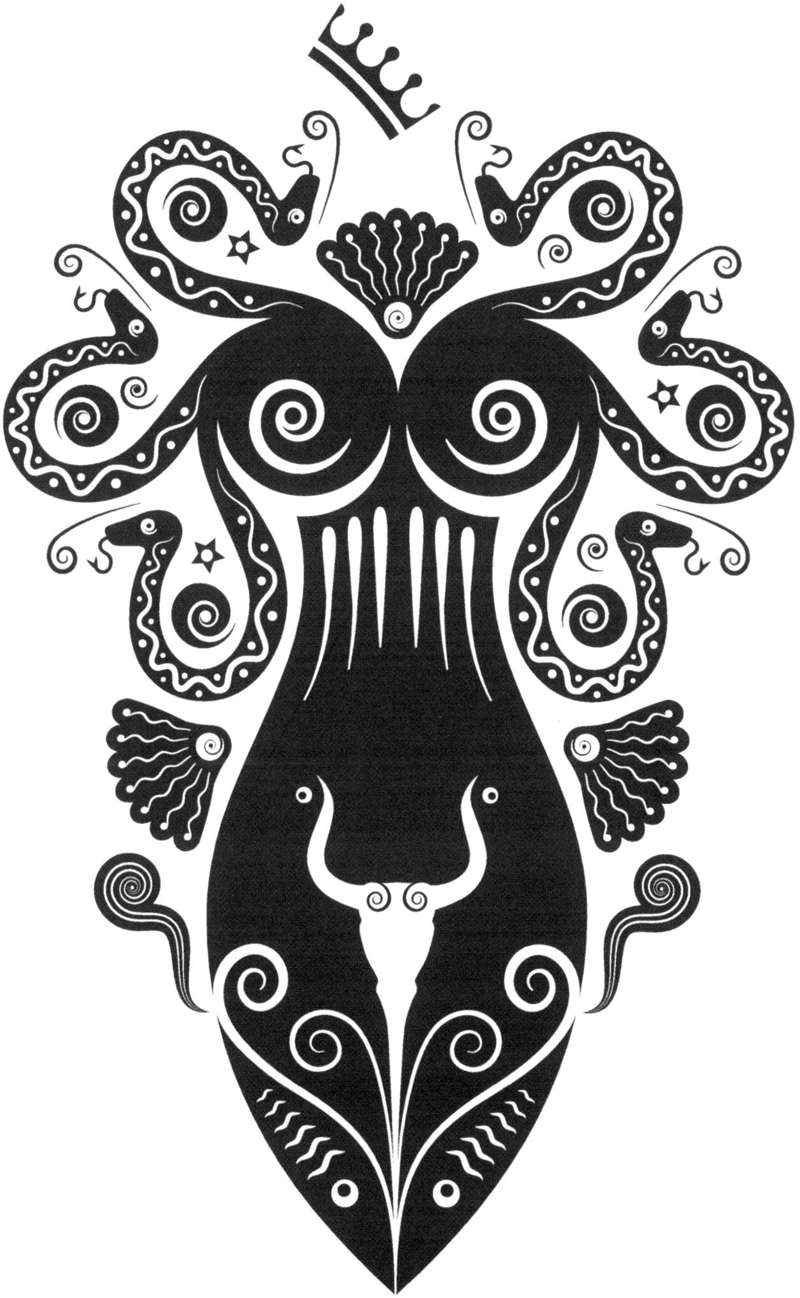

"Forgive me, I didn't mean to diminish you," said the merchant.

"There is nothing to forgive," said the queen, "to be appreciated just as a woman feels liberating. But I still have to keep up appearances, especially on first encounters. I could have met you at the entrance as your customs dictate but that would have offended my people. When a monarch, no matter how powerful, provokes her subjects, there are always consequences. So you'll have to wait for me to descend and then kiss the ground before my feet, as our traditions require."

"I understand," said the merchant.

"I'm sure you do!" The queen regaled him with another smile. "I can see you even make an effort to marvel at my sight. I appreciate that. Getting the pacing of this descent right is difficult. I began practicing when I was fifteen. My young self found it extremely boring. But I soon realized the trick was to maintain a certain discipline. Boredom is a choice. If you succumb to it, you get the pacing wrong. Just like with your ritual. How was it called?"

"Handshake," said the merchant.

"Right," said the queen, still descending. "The efficiency of your rituals is intriguing. Everything seems optimized for time. As if you don't have enough of it. Or perhaps you save it for something more important, something that remains secret from the public eye. What do you do at night after an efficient day?"

"The night is a time for rest," said the merchant.

The queen reached the bottom of the staircase. "That's it? Just rest?" she said. "I thought your nights were a bit more entertaining."

"A lot of people think so," said the merchant as the queen approached him, "but the Great Book says that the secret to success lies in relentless moderation."

"I hope you'll find our meeting efficient. But first we must complete the rituals," said the queen.

"To hear is to obey!" said the merchant, got down on his knees, and kissed the ground before her.

"Rise, my guest!" said the queen and extended her hand towards him. "Now teach me how to do a handshake."

The merchant had traded goods of unmatched quality. He had seen the finest furs from the North, delicate cotton sheets from the South, and silken robes as ethereal as the first rays of the eastern sun. Nothing could compare to the softness of her skin. Rings of rose gold encrusted with emeralds graced her fingers. Bracelets crafted from sapphire beads hung around her wrists. Yet all of them felt coarse and undeserving of her flesh.

An abrupt handshake took him out of his trance. It was firm, albeit a bit forced.

"How was it?" asked the queen.

The merchant, still short of words, nodded in approval and cleared his throat.

"You must be thirsty," she said and clapped her hands. The four women that welcomed him at the entrance appeared again. The first carried a glittering black cube, the second—a tray with a steaming kettle, the third—two cups with sugared edges, and the fourth—a plate of sweetmeats.

Distracted by the embarrassing memory of his first encounter with the women, the merchant didn't notice when the interior of the tent changed. The columns and the staircase were gone. Crimson carpets covered the marble floor, and a large sofa draped in snow-white fur stood in the middle. The first woman stepped forward, laid the cube in front of the sofa, and tapped twice on it. The cube started hissing. Its top opened, and various click-clacking contraptions sprang out like a swarm of crickets with glittering metal legs and throbbing bodies. The merchant had never seen creatures of this kind. They moved like insects, yet looked like pieces of jewelry, half-alive and half-dead. With remarkable precision—as if driven by an invisible puppet master—they joined together and split apart until finally, in the most amusing way, their bodies fused into a polished mahogany table. When the transformation was complete, the other women left the things they were carrying on it. The queen dismissed them with a silent nod and sat on the sofa.

"Have a seat, my guest!" she said and tapped the cushion next to hers. "You must have a lot of questions."

The merchant was without a doubt amazed by the strange transformations he witnessed, but he hid his emotions, for he remembered a passage from the Great Book that said:

It is easier for a camel to go through the eye of a needle than for the visibly impressed to conduct a profitable deal.

After she poured tea in his cup and offered him sweetmeats, the queen told him about her country. She ruled over a queendom hidden from the world since ancient times, way before the founding of Abharazarhadarad. People there lived in perfect harmony. Unlike the rest of humanity, they didn't have to produce their own food, build houses, or do any chores. All those unpleasant tasks were performed by wondrous tools called *automata*.

Free from the mundane duties of everyday life, her people developed a taste for luxurious goods and experiences that surpassed all other cultures on earth. Nevertheless, this constant indulgence had a downside, admitted the queen. Even the greatest pleasures degrade when experienced too often, so she, by popular demand, decided to open her queendom to the world. This was why she came to Abharazarhadarad, searching for new goods and experiences. As she was telling her story, the queen kept refilling his cup with tea. He noticed that every sip tasted differently, as did every bite of the sweetmeats. Those were samples from her vast catalog, insisted the queen, carefully selected—from light aromas that barely caressed the palette to more pronounced flavors that invaded the entire body and could trigger goosebumps. If consumed in large quantities, they could even cause bouts of relaxation, followed by sensations of strenuous bliss. The merchant listened to her carefully and took notes, as it was customary during trade negotiations, for it was written in the Great Book that a businessman without a notebook is like a smith without a hammer. He drank and ate with the queen until the early hours of the night and after he tasted all the samples, he thanked her for the hospitality and prepared to go home.

"It was a long day," said the queen, "are you sure you don't want to stay over? The streets of Abharazarhadarad must be full of dangers at night."

"Your generosity is unequaled, but I respectfully decline," replied the merchant, "The sooner I get back home, the faster I will be able to calculate your estimates."

"As you wish. I am in no hurry to trade," said the queen, "but I enjoyed your company so much I can't wait to see you again. Come back tomorrow at the same time!"

The merchant knelt to kiss her feet. The queen shook his hand in return, and he headed home. He summoned his advisors, who came in a rush, dressed in their pajamas.

"I met the Queen of the Orient," said the merchant. "She has stockpiles of exotic goods that I've never seen before. Undoubtedly, it will be difficult to create demand for them without a significant investment. My advertising branch is already over budget. The risk of failure is substantial."

"It is most certainly so, sire!" agreed the advisors. "Praise be to the One who brought us the gift of caution!"

"However," continued the merchant, "I made some calculations on my way back, and by a conservative estimate, a successful outcome will help me beat the predictions of the Supreme Board for the next financial quarter by at least ten percent. Therefore, I think that trading with her is a good idea."

"Your insight, sire, remains unsurpassed, as usual!" proclaimed the advisors in one voice.

Content with their advice, the merchant dismissed them and got to work. He lit a candle and recited a praise to the Goddess three times, as customary. He consulted the Great Book, verse by verse, strictly adhering to the laws of numerology, writing down the extracted values. Then he analyzed the positions of the planets and their relation to the brightest stars, and divided everything by the diameter of the curve formed by the shadow of the earth on the surface of the moon. When everything was ready, he took a pair of dice, sprinkled them with holy water, and threw them once per every item he had in his list. With remarkable calligraphic skill, he wrote down the estimates on a piece of vellum. It was already dawn when he put the last stroke and went to bed.

He woke up at noon and summoned his advisors. They came as fast as they could, still chewing their lunch.

"Last night, when I was with the queen," said the merchant, "I saw a strange object: a black cube that unfolded and, with the help of sophisticated contraptions, turned into a dining table. I suspect it was a staged demonstration of exotic technology in order to impress me and weaken my negotiation position."

"It was most certainly so, sire!" agreed the advisors. "Praise be to the One who brought us clarity of mind!"

"However," said the merchant, "The same black cube appeared in my dream and instead of a table, it turned into a pile of gold cuboids. I am now convinced it is an omen from the Goddess and have therefore decided to ask the queen to sell it to me, whatever its price might be."

"Your insight, sire, is beyond comparison!" concluded the advisors in one voice.

When the merchant visited the queen again and showed her the estimates, she praised his business acumen and the beauty of his calligraphy. Right before he was about to leave, he shared his interest in the cube. Could she by any chance consider selling it?

The queen was surprised. Didn't people in Abharazarhadarad have enough tables? Or were they easily captivated by shape-shifting objects? If only she had known, she said, she would have brought more of them, but neither her nor her vizier thought there could be a lot of demand for a cube that unfolds into a table because, to be honest, it was a bit superfluous, yet who was she to judge the values of other cultures. But what about the infusions of lilac poppies, she asked. She could consider offering an appetizing discount if the merchant ordered a large amount. Other prices could be tweaked as well, she said, although not by much. After all, there were transportation costs and a caravan of elephants crisscrossing a desert was a logistic challenge of epic proportions.

The merchant assured her that according to his projections, the tea would be a resounding success on the market, and the quantity he was willing to trade was a matter that could be further negotiated, although his instinct told him that lilac poppy wouldn't be as popular as the turquoise variety because blue hues were in fashion this season. However, he said, all this is a separate issue that shouldn't be bundled with his inquiry about the cube. The reason for his sudden interest in it was because he believed it was his duty as a good businessman to explore possibilities that might seem illogical and strange, but could ultimately generate enormous profit for both sides. He was sure, he said, that the queen, insightful as she was, knew that trading was not a zero-sum game, and people's propensity for amusement was practically unlimited. With proper guidance and a little bit of luck, one could double, even quadruple, the value of any object overnight.

The queen agreed that a bit of unorthodoxy was always welcome in deal-making, but when it came to the price of the cube, she hesitated to name one.

"You might find it silly," she said, "but I have always struggled with prices. Have you asked yourself why is gold so precious and steel so cheap in comparison? Certainly it should be the other way around. Gold is so fragile, and steel so powerful."

"We all struggle with such questions," replied the merchant. "But it is this uncertainty itself that makes trade possible. The Great Book says different people want different things at different times with different urgency."

"Maybe I lack the patience to understand other people's needs," said the queen, "or perhaps I don't have the talent to trade at all."

"Theory can be overwhelming. But in most practical cases, trade is best conducted when the participants focus exclusively on their own needs."

"In this case, I know exactly what I need," said the queen, "but if I admit it, you might take me for a fool."

"I wouldn't dare," said the merchant. "It's not my job to judge people, but to find a way to fulfill their desires, strange as they might be."

"Very well then. I will trade the cube for a kiss," said the queen. "Would you agree?"

A kiss? The merchant expected something eccentric, like a cursed gem stone or a forbidden manuscript. But a kiss? How can someone even consider trading something so ephemeral? Unless the queen was trying to make him look like a fool. Of course she was, he thought. To her, his request must have looked so peculiar that she couldn't resist a joke. He started laughing.

"I'm not joking," said the queen. "The moment I feel your lips touching mine, the cube is yours."

"I don't understand why the kiss of a stranger is worth so much to you," said the merchant.

"Is your kiss worth less than a table?" asked the queen. "Perhaps you underestimate yourself."

"I'm just not used to putting prices on such things," said the merchant.

The queen moved closer. "We're both trying out something new. Perhaps we should improvise?"

"It is written in the Great Book," said the merchant, "that improvisation is one of the three sacred paths to success. For every time we…"

The queen's tongue swirled between his lips and silenced him before he could finish the sentence. The kiss caught him off-guard. No Abharazarhadaradian woman would dare to kiss a man this way. He blushed. That couldn't be good for business.

"It's yours," said the queen, holding the cube in her hands. "Take good care of it!" Her face was glowing, more beautiful than ever.

The merchant thanked her profusely, went back home and summoned his advisors. He laid the cube in front of them and tapped it twice. Nothing happened.

"I don't understand," he said, "Yesterday I saw it unfold into a table."

"We are most certain you did, sire," said the advisors. "Praise be to the One who witnesses all our deeds and holds us accountable for them!"

"However," said the merchant, "since I don't quite understand how it operates, I shall return to the queen's camp tomorrow and ask for precise instructions."

"Your insight, sire, is magnified by your humility!" proclaimed the advisors in one voice.

On the following day he went back to the camp but discovered an empty field. There was no trace of the queen and her servants. He asked around if somebody knew when the queen had departed, but people replied they hadn't seen anybody camping here in a long time. They were wrong, he told them, just yesterday on this same spot there was a camp that belonged to the Queen of the Orient, a woman of unsurpassed beauty and wealth. She crossed the desert on a caravan of seventy two camels and thirty six elephants. He signed a trade contract with her.

That was impossible, said the people. Elephants couldn't travel through deserts, and a journey all the way from the Orient would be challenging even for a camel.

"I must have been dreaming," thought the merchant, "but if that's true, the cube shouldn't exist either."

Yet when he got back home he saw it standing right where he left it. He tried to open it again. Nothing moved. How could he be so careless, he thought. He should have asked for instructions. He should have even negotiated a return policy. Every contract he ever signed had a reclamation clause. If the product malfunctioned, he could always get his money back. Except this one cost him a kiss from the most beautiful woman he had ever seen. He remembered her face, the sweet smell of hyacinth and myrrh, the softness of her skin, the taste of her lips. His heart was pounding like a drum. His knees weakened, and he collapsed on the floor.

Three days passed before his advisors, alarmed by his absence, found him. He hadn't slept or eaten. Kneeling on the floor with the cube in his hands, he was calling his queen, the beautiful, the generous, the majestic! They took care of him, bathed him, and made him drink an infusion of chamomile and wild honey. When he finally fell asleep, they took the cube and locked it in a safe.

"Come back to me," he cried in his sleep, his voice shrieking like a wounded animal.

"Come back to me," he begged her, over and over, as his pupils trembled underneath his eyelids, trying to escape the nightmare of the loss he felt. There was a gaping abyss where his heart once was. It would never be whole again, not while she was gone.

One by one, the best doctors in Abharazarhadarad came to see him. Then they came again in groups of two and three. They tested theories, tore them to shreds, only to start over. It was an obsession of the mind, one said. Nonsense, countered a second one, it was the heart, and it wasn't obsession, but infatuation. I beg to differ, said a third, it was neither obsession nor infatuation, but sheer madness and its cause lied in the stomach, for he complained of strange rumbling and a sense of weightlessness. Well maybe they could reach a compromise, proposed a fourth, why not call it obsessive gastro-cardiac disorder? Bullshit, shouted a fifth, scientific terminology was not a matter of compromise but of factual truth. A truth that was beyond obvious—the man was just exhausted. After observing their bickering for weeks, the patience of the advisors reached its limit.

"In the name of the Goddess," they said in one voice, "you should all go away because you are worse than charlatans."

On the next day a word came to them that a wise traveler from the North was entering the city. His name was Isidore of Clonfert. He was born on an island full of cows and greenery, which he left at a young age in search of enlightenment that only a warmer climate could bring. By the time his ship arrived in Abharazarhadarad, he was already past his puberty, which he spent on the dock, reading romantic poetry by transcendental philosophers. During his brief stay in the city, he had already managed to negotiate a trading treaty between two mortal enemies and cure the gambling addiction of an alcoholic. The advisors welcomed him with great hope. After Isidore examined the merchant, he concluded that the man had fallen in love.

"No wonder the doctors had a hard time diagnosing his condition," said Isidore. "Love is notoriously elusive and doesn't conform to rigorous definition. It is often contracted through the eyes, but it is most viral when it enters through the mouth. Symptoms can start with tickles on the back of the neck, spread to the shoulders, causing shortness of breath, enter the stomach and obliterate the victim's appetite, and from then on, result in constipation with sudden bursts of sadness and despair. In some cases, with proper rest and adequate care, patients recover on their own."

"We understand," said the advisors in one voice. "Praise be to the One who brought you to our city to instill hope in our hearts."

"However," continued Isidore, "once it enters an advanced stage and spreads beyond the stomach, its outcome can be deadly. This type of love becomes more powerful than any drug ever invented. It can be cured only by itself, like fighting fire with fire. Therefore, the merchant must be subjected to seduction by a third party. If the seduction is successful, the poison in his blood will be neutralized, and he will avoid the woeful fate that is bestowed upon all abandoned lovers."

"Your knowledge, young man, is nothing short of remarkable," said the advisors in one voice.

"Now if you excuse me," said Isidore, "I must continue on my way because I'm on a journey of a lifetime and I can't afford to arrive late at my destination."

Following Isidore's advice, they published an advertisement in every newspaper in Abharazarhadarad. It said:

A rich man of unrivaled wisdom is looking for the love of his life. Further details available upon request.

Seventy two girls and thirty six men applied. One by one, they came to see him, each trying to seduce him. They kissed his mouth and caressed his neck. They massaged his chest and whispered sweet nothings in his ears. Then they came again, in groups of two and three and made him indulge in every delight the human body could experience—from silk bondage to double penetration. They tried different positions and invented new ones—all in vain. It was a lost cause, said the woman with the most beautiful breasts in Abharazarhadarad. She had never seen a man who could resist her tight embrace for more than five minutes without ejaculating. Her breasts were indeed irresistible, said the most hung man in the city, but what was even more surprising was the merchant was indifferent to his legendary curved penis that looked like a desert knife and could cause an instant orgasm in women and men alike. Soon, confusion ensued, and the patience of the advisors reached its limit.

"For the Goddess's sake," they said in one voice, "all of you should leave because we've seen enough and it's clear to us that he cannot be cured this way."

However, on the next morning, the merchant appeared calm and happy. He thanked his advisors for their care and assured them he was now content because he had found reason again. He ordered them to send expensive gifts to everyone who participated in his treatment, from the doctors who struggled to diagnose him, to the people who tried to seduce him.

Later that night, when the advisors, relieved by the good news of his recovery, went to sleep, the merchant broke the safe where the cube was hidden and headed to the desert.

He's still roaming the sands today, for it is written in the Great Book that people whose hearts are stolen know no rest and time has no power over them. They neither age nor tire, unless—by the mercy of the Almighty Goddess—they reunite with their loved ones to become whole again.

Original Bliss

THE LAND OF OOH'AH wasn't popular with travelers, for it was surrounded by thick forests of *Acrifolium gigantea*, venomous cacti whose thorns could kill an elephant with a single scratch. As one would imagine, the people who lived there were called ooh'ahians. They considered themselves the purest race under the sun, not because they were better than everybody else, but because their lands were located exactly in the earth's middle, where all directions converged into a single dot called *The Point of Emergence*. It was from this point that life exploded into existence eons ago, as accounted in their holy book *The Scroll of Ooh*.

Like a zit on the face of the Multiverse, The Point of Emergence—hallowed be its divine protrusion—squirted matter of all varieties in four consecutive eruptions that lasted four days, four nights, and a couple of extra minutes because the Multiverse (of which time was merely a meager aspect) had never been, is not, and never will be bothered by precise deadlines.

The first squirt brought the viscous alpha particles and all the elements in order of softness, each begotten by its predecessor: gases, liquids, gooey gels, crumbly stones, basalt, diamonds, and graphene.

The second squirt brought all the plants: grasses, shrubs and bushes, along with the small trees, then the medium ones, and lastly—those that were larger than everything else described so far.

The third squirt brought the animals. The small herbivores jumped right through, closely chased by the small predators, who feasted on the weak and sickly. Then the medium herbivores came out, saw the small predators and mocked them condescendingly.

"Your mouths are too small for our big bones," they said, "and your teeth—too fragile for our thick skin."

Alas, while they were indulging in ridicule, a bunch of medium predators sneaked out, attacked them, and many were eaten before they could stop giggling. When the largest herbivores appeared, they saw all the carnage, shook their heads in disapproval, and vowed to never crack a smile, lest some large predators came out of the Point of Emergence to gut them. This is the sole reason why, unlike monkeys, hippopotamuses don't have sense of humor and nobody enjoys their company, much less their flesh.

The fourth squirt began with a thunderous rumble, and everybody got scared the world was about to come to a premature end, when—lo and behold—out of the prolapsed rupture appeared the head of Ooh. Ooh was a sapient being who was male, female, and everything in between, and who, for the sake of political correctness, from now on will be referred to with the pronoun ze. Ooh looked at zimself and, overtaken by desire, ze lustfully made love to zis own body. Nine months after, the first humans popped out of zim, and they were a man named Ah and a woman named Meh. Their birth—besides other random conclusions—established without a doubt that life can only spring into existence through tight openings.

When Ooh looked at zis children, zis heart was overcome with sadness. "Half of their genitals are missing," Ooh lamented. "What did I do to deserve this misfortune and beget such abominations?"

The Multiverse didn't grant zim with an answer.

In an act of defiance, Ooh swore that no matter how repulsive zis children looked, ze would protect them from the churlish cruelty of life. Ooh created for them the most beautiful garden, and in it, ze put trees of all varieties: some bloomed in gorgeous colors, some had needles instead of leaves, and there were others whose trunks were so twisted that when the wind shook their branches, they looked like dancing giants whose feet were stuck in mud.

And Ooh commanded zis children saying, "Of every tree you can eat freely, and—should the need arise—frolic from branch to branch; but of the tree of the knowledge of good and evil you mustn't eat, for its fruits ferment before they ripen, and once you taste them, you will realize how incomplete you are, and your hearts will break like icicles shatter when they hit the pavement."

Thus despite the harshness of life, the humans spent their days in perpetual bliss caused by sheer ignorance.

One afternoon, when Ooh was having a siesta, Meh sensed a pungent aroma in the air. It was sweet and sour, and it roused her appetite, so she went looking for its source. Her nose led her to the tree of the knowledge of good and evil. On its lowest branch hung a plump fruit. Its skin was cracked, and out of it oozed thick sugary juice. Meh remembered Ooh's words, yet she was too ignorant to consider the true cost of

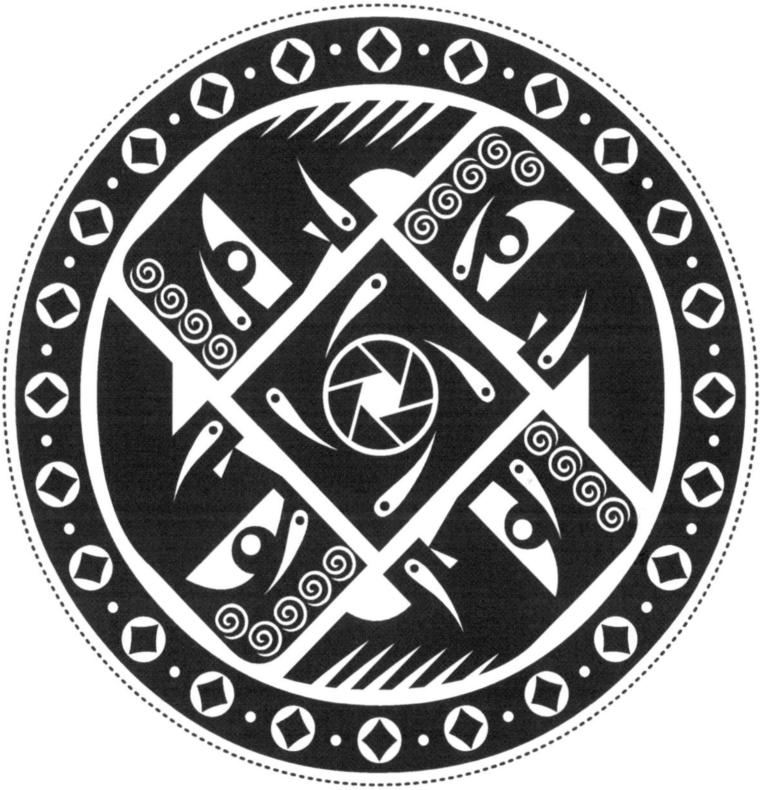

disobedience. She took a bite. The alcohol in the fruit enlightened her soul and revealed to her the knowledge of good and evil. As juice dripped all over her breasts, she looked down and froze in terror.

"Oh no," she cried, "I am missing a penis!" Devastated by her newfound disability, she sat down and wept for a whole day.

When she returned home to her husband, she told him what happened and he rolled up his sleeves to give her a good beating, as prescribed by the holy scriptures.

To his surprise, she showed no remorse. Instead, she grabbed his arm defiantly and said, "You know, I think you should stop beating me every day because that's an evil thing."

"I don't understand," replied Ah, "what does the word evil mean?"

"Take a bite of this fruit and it will dawn on you," said Meh.

Ah, who by this time was rather hungry, bit into it without much thinking.

When Ooh found out about this, ze condemned Meh: "Vile woman, by disobeying my advice to stay away from the tree of the knowledge of good and evil, you have brought tremendous anxiety upon yourself and your husband. From now on you will see the world as it is and because of this you'll be chronically dissatisfied. Your joys will be transient, your sorrows—soul-crushing, and the awareness of your impending end will give you recurring nightmares."

Then Ooh banished them from the garden, for they didn't deserve zis protection anymore. They set off on a journey to find a place to live, but just like Ooh predicted, nothing could satisfy their demands: The beaches were too windy, the mountains too cold, the deserts too dry, even the meadows in full bloom were infested with buzzing insects that didn't let them nap in peace.

What happened next is a matter of debate. During the first ecumenical council of the Most Holy Church of Ooh, two irreconcilable theories caused a schism between post-reformist and neoörthodox priests. The seed of the uncertainty was sown a century and a half before the council, when the Crypt of Faith—where all holy scripture was diligently preserved—was transitioning its catalog from old-fashioned marble plates to the newly invented paper format. One Monday morning a scribe named Benny, who had been restlessly partying all weekend and could barely keep his eyes open, reached out to grab his coffee mug, missed it, and hit a bunch of marble plates that fell off his desk and shattered on the floor. Among them was the story of the first humans, carved out in stone verbatim, exactly as the Divine Spirit of Ooh recited it to the epileptic prophet who invented the chisel. As it hit the ground, the lower part of the marble plate turned to a mess of glittering shards, and half of the story was instantly lost in the bottomless abyss of universal entropy.

From this day on, Benny became known as Saint Benedict the Distracted. He was traditionally pictured on icons as a slender man with a fuzzy gaze, holding a chalice with hot coffee in one hand and a half-bitten croissant in the other. Sure enough, two pious librarians named Lucius and Maurucius rushed to scribble an account of the story from memory, lest it became completely forgotten. Their versions became known as the *synoptic gospels* and despite being profoundly different in tone and spirit, each claimed absolute veracity to the original, a logical conundrum that, once dressed in religious doctrine, became known as the miracle of *doubletruth*. Lucius was an amateur botanist raised by a dominant mother, who loved him so much, she breastfed him until he was fourteen years old. Maurucius was a womanizer with a pronounced romantic streak, who fooled himself he could commit to a single woman once he finds a stable job and a reliable pension plan. Naturally, each librarian interpreted the story from his own point of view, and soon people realized that the veracity of second-hand sources could always be questioned.

As time passed by and people's faith degraded under the strain of pragmatism, their beliefs got poisoned by logic. The harmonious relativism of the old days was coming to an end and doubletruth was declared obsolete. Society split in two factions: the neoörthodox stuck with the gospel of Lucius, since his writing was full of meticulous details and oozed respect for parental figures, while the post-reformist embraced Maurucius because of his poetic flourishes and loose storytelling techniques.

According to the neoörthodox interpretation, it took forty years of wandering until the first humans realized that life was not about getting what you want, but about accepting what destiny had in store for you. Full of shame and regret, Ah and Meh returned to beg for Ooh's forgiveness.

"Have you journeyed to the springs of the sea or walked in the recesses of the deep?" asked Ooh.

"We have," said zis children, "and still, we could get no satisfaction."

"Have the gates of death been shown to you?"

"Yes," said zis children, "and we were terrified and broken-hearted when we gazed upon them."

"Have you entered the storehouses of the snow or seen the storehouses of the hail, which I reserve for times of trouble, for days of war and battle?"

"To be honest, we were about to go there," said the humans, "but we decided against it, because it was so cold that our limbs shivered and our teeth were clacking uncontrollably. Regardless, we are sure that had we gone there, we would still have not found what we were looking for because the reason for our troubles was our recklessness and the offense we caused you. Therefore we abhor ourselves and repent in dust and ashes."

"When you ate from the tree of the knowledge of good and evil, you became the masters of your own destiny," said Ooh, whose burning anger was subsiding. "Now the only way to restore your innocence is to eat from the tree of the bound will."

"Strange, I don't remember ever seeing that tree blossom," said Meh.

"That's because it bears fruits only when necessary, and the first ones are just ripening as we speak," replied Ooh.

The garden was filled with awe-inspiring trees. Near its entrance was the tree of missed opportunities whose blossoms faded before their buds opened up. Just a few steps away to the right was the tree of contrarian trickery. It had flowers instead of leaves and leaves instead of flowers. Further ahead one could hardly miss the tree of misplaced affection, whose pollen was too heavy to be carried by the wind, and its scent was too bland to attract even the hungriest insects. Right next to it, the tree of fatal attraction produced such sweet smell that the bees nearby overdosed on its nectar and entered a cataleptic state of hallucinatory satisfaction, from which they never recovered because A) they found this chemically-induced plane of existence more enticing than real life, and B) their real life really sucked.

Further down there was the tree of submissive arousal whose flowers refused to open unless someone repeatedly whispered vile obscenities like *Pinch my stigma and slap your stamen all over my ovary*. This tree could only produce fruits if its trunk was beaten with a leather whip, and the harder the blows were—the bigger the harvest. Across the lane was the tree of unnecessary drama, surrounded by a patch of grass in pristine condition because no one wanted to picnic under its shade and listen to the constant chatter of complaints coming from its leaves. In the middle of the garden one could find the mutilated remains of the tree of eternal life, whose fragile trunk was cut by ignorant vandals looking for wood for their camp fire.

However, nothing could compare to the tree of the bound will. Its twisted branches were entangled like copulating snakes. Its leaves had the color of ash, and when a gust of wind had the misfortune to pass by them, they hissed like stray cats who hadn't eaten for a week.

Even though they had traveled far and wide, the humans had never seen anything as repulsive as the fruits of the tree of the bound will. They hung on it like metastasized tumors. Those ripe enough to fall never reached the ground. They hovered right below the branches because the very force of gravity refused to act upon them and draw them to the earth, lest their filth contaminated it. The skin of those fruits was rougher than sandpaper and once cut, it revealed a mushy flesh laced with toxic foam, whose stench was more foul than that of excrement, while its poisonous fumes stung the eyes and made the nostrils itch.

Meh was so repulsed that she vomited every bite, and Ah fainted from the smell before the fruits could even touch his lips. A whole week passed, yet the humans, covered in sweat and vomit, still struggled in vain to ingest even a tiny piece. When Ooh saw them gasp and toss around like fish in a dried-out lake, ze pitied them and brought a bag of spices to tone down the wretchedness of the redemptive meal. Ze sprinkled cinnamon and mint, cumin and fenugreek, dill and nutmeg, pepper and ginger. Nothing helped.

Finally, Ooh made a dressing from squashed tomatoes, which he called ketchup, and the humans swallowed the fruits without struggle. Their stomachs rejoiced in great relief. Their souls, cleansed from the wickedness of knowledge, embraced their restored ignorance like the lips of a newborn baby clutched to a well-rounded tit. They lived happily ever after, for happiness is mostly bestowed upon people who are deprived of curiosity.

The post-reformists begged to differ. No, they said, the first humans didn't return to Ooh with bowed heads. On the contrary, it was Ooh who went searching for them because after ze chased them out, ze experienced an unnerving feeling, which ze ultimately called *loneliness*. It was this feeling that helped zim come to terms with zis own responsibility for the disabilities of zis own children.

Full of remorse, Ooh spent forty years trailing their footsteps until ze finally caught up with them and, with tears in zis eyes, ze fell on zis knees and asked them for forgiveness: "Oh children of mine, I have betrayed you, blinded by perfection and confused by my inability to accept you as you are. It wasn't until I felt your absence when I realized that without you my soul was incomplete. For this, I abhor myself and repent in dust and ashes. Come back to me and let me atone for my sin by granting you the gift of sex, so through the act of copulation you become whole again."

And as ze watched Meh and Ah lay together, zis heart rejoiced and found peace again.

The Book of Love

AS EXPECTED, THE GREATEST LIBRARY on Earth was located in the Kingdom of the Word, since its inhabitants valued books more than they valued gold (or human life for that matter). The library collection was so vast, its printed catalog was three meters wide, ten meters high, and weighed more than a ton. It took ten people to lift its cover. Each year the amount of its pages increased with astonishing speed. Many librarians feared the catalog would soon grow so heavy, it would become unusable—a doomsday scenario known as the *knowledge singularity*. Common people paid little attention to such catastrophic forecasts, and unapologetically indulged their thirst for knowledge. Any writing longer than a standard sheet of paper was considered a book and had to be handed to the authorities for assessment. If it was deemed valuable, the original was confiscated and its author received a copy, accompanied by a letter from the king that said:

> *Dear citizen, one or more of your works have been certified as sufficiently valuable to be preserved on the shelves of our Library of Superb Enlightenment. How awesome is that? I, your King, guardian of wisdom and destroyer of ignorance, hereby dispatch my heartfelt regards!*

The king was less polite with people who refused to hand over their writings. They were sentenced to slave labor in the royal paper mills. The punishment for destroying a book was even more severe—a lifelong exile on an island swarming with poisonous chameleons. If the destroyed book was exceptionally valuable, the punishment was death—the offenders were sacrificed to Clearchus, the Librarian God, whose autobiography occupied a prominent space in the center of the library.

As the story goes, he created the world while scribbling with his divine pencil on the Plane of Existence that—in the grand scheme of things—resembled a giant sheet of paper. His autobiography began with the words *Oh gosh, what did I do now?*

Like all demiurgic deities, Clearchus had no clue what he was doing. The act of creation was just a hiccup of his restless mind—a fact he openly admitted. He insisted that all things acquired meaning posteriori and any predestination was a deceptive illusion caused by people's fear of the unknown. His relativistic philosophy inspired a religious cult that had no established dogmas and was exclusively preoccupied with the acquisition of knowledge. His followers believed that the more they knew about the world, the more they filled it with meaning.

One day a traveler arrived at the border and requested a transit visa. It was freezing cold and the customs officials cordially invited him inside. They collected his passport and—following an ancient custom that many travelers found pleasantly peculiar—offered him milk and cookies. The traveler was seated on a plush sofa that was so comfortable, he would have certainly fallen asleep, if a clerk pushing a desk on squeaking wheels hadn't appeared out of the blue.

"Welcome to the Kingdom of the Word," said the clerk and positioned the desk right in front of the traveler. "I'm the chief of the Transit Permits Department and I'm here to asses your visa application."

"It's a pleasure to meet you," said the traveler. By the way, these cookies are delicious."

The bureaucrat smiled politely and pulled out an application form. "Would you state your name for the record, please!"

"Isidore of Clonfert."

"Do you have any books in your possession, Mister Clonfert?"

"A small one, handwritten," said Isidore after a brief hesitation.

"Its value, please!" asked the bureaucrat dryly.

"It's a gift. Needless to say, for me it's priceless, but I doubt the general public will find it interesting."

"No book is priceless," said the bureaucrat, "for if it is, it must contain the knowledge of everything, everywhere, and everywhen."

"Oh, of course not! It's priceless for me personally because it's a gift from someone special."

"I'm afraid I don't understand," said the bureaucrat, "but rest assured there is a way to determine the exact value with a few simple questions. In the meantime, would you like more milk? The process might take a while."

"I'd love a second cup, thanks!"

The bureaucrat pressed a button on his desk, and an assistant carrying a beautiful porcelain jug came in.

"Would it be too much if I ask for extra cookies, please? I can't believe how delicious everything is!" said Isidore.

The bureaucrat nodded and pressed another button. Another assistant carrying a plate with cookies appeared.

"Perhaps you could share the recipe," said Isidore.

"I will file a request to the culinary department, but it will have to wait until I process your application," said the bureaucrat. "Please hand over your book to me."

Isidore pulled out a small rugged book whose pages were all bent and yellow. There was a coffee stain on the cover. The bureaucrat took it and placed it on his desk carefully, as if it was an ancient manuscript that could fall apart any moment. Then he opened a second drawer and took out another form. Isidore took a sip of milk.

"Please provide short but descriptive answers to the following questions," said the bureaucrat: "What is the theme of the book?"

"Love," replied Isidore.

"In what form is the theme developed?"

"Poetry."

The bureaucrat raised an eyebrow and flipped several pages. "Very well. Does it rhyme, and if it does, is it A) perfect rhyme or B) general rhyme; and if it is A) perfect, is it A1) masculine, A2) feminine or A3) dactylic; and if it is B) general, is it B1) syllabic, B2) imperfect, B3) weak, B4) semi-rhyme, B5) oblique or B6) head-rhyme?"

"I have no idea, to be honest," replied Isidore while chewing on a cookie. "I've never thought about it. The person who wrote it wasn't really a poet."

"What was his occupation?" asked the clerk.

"A carpenter," replied Isidore.

"A carpenter? Who writes poems?"

"Yes," said Isidore, "Sometimes inspiration moves in mysterious ways, doesn't it? One day you're cutting trees, the next one you write poetry."

"Perhaps that's why you struggle with the value of this book," said the bureaucrat. "I would be equally confused under such circumstances."

"I'm sure I can answer at least some of your questions if you hand it back to me. It's been a while since I last read it. I don't know the poems by heart," said Isidore.

"No, I will read it to you," said the clerk. He cleared his throat and began reciting with a flat, emotionless tone:

My love,
How hard words come to mind,
Yet how eager is the mouth to utter them.
And how their meaning eludes us
When they are overloaded with feelings.
Like handicapped donkeys they stumble,
Unable to carry the burden of our hearts
When we are apart:
When our eyes are wide open
But our faces are nowhere to be seen,
When everyone else is a stranger
And hope is spread thin
On a world that has no meaning whatsoever
Without you

"Are there any missing pages?" asked the clerk. "This doesn't feel like a beginning."

Isidore was silent, staring at the edge of the desk.

"Excuse me, sir!" said the clerk. "Is everything OK?"

"Oh, yes. Definitely!" replied Isidore. "I'm sorry, the verses brought back some memories and I didn't quite hear your question."

"I was suggesting that some of the initial pages might be missing because the poem begins too abruptly," said the clerk. "That's a bit jarring, not to mention that the language itself is confusing. It's full of juxtapositions and it implies the meaning of life depends on a single person. I'm not sure I have encountered such a premise even in some of our epic science fiction novels."

"There are no missing pages," said Isidore. "And there is no particular order to the poems. As for their meaning, where I come from people say that poetry works best on an empty mind and a full heart."

"The empty mind is a dangerous thing, Mister Clonfert," said the clerk. "It opens the door to chaos and transgressions."

"So does love," said Isidore. "Who hasn't been tempted at least once in life to suspend their reasoning? Yet we survive, somehow."

"Some of us do. I'm proud to call myself a survivor," said the clerk and pointed to a purple ribbon on his suit. "This is the Knot of Reason. It's a medal given to those who have overcome intense emotional turmoil. I spent five years in a rehabilitation center battling anguish and despair because I was fixated on a person who didn't respond to my feelings. Many of the people I met there, however, never got out."

"I'm sorry to hear that," said Isidore.

"Don't be. We're all personally responsible for our own feelings," said the clerk dryly. "This poem seems to suggest the opposite. Coming from an unprofessional, that's hardly a surprise. I don't think it's even necessary to explore the quality of the rhyme. But the message contained inside will serve as cautionary evidence that poetry is best left to poets."

Isidore sighed. He was about to start an argument, but got distracted by a cookie that looked especially appetizing.

"Let's move on to the next poem," said the clerk.

> *My heart breaks when I see you*
> *Curled up on the other side of the bed.*
> *So far, your warmth is just a distant memory*
> *In the silence of the early hours.*
> *Come back to my arms, lay your head on my chest,*
> *And let the beat of my heart lull you to sleep.*
> *My body will ache under your weight*
> *And my joints will be deprived of comfort*
> *And the sweetness of that pain will heal the damage*
> *Caused by the loneliness I felt*
> *When I saw you turn your back to me*
> *While you were sleeping.*

"Now this is something else!" said the clerk.

Isidore stopped chewing. "Did you really like it?"

"I loved it!" said the clerk.

"It brings back so many memories," said Isidore. "When I was born, my mother visited a witch who told her I would leave home when my beard started growing. I would become a great traveler, she said to her, the first one to cross the world from end to end! My parents never doubted the prophecy and did their best to prepare me. I never heard them say the words *I love you.* They did love me, of course, but they knew journeys like mine don't end where they begin. The more attached you become to people, the more you suffer when you have to let them go. So they kept their distance. I still remember my mother's words when we said goodbye. *Don't look back,* she said. She was afraid that if I did, I would see her crying."

"This is a compelling story, Mister Clonfert!" said the clerk. "You should consider writing a book about it. Our library doesn't have a lot of entries from your country."

"Maybe someday, at the end of my journey," replied Isidore. "But that's not why I'm telling you this story. You see, where I come from, if you have a destiny, you can't do much but accept it. People are just not used to question those things. But as you travel and you gather experience, doubt starts to creep in. First you doubt your senses, then your judgment, and finally, your destiny. Two years ago I met the man who wrote this book. We fell in love, and overcome by passion, I started doubting everything. Perhaps my real destiny was to spend my days with him? Yet settling down would have made the sacrifice of my parents meaningless. In the end, I continued with my journey. And I broke his heart."

"Ah, the irresistible allure of the unknown!" said the clerk. "It makes the world go round."

"Indeed it does," said Isidore, "but sometimes I think life would be so much better if the world stopped spinning."

"He must have been an interesting person, that carpenter," said the clerk. "Such a talent for juxtapositions! The first poem is a bit sloppy but this one is delightfully bizarre. Feeling abandoned by a person that is sleeping next to you is such an extravagant emotion. It could spark a whole new field in speculative psychology. Mister Clonfert, I think the value of your book is much greater than we expected and..." the clerk leaned in, as if there was someone else in the room who could overhear their conversation, "I shouldn't really tell you this, but I can almost guarantee it will be confiscated. This is good news for your visa application."

"Confiscated?" said Isidore. "Why?"

"It will be preserved in our library for the benefit of the entire human race. Needless to say, you will receive an exact copy as a sign of gratitude."

"You don't understand," said Isidore, "A copy of this book won't have the same value for me."

"Of course not. It will be printed on high quality paper with water-resistant ink. I'd say this is your lucky day," said the clerk triumphantly. "More milk?"

"No... I mean yes, I want more milk, but I can't give you the original. It has his fingerprints, his handwriting. Out of the question!"

"In this case I'm afraid you will be denied a visa," said the clerk. "Why?"

"If you set foot in our kingdom with a book you refuse to hand out, you'd be sentenced to slave labor for the rest of your life. Is this a choice you're willing to make?"

"Definitely not!" said Isidore and stood up. "I'll find another way. Thank you for the milk and cookies."

The bureaucrat shrugged and handed back the book.

Isidore left and swore to never come back. He tried to circumvent the kingdom, but found a scorching desert to the south and impenetrable glaciers to the north. After six months of fruitless search for an alternative route, he returned to the border.

"It's good to see you again," said the clerk, "Can I offer you a cup of milk?"

"Just take the damned book and let me pass," said Isidore.

Thus the greatest love poetry ever written was cataloged and preserved, so it could inspire lovers around the world until the day of The Final Exam, when Clearchus will come back to Earth to test and grade everyone according to intelligence and merit. Glory be to His Librarian Excellence!

Sophisticus the Wise and Occam the Barbarian

The Wings of Love

LONG TIME AGO, IN WHAT IS NOW the Margraviate of the Windswept Hill, lived a prophet named Vulnicurus who preached that love—and love alone—could tame the vile instincts of the human heart and bring peace on Earth for all eternity. One day, as he climbed on a holy tree to deliver a sermon about the merits of promiscuity, he suddenly disappeared without a trace. After a brief kerfuffle, people concluded he must have ascended to Heaven. From that day on, they took his teachings seriously.

Back then, the hill that rose in the midst of those lands was inhabited by giant birds called rukhs. Those who were unlucky enough to see their nest up close swore than it floated right above the needle-sharp top of the hill, suspended in the air by some kind of demonic power. Alas, what appeared as the work of the devil was just sophisticated engineering. The rukhs were masters of construction, and their drive for perfection was no doubt aided by their saliva, which under certain conditions acquired the quality of a powerful adhesive. Even today, long after the birds became extinct, the nest stands in its place as a testament to their ingenuity and skill. The rukhs fed on small insects like mosquitoes or fig wasps, although they could also enjoy an occasional bumble bee if life was generous enough to send one their way. They laid eggs once per century. Unlike their parents, the chicks were carnivorous and required constant supply of meat. It was for this reason that from time to time the rukhs snatched a human.

Such was the fate of Vulnicurus and many others like him, although nobody was aware of the truth. In the realm of human reality, which doesn't always overlap with the factual world, the victims of the rukhs were still alive, suspended in perpetual heavenly bliss. Many of them were forgotten, but the memory of Vulnicurus lingered long enough to evolve into a proper religious cult. His teachings about the soothing power of love muddled the minds of future generations, right until present days, when the margraviate was threatened by a barbarian horde advancing from the East.

Harbinger of Doom

BY A PRANK OF DESTINY the invasion happened during the reign of the most enlightened margrave in history—Sophisticus the Wise. When he received the horrifying news, he wrote a cordial letter and sent his best diplomat to deliver it to the barbarian horde. He signed off with *love and kisses,* as it was customary among aristocrats of his standing. Strangely, his request didn't dissuade the barbarians from pillaging every village and murdering every soul that crossed their way. If anything, the gallantries of the margrave had the opposite effect: The diplomat was ritualistically raped by the barbarian leader, who sent back the following reply:

Shiver, oh, submissive infidel with a ridiculous name! The anxiety that inspires your pleas is nothing compared to the terror you will feel when you witness my army blacken your horizon. And when my vermilion breastplate blinds your eyes, you will bow down in awe of my power and willingly fall on your knees to offer me your head for I am Occam the Barbarian! I killed a python with my bare hands when I was five. I broke the neck of a horse when I was ten. I strangled an elephant when I was fifteen. At twenty, I impregnated thirty women in a single night, and when I was done I still had an erection, and each one bore twins, except the last one, who gave birth to triplets. No god can subdue me. No man can defeat me. Neither poison nor magic have power over me. I rubbed this letter on my hairy armpits, so you can taste my sweat and tremble from the pungency of its odor. Don't ever call me your brother, and if you insist on kissing me so much, the only part of my body suitable for your lips are the soles of my feet.

The word *barbarian* meant *a bearded man with huge muscles and a crotch to match* and came from the Great Multilingual Age, when—shockingly—every tribe on Earth spoke a different language and lived in perfect harmony with its neighbors. Eventually God, who created humanity for his personal amusement, became bored by this idyllic state of affairs. He decided to stir things up by sending people the curse of the common language. Suddenly, everyone could understand everybody else, regardless of race or distance. Links between different tribes were established, goods and ideas were exchanged, and some people even started to intermarry. Philosophers spoke of a new age called *globalism*. From now on, they said, everybody's opinion would have the chance to be universally appreciated.

Nobody thought about what would happen if that same opinion was universally criticized. Soon people realized that some egos were too fragile to bear the burden of global exposure. For every celebrated thinker there was another whose ideas were ignored or even ridiculed. A decade after the creation of the common language two cooks, who lived on the opposite sides of the world, started an argument about the best recipe for scrambled eggs. In the middle of the heated debate, one of them called the other *fool* and sparked the First Whole Wide World War of Words (often abbreviated as wwwww1). It lasted half a century and left the common language in tatters, adding a plethora of unpleasant vocabulary like *idiot, moron, dumbfuck, cocksucker, teabagger,* and *titwanker*. A deranged general unleashed the most offensive word ever invented—*cunt*—on his enemy's capital, killing half of its civilian population.

God was very pleased with the results.

Sophisticus wasn't aware of the etymology of the word *barbarian* and assumed that Occam was just a confused young man.

"I feel so sad about all the pious people this savage warlord has murdered," he said to his closest advisor, "but what truly breaks my heart is his own tortured soul. A person with such a foul mouth must have never experienced love and its healing powers. His heart must be overflowing with suffering because—as the prophet Vulnicurus taught us when he preached from the Tree of the Exalted Departure—hubris and cynicism are the unequivocal manifestations of emotional self-sabotage. It is therefore our duty to show this man the value of meekness and compassion. Prepare a gift of our best treasures and don't skimp on the quantities! Let's lavish him with diamonds, rubies, gold, pearls, and amber. Throw in abundant quantities of delicate perfumes, fine textiles, and our most sophisticated musical instruments. Let's make a gift that is irresistibly delightful for the senses. I want you to bring it to him personally, so you can witness first hand how quickly aggression turns to meekness. When everything is done, bring him to me, so he can apologize for his crimes. Needless to say, I will immediately forgive his sins, in a gesture of unsurpassed compassion, even before he has finished pleading."

"Your Highness, excuse my unsolicited flattery, but I must say that such an elaborate plan can only come from a true genius. In fact as you were describing it, I got goosebumps all over my neck and shoulders," said the advisor and set off to work.

On the next morning, news arrived that the barbarian horde was advancing with alarming speed towards the capital, but the margrave was so confident in his plan that he dispatched his advisor with plenty of pomp and circumstance, and then immediately initiated preparations for a triumphal procession. In just a week, all streets were decorated with victory banners, buildings were repaired and their facades repainted, and a huge poster with the inscription *We love you, Occam!* and a subtitle *Let's put the past behind us!* was hung on the terrace of the royal palace. When the time came for the caravan's return, the whole population went out of the city gates to welcome the defeated enemy. A human silhouette appeared on the horizon, and everybody started cheering. To their disappointment, the lone figure turned out to be not an exalted barbarian, but the margrave's advisor. He looked rather distraught.

"These people are monsters!" he shouted as blood spouted out of his mouth. "Monsters without hearts!"

Panic erupted among the masses. Everybody rushed back to the city gates with such mindless anxiety that even mothers ran over their own children, for sometimes the instinct for preservation becomes stronger than love and reduces the human being to a beastly automaton.

Sophisticus, exulting in his pride, concluded that the failure of his plan was his advisor's fault: "You clearly must have done something wrong and annoyed this poor warlord. I can only blame myself for not realizing how unfit you were for this task. But what's done is done. You're fired!"

"Your Highness," replied the advisor. "I know it's hard to believe, but this Occam is like no one we have ever seen before. He's neither confused, nor misguided. He doesn't care about love. He doesn't care about beauty. He threw all the precious stones I brought into a river and used the textiles as diapers for his horses. I was only able to escape because they all got drunk on the expensive perfumes."

"Are you so devoid of dignity that you would rather spread lies about a fellow human being? Get out of my sight before I lose my patience!" said Sophisticus.

The failure only increased the margrave's determination to deal with the barbarians once and for all. But this time he had an even better idea. He quickly summoned his librarian-in-chief.

"I'm sure that the gifts I sent were irresistible, and had my advisor not botched everything, we would have had this Occam guy at the dinner table, laughing and dancing, and most likely enjoying the caresses of our most beautiful virgins," said the margrave. "But let's use this second opportunity to achieve the impossible and make an already brilliant plan even better. Assemble a collection of our most precious books, particularly those that are rare and cost a fortune. You will have the great honor to bring them to the barbarians and witness how, when given a chance to educate themselves, ignorant wildlings transform into civilized, empathic beings, for which I frankly envy you because it is an opportunity that comes once in a lifetime."

On the next morning, news arrived that twenty three villages and twelve merchant outposts were brutalized by the advancing horde. The few survivors told stories of unspeakable horror and noted that a strong smell of expensive perfume preceded every attack. The stench of patchouli brought crucifixions, basil and chamomile—pillage and fire, and when the air stank of roses, it was a certain sign for an impending mass rape.

"Don't despair," said the margrave to the nervous population gathered to witness the departure of the librarian-in-chief. "Once we unleash the weapon of knowledge upon these so-called barbarians, they will embrace the teachings of Vulnicurus and become as meek as we are."

Three days later the librarian-in-chief returned, wearing nothing but a loosely sewn skirt made of vellum sheets, ripped from a five-hundred-years-old manuscript with fertility prayers by Vulnicurus. His body smelled of roses.

"Just to think that I put such high hopes on you," scolded him Sophisticus. "It seems that incompetence is endemic among state employees."

"Indeed it is," a familiar voice replied. The crowd opened up and made way for an old man, whose shaking hands clutched to a golden cane. "I have been repeating this forever, Your Highness, yet nobody listens!"

"Holy Father, it's a blessing to have you among us," said the margrave and bowed respectfully.

"I'm afraid the blessing is not reciprocal because for me it is sheer terror to have you all as my flock ever since the day I was elected to serve as your Pope," said the old man. "Every night I pray to Vulnicurus to tell me what did I do to deserve this burden. And every night he remains silent because he knows it's not fair."

"Please forgive our trespasses, Holy Father! You must know we always mean well and act to the best of our abilities," said Sophisticus, who was used to the complaints of the old man.

"I have a dream," said the Pope with a soaring voice, as if the vitality of youth once more took hold of his frail body, "I have a dream that one day people will stop doing their best and will start doing what's *right* instead. I have a dream that at the end of that day, when they go to bed to make sweet love to their husbands and wives, they won't think of life as a one-way ride from sloppiness to perfection, but as a long winding road, full of twists and pitfalls. I have a dream that we will remember the words of Vulnicurus: Good intentions often lead to Hell, while the road to heaven is through constant vigilance."

"How clear are the words of the prophet when they come from your mouth, Holy Father," said the margrave. "We will forever be in debt to you for constantly reminding us of the right path, for just like sheep, we are easily distracted, and if left without a loving shepherd, we will most certainly perish. Please help us overcome the threat of those barbarians and return to our daily routine of worship and leisure!"

"Very well," said the Pope. "Prepare my private carriage. I shall depart at sunrise to speak personally with this Occam, for—as evidenced by what just happened—it is clear that my persuasiveness is a great weapon that should not be spared in the struggle against this savagery."

On the next morning, news arrived that the second largest city in the margraviate was obliterated by the barbarians. They bombarded it with burning books, mounted on improvised trebuchets and hurled over its impenetrable walls, until all the streets were set alight, and the entire population suffocated. Neither Sophisticus, nor the Pope took the tragedy to heart. Both had their minds fixed on the future and the inevitable conversion of the savages. The only thing they didn't agree about was who should take the credit for it, but this was a discussion that could wait until the threat was thoroughly eliminated. If the old man was too stubborn or made a lot of noise, Sophisticus could always bribe a couple of cardinals and initiate a vote of no confidence in the Holy Synod.

The Pope departed with the usual fuss about how unfortunate he was to carry the burden of a spiritual leader. The four horses that drew his carriage had no complaints, because lamenting destiny was a human specialty. Three days later they came back drawing an empty carriage. There was a tiara and a sheet of paper left on the passenger seat with the following message:

> *People of Windswept Hill, it is my duty to inform you that I, with great relief and enthusiasm, willingly renounce the title of Pope. I have finally found my true purpose in life, and it is to spend my days with those who you unjustly call savage, for among them I find true appreciation and they treat me with respect. I won't miss any of you.*

"I should have known he was just looking for an opportunity to betray us, and his moral pleas were a devious facade," said Sophisticus, "but then again, if I were able to predict such cynical behavior, I would have been a cynic myself."

The next morning, the usual news about rape and pillage reached the capital but this time the barbarians also laid a perpetual claim on the land, insisting it was promised to them by a prophet called Valkyrius, which sounded suspiciously similar to Vulnicurus if you said it with a full mouth.

Gloomy mood descended on the margraviate. People removed the street decorations, locked themselves in their homes, and began praying anxiously. A homeless beggar started preaching that the end of days was near and Occam was the reborn Vulnicurus, who returned to Earth to punish those who strayed from the path of righteousness.

On the next day, a young traveler from the West entered the city and asked for an audience with the margrave.

"Dear stranger, I am flattered beyond compare that you decided to pay me a visit," said Sophisticus, "however, I'd urge you to swiftly gallop back to where you came from, for this city will soon perish from the face of the earth. For ages it has sheltered tender souls who seek refuge from gratuitous condescension and bristling ridicule, but a horde of stinky savages that can't tell the difference between a bathtub and a jacuzzi—much less appreciate the value of hospitality, for which we are extremely famous—is swiftly approaching and will soon put an end to our civilization."

"Your reputation for hospitality—or eloquence for that matter—doesn't do you justice, Your Highness," said the young stranger. "Please allow me to introduce myself. My name is Isidore and I come from the far-away island of Clonfert. I'm an explorer by profession and a traveler by consequence. I heard about the threat that has befallen you and came to witness it first hand. The demise of a civilization is a rare event, and someone needs to document it for posterity."

"I have never seen such reckless curiosity in a man before. If circumstances were different, I would have found it alarming. Alas, the awareness of my inevitable doom makes me indifferent to most things. There's a sense of peacefulness when you know the world is ending and everything you have ever valued will forever disappear without a trace."

"Perhaps I can reignite your joie de vivre if I tell you a couple of interesting stories," said Isidore.

"I have nothing better to do but sit and wait for the ultimate oblivion," said Sophisticus and reclined on his throne. "If you prefer to recite fairy tales until a barbarian slits your throat mid-sentence, so be it."

"Very well," said Isidore, "Here's a story from my homeland of Clonfert that, without a doubt, will bring a smile on your face."

Róisín and the Shepherd

ONCE UPON A TIME, SO FAR BACK that the sun rose from the West and set to the East, a humble shepherd lived on the island of Clonfert. One day, as he was frolicking on the green meadows in the company of his sheep, he tripped on a large stone and hit his head on a pot of gold that was hidden under it.

"How interesting," he said to himself after the throbbing pain from the impact subsided just enough so he could think straight, "today I learned that—unlike what I've always imagined—great wealth doesn't come for free, but is achieved through great pain and suffering."

He took the pot of gold home, pressed a bag of ice on his swollen head, and started making plans how to spend all this wealth in a responsible manner. For quite some time he had been laying eyes on his beautiful cousin Róisín, who, despite being sixteen years old, was still single due to her pickiness and stubborn character. Her room was right next to his. He had never seen a man enter inside, although sometimes at night, when the entire village went silent, and insomniacs could hear the buzz of the stars in the night sky, a strange moaning occasionally sneaked through the wall. It tickled his imagination with such intensity that in the mornings he often woke up with a painful erection. Róisín was either the daughter of his mother's reclusive sister (according to his grandparents) or the illegitimate child of his father's brother with

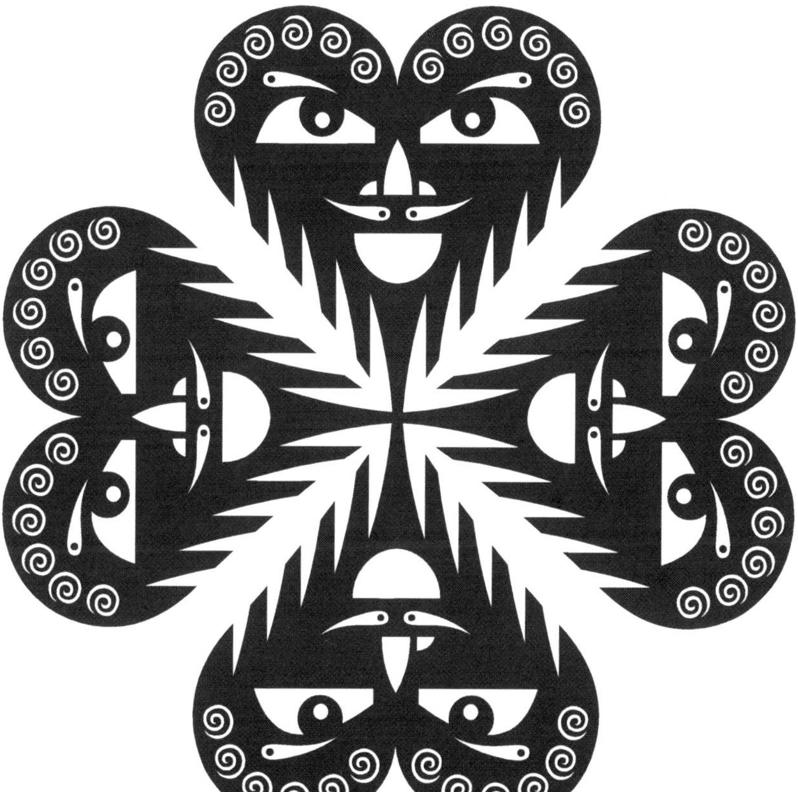

an unlicensed sex worker (according to a well-informed neighbor). Her curvy body made him choke on his saliva, and he used every opportunity to catch a glimpse of her glorious features—a bittersweet endeavor because carnal desire cannot be quenched by detached observation. Rumor had it she could crush whole almonds with her perky breasts. They always jiggled up and down when she walked, and when she got into a hurry, they went into a bouncing frenzy that haunted the fantasies of those who had the privilege to behold them.

Perhaps now that he was financially independent, Róisín would finally agree to marry him? He let that thought marinate a little bit, then poured himself a glass of whiskey to wash down the ensuing anxiety. At worst, she would beat him up with her broom, something that—despite the pain—excited him sexually.

When he woke up the next morning, he put on his best clothes, and was just heading to Róisín's room when the doorbell rang.

"Hello," said the creature that stood on the porch. "You stole something from me. Give it back!"

"I did no such thing, little green man," said the shepherd. "And I have no idea who you are or what you are referring to."

"Spare me your posturing, you naughty drunk," replied the creature. "Didn't your mother tell you not to steal a leprechaun's pot? Because of you, I had to go out to piss twice last night. I need it back. My wiener almost froze in the cold."

"What? You urinate in that pot?" said the shepherd and instinctively rubbed his hands on his shirt.

"See? I knew you had it!" said the leprechaun. "Of course I piss in it, what else do you think I use it for."

"For storing gold, perhaps?" said the shepherd.

The leprechaun was an eye roll away from losing his patience. "Look, *perhaps* you were too distracted when people read you bedtime stories. But if you paid even the slightest attention, you would have learned that leprechauns piss gold."

Another interesting fact about leprechauns was that if someone took their pot of gold, they couldn't take it back by force because of an obscure clause in an antiquated law regulating the possession and use of magical objects. It stated the following:

Any object derived from magic and/or considered essential to the practice of magical activities shall be automatically leased to the person in whose pocket it resides, notwithstanding race, gender, sexual orientation, or class. In the case of absence of pockets or compartments of similar functionality and size, the lease should apply to the person who fulfills the following conditions in the exact specified order: 1) the person is the last one who has had physical contact with the object, and 2) the person is the only one who knows the whereabouts of the object. If the person knows the whereabouts of the object but hasn't been in physical contact with it, he or she has to notify its supposed owner within a reasonable timeframe and amicably facilitate its return.

Many leprechauns had gotten in trouble after they lost their pots. One named Siobhan of Slutsend died from a bladder infection because she refused to marry an elderly gentleman who hid her pot under his bed. Songs about her dire fate are still sung in the forests of Clonfert, the most heart-wrenching among them being *Oh Siobhan, thy pipes, thy pipes are clogging*.

The shepherd would have gladly returned the pot if the gold inside wasn't so essential to his plan of charming Róisín.

One of the ironies of life is that far too many men have been accused of greed when the only thing they ever wanted was to impress someone dear to their hearts.

After several attempts to reason and one thinly veiled threat, the leprechaun changed tactic.

"Fine, young fella! I see you are as stubborn as a mule. The time has come to make you an offer you won't be able to reject."

"And what would that be?" asked the shepherd.

"If you give my pot back, I will make one wish of yours come true," said the leprechaun and grinned.

"One wish?" asked the shepherd, as if he was trying to figure out whether it was enough.

"That's right."

"And that wish could be anything?" asked the shepherd.

"Anything," said the leprechaun, "besides the obvious smartass bullshit that some people think they can get away with. Like, umm, my only wish is that you grant me three more wishes. That's a classic!"

"Deal!" said the shepherd. "I wish to marry my cousin Róisín, who is very beautiful and..."

Without waiting for him to finish, the leprechaun clapped his hands and everything changed. Something heavy landed on the shepherd's head and when he reached out to remove it, he hit himself with a strange object that he didn't know he held in his hand.

"Careful with that scepter," said the leprechaun.

"What's that thing that fell on my head?" asked the shepherd.

"A crown," said the leprechaun.

"Why the hell did it fall on my head?" The shepherd threw the scepter on the floor and took off the crown.

"You wished to be a king and I fulfilled your desire. Now give me back my pot," said the leprechaun.

"I didn't wish to be a king. I wished to marry my cousin," replied the shepherd.

"Oh! I see. I'm sorry, I must have misheard," said the leprechaun.

"Listen, you little green rascal," said the shepherd and grabbed the leprechaun by the throat, "tell me exactly what is going on or I swear you'll never see your pot again."

"Please don't hurt me! It's been such a long time since anyone asked me about something different than becoming a king that I have forgotten how to fulfill those wishes. I know this wasn't what you wanted, but come on, you have to be a real asshole to complain about it. Just look around you!"

The shepherd turned his head. The humble house was transformed into a beautiful palace. A cheering crowd of people was gathered in front of it. When he saw their faces, he immediately recognized his sheep, meek and obedient as ever. The idyllic atmosphere calmed his anger. He gave back the pot to the leprechaun, who disappeared into the forest.

The shepherd might not have gotten what he wanted from the leprechaun, but, being a king, he introduced a law, according to which all citizens named Róisín were free to marry anyone they wanted, except in the unlikely circumstance when one of their cousins becomes a king. Should such a thing happen, said the law, they must marry him instead. Róisín didn't give up her freedom so easily. She hired a lawyer who filed a suit on the basis of preferential discrimination:

> *My client states that, while she is smitten by the generous privilege this law bestows on her humble persona, by no means she could claim or accept the title of queen simply based on her given name—an attribute that she had no control of and that, truth be told, she doesn't really like that much because 1) it's a peasant's name, and 2) she always wanted to be called Deirdre.*

Law experts fought for years trying to determine whether her complaint had any merit. When the king bribed the judge who was in charge of the case, Róisín took matters to an appeals court. As it became clear that even monarchs are not powerful enough to get what they want, the king withdrew the law with the following public statement:

We live in an unfair world. Our most noble yearnings are met with indifference and ridicule. Throughout my life I've never asked for anything else but to wake up every day next to my beloved cousin, who is—and always will be—the most beautiful woman in the world. Like all fools, I've always hoped this dream might come true, that I could earn her love. As I withdraw this law and face the consequence of ultimate despair caused by my shattered heart, I apologize to all involved parties.

When Róisín read this, she called her publicist and dictated the following message:

Your Majesty has always possessed the cunning mind of a gifted shepherd, a quality that now serves you well in your role as a king. Yet, by some twist of fate, or a personality glitch, when it comes to emotional matters, your legendary shrewdness gives way to pathological shyness that prevents you from letting other people know what you want, when you want it, and for how long. Had you ever spoken to me directly and revealed the way you felt, you would have found out that I was—and still am—quite fond of you.

When he heard this, the king went to his cousin's quarters, knelt in front of his beloved, and asked her to marry him. She gladly consented. They had many children, some of which were inexplicably deformed, and ruled in peace and harmony until the coming of the Trondheim monster.

Interlude: Monsters Are No Laughing Matter

"THAT'S A FUNNY NAME for a monster! How did it look like?" said Sophisticus.

"I can assure you, Your Highness, this monster was no laughing matter! As for its true appearance, no one knows for sure. It's one of those things whose look is long forgotten, but whose name survives because it instills fear in everyone who utters it," replied Isidore.

"Trondheim... Trond. Heim. Hmm. It just doesn't roll in a scary way to me," said Sophisticus, shuffling the syllables in his mouth as if he was tasting wine. "It feels like the name of an exotic circus animal. Or—and that's even better—it could also be a verb describing uncoordinated movement through rough terrain. Trond-heim-trond-heim-trond... Do you see where I'm going with this?"

"I see your point, but take my word, you'd feel a lot different if you were from Clonfert," said Isidore. "Surely you must know that fear, like all feelings, can be culturally conditioned. I once visited a country where people lived in constant fear of rabbits. What was worse, nobody knew why. Whatever caused it, it happened so long ago, everybody thought their phobia was a most natural thing."

Sophisticus burst into laughter. "That's even funnier! Ah, I haven't cracked a smile in weeks. It feels so refreshing! Please tell me more about this circus monster!"

"In Clonfert," continued Isidore, "there are several theories about the nature of the Trondheim monster. The first one speaks of a giant dragon who came from the South to settle on our island after its natural habitat was flooded due to climate change. The second states that the monster itself never existed, and what caused the extensive devastation was an invasion of savages, who came from the North on flat boats that could float in the air as easily as they sailed on water. They were called the Trondheim Armada, and because of this, some historians theorize that Trondheim was actually the name of their hometown. Whatever the case, all experts agree that there isn't anything scarier on Earth."

"Oh, if only the diplomats hadn't left the city! I'd gladly invite the ambassador of the Kingdom of the Word for tea and then casually mention this story while I pass the sugar," said Sophisticus. "His fellows back home would turn every page in their moldy library in search for references. Do you know how much paper they hoard in that humid disease-incubating vault? Each year ten percent of their staff fall ill because their immune systems can't cope with the rapidly mutating bacterial gunk that grows on the pages of their most treasured possessions. I once negotiated the extradition of a renegade aristocrat who took refuge in their capital. All I had to do was send them an ancient manuscript my people dug out when they were fixing a broken pipe under the wine cellar. It was at least ten centuries old. Imagine all the people that touched it. I bet half of them never washed their hands after they went to the toilet. And those freaks took it and thought I was heartbroken to give it up! Oh, I miss the good old days so much!"

"Their passion for knowledge is legendary," said Isidore.

"Listen, can I offer you a beverage? I'm sure there are some supplies of wine left in the cellar," said Sophisticus.

"I'd love a glass of wine, Your Highness," replied Isidore.

The margrave clapped his hands. A servant appeared.

"Bring us some wine, with crackers!" said Sophisticus. "In the meantime, dear guest, please continue with your fascinating stories!"

The Greatest King that Ever Lived

IN THOSE SAME ANCIENT TIMES, when the sun's path in the sky was reversed, another legendary king lived on the island of Clonfert. His kingdom was located on the eastern shore, which now of course lies to the West. The king was groomed to rule since his conception, for his mother was manically ambitious and didn't miss a single government briefing while she was pregnant. She was certain the child in her womb was paying attention to every minute detail that was discussed, be it foreign policy, social security, healthcare, or military spending. And it was indeed true. As he transitioned through various embryonic states that firstly resembled an amoeba in distress, but quickly progressed to slender amphibian and humanoid rodent, the future king absorbed so much knowledge that at the moment of his birth, he promptly requested a meeting with the foreign minister to address an international crisis, concerning a flock of sheep that illegally crossed the border in search for greener pastures. Due to his unsurpassed talent, the king was deeply respected by his subjects, who were always obedient because they knew that even if they turned the world upside down, they wouldn't find an aristocrat so dedicated to their wellbeing.

While the king took all matters of government to heart and excelled at everything, his real passion was the army. Unfortunately, he ruled in times so peaceful that most people couldn't find a good reason to quarrel about politics in the pubs, much less pick up weapons for a cause that called for any kind of bloodletting. To quench his thirst for battles, the king staged elaborate spectacles where, split into opposing camps, his best men stormed mock fortresses, looted mock granaries, and kidnapped mock virgins. And because it was all make-believe, everyone went home in one piece, smiling and content. Yet occasionally, a strange thought flickered through the king's mind. How wonderful it would be, it whispered, if one day instead of ketchup, his sword got splattered with real blood.

He picked his wife among thousands of virgins who competed in a grand tournament for knitting, small talk, and diaper change that lasted three days and three nights. She was modest, meek, and spoke only when she was spoken to. Her beauty could disarm thousands of skeptics, who would swear loyalty to her husband the moment they saw her smile. Such irresistible charm earned her the title *Queen of Hearts* and her fame spread far away from the shores of Clonfert.

One day, as the queen was resting on her balcony surrounded by her pets, she heard a rumble coming from the sea. When she peeked over to see what was going on, she saw the strangest thing: a giant wave was rising over the horizon, and right above it floated a black ship with three rows of paddles on each side. They moved in perfect harmony, spurred by the rhythm of a powerful drum and chants that echoed in the air like the cries of angels waving swords.

Usually, when the queen looked down from her balcony, the first thing she saw was a cheering crowd, and she developed a habit of blowing kisses left and right, to everyone's delight. With time, this gesture became a reflex—like sneezing while inhaling ground pepper—so it wasn't at all surprising that the moment she laid her eyes on the strange ship, she quickly pressed her fingers on her plump lips and sent it a most tender kiss. She expected an acknowledgment, like a simple *I love you* or a polite *You look fabulous today, Your Majesty.* When she didn't receive an answer, she shrugged and went back inside because she was knitting a sweater that was already three days behind schedule.

"Whatever this thing is," she thought, "the king will take care of it once he comes back from hunting."

Her subjects were also surprised by the unusual sight. Back then the seas were calm because the earth didn't yet rotate around its axis. "Whatever this thing is," people thought, "the king will take care of it once he comes back from hunting."

When the king finally came back from hunting, he witnessed a sight that sent shivers up his spine. The streets were covered in mud and littered with corpses. The only thing still standing from the palace was a wall from the royal chambers. Pinned on it was a note that said, "Hey sissy, I'm the Trondheim monster and I'm wearing your sweater. Come see how it fits my body!"

"Alert the entire population and summon all armies," said the king to his generals, "We're finally at war!"

Thus the king unleashed the greatest mobilization his country had ever seen. Young and old, male and female, rushed to the production lines. For three months everybody worked tirelessly to build the greatest war machine the world had ever seen. It was ten times taller than an oak tree and wider than the thickest city wall. After the engineers finally mounted a saddle on it, the king impatiently hopped on its back and pulled the bridle. The machine neighed loudly.

"My fellow Clonfertians," said the king, "you have constructed the greatest weapon! I promise I shall not rest until I find this monster, avenge all of you, and bring you its testicles!"

The king pulled the bridle again and the machine took to the sky. For three days and three nights he flew over the ocean until he spotted the Trondheim monster sailing back home with all its loot. He descended upon it with the rage of a thousand men, screaming and cursing, slashing and pounding, kicking and hammering. Tainted by blood and sweat, the waters of the ocean started to boil. A giant wave, taller than a mountain, circled the entire globe three times. Tugged by its power, the earth started spinning around its axis and so it continues to this day, although with an ever decreasing speed because a battle this epic hasn't happened ever since. The spin of the earth caused the sun to rise from the opposite side—a most uncomfortable side effect because it messed up people's circadian rhythms and rendered all maps obsolete. In a blink of an eye, East Clonfertians realized they now lived in the West and suffered an identity crisis, from which their culture never recovered. West Clonfertians, being the butt of sunset jokes for millennia, now faced the sunrise and gladly embraced the privilege to live on the right side of geography, and—by extension—of history itself.

The war machine plunged its fists into the body of the Trondheim monster and inflicted such pain that the creature spat an avalanche of obscenities at the king, each more offensive than the previous, hoping to weaken his resolve and crush his spirit. Alas, it was in vain, for there wasn't a man more thick-skinned than the legendary monarch. When the monster realized that its ammunitions of insults were useless, it threw them overboard, spread its venomous tentacles and swung them at the king. Like whips they cracked and sank their hooks in the machine's neck, leaving it gasping for air, tossing and turning. The king grabbed the bridle tightly with one hand, pulled out a spear with the other, and plunged it deep in the monster's eye. A mighty scream pierced the sky and the creature's paddles parted the waters as they splashed down in an excruciating spasm, revealing a rocky bottom infested with fluorescent crustaceans. The monster's tentacles loosened their grip. The machine took a gulp of air and came back to its senses. It grabbed the monster with its clamps and lifted its body so quickly that a giant whirlpool opened beneath it, as if someone pulled out a plug from the bottom of the ocean.

"Take this," shouted the king and pressed a red button on the machine's head. The sky filled with thunderbolts and lightnings, and it all became very, very frightening. The machine swung its clamps and—roaring with the strength of thousand giants—threw the monster far beyond the horizon. A streak of its dripping blood tainted the water and poisoned all living things that swam nearby. The king spurred the machine and followed the trail of dead creatures. He found the wounded monster stuck in a shallow bay, dismounted the war machine, and took out his sword.

"Abomination of nature," he shouted with his manly voice, "expose your testicles to me, so I can castrate you and hang them on the throne of the queen you murdered!"

"Oh, mighty monarch," replied the Trondheim monster with a soft, submissive tone. "You have full dominion of all my body parts, for it is clear without a sliver of doubt that you are the strongest of all men. Yet strength is nothing but arrogance when it's deprived of the ennobling power of pity. Therefore, I beg for your mercy! I assure you that this gesture will make you even more famous than taking my testicles as a trophy, for I will serve as your obedient slave until the end of my days! I killed many of your people, but your queen is still alive and she resides safe in my belly, where she is treated with respect worthy of a royal. My servants are at her disposal day and night to console her and entertain her. They even give her a rub when she gets bored of eating too much cake. When we reach the safety of the dry land, she will disembark my insides and take her rightful place next to you. I'm certain that she'd be a better company for your throne room than a pair of old shriveled testicles that can't speak even when they are spoken to."

"As much as I'm tempted to emasculate you, I must admit your words make sense," said the king. "So I shall chain you and drag you back to my kingdom where you will work in my kitchen during the day and take care of my chamber pot during the night. And you better pray the queen has already finished knitting my sweater. I'm getting cold from all this splashing around and if I catch a flu, you wouldn't like my temper."

Thus the king tied the monster, mounted his war machine, and dragged

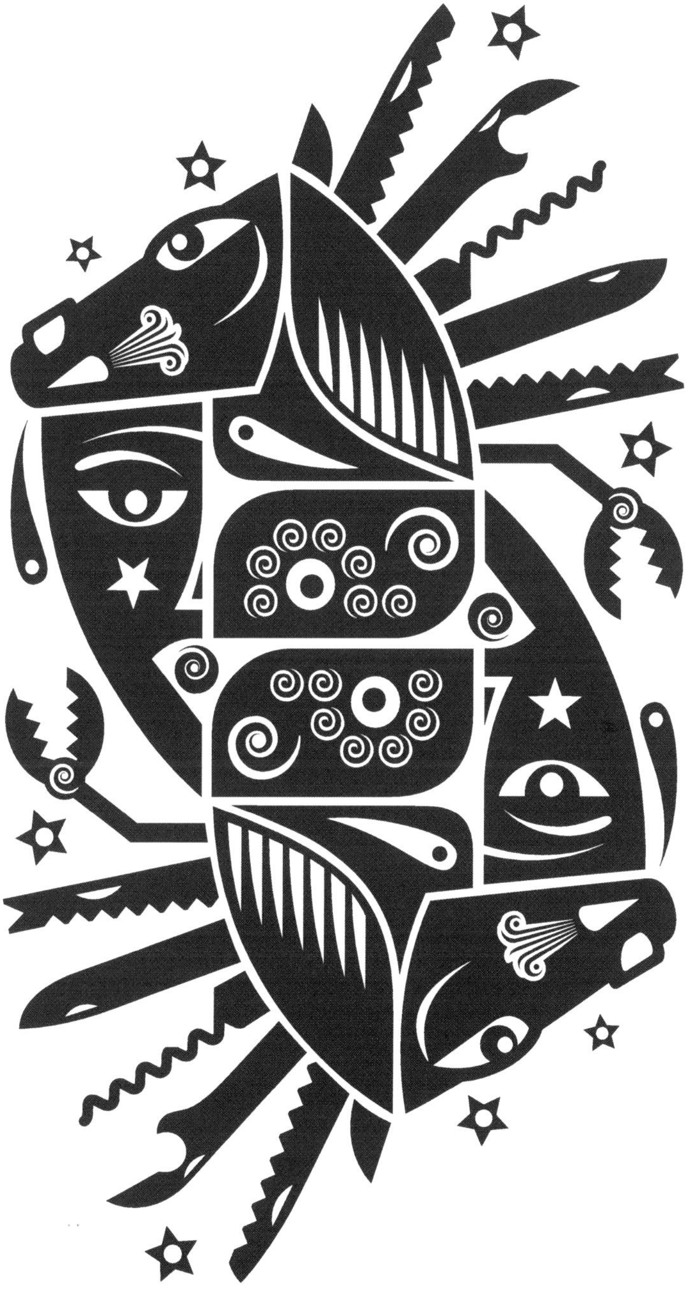

its enormous body out of the shallow waters. When they reached the deep ocean, the monster suddenly opened its cavernous mouth, and out of it emerged a powerful hurricane. It swung the war machine so high, the king could see the curvature of the earth, and right then and there, the mighty monarch sensed his impending defeat.

As he fell back down through the stormy atmosphere, his coiffure ruined by the wind, he said, "Oh, what a shame! I was blinded by my own hubris. Had I emasculated this monster, I would have remained alive, albeit less famous."

He barely finished his contemplation when the monster caught his body with its tentacles and slowly dragged him underwater.

"Puny human," it said, "did you really think I'll let you die so quickly? Don't you know there's no greater pleasure than watching the spark of life shimmer out like a candle in the wind?"

That was the end of the greatest monarch that ever lived. Trapped inside the belly of the monster, the kidnapped queen watched her husband's demise. As his lungs slowly filled with salty water, she wiped her tears, blew one last kiss, and continued knitting.

Epilogue: In vino veritas

"FOR THE LOVE OF VULNICURUS!" shouted the margrave. "Suddenly when I hear the word Trondheim, I get sick to my stomach."

The door opened and a servant holding a silver platter entered the throne room. "The wine, Your Highness!"

"Oh, your words are nectar for my ears! Serve it swiftly before my insides shrink into a singularity," said Sophisticus. "I've just been told the most repulsive story ever."

Sophisticus rashly dismissed the servant and opened a closet near the throne. He reached behind a row of hanging clothes and took out a small flask.

"Let's spice up this wine!" he said.

"What's this?" asked Isidore.

"Lilac poppy tincture. It lightens my mood in moments of severe despair. I got it from a vagabond queen that passed by not so long ago. She was quite something, that woman. Unfortunately, at my age, I could barely keep up with her, if you know what I mean." Sophisticus grinned, reminiscing about their encounter. "I had to let her go. A woman of such beauty needs a lover that can chase her around the bedroom, not a father figure that falls asleep before dinner. My advisers were all too happy when she went away. They said she was distracting me from my duties. Sometimes I think they are closeted atheists, because if they ever read the scriptures, they would know the whole point of love is to distract from the mundane."

"I wholeheartedly agree," said Isidore.

"You're a wise young man, aren't you," said Sophisticus, "Here, give it a try!"

He handed the flask to Isidore, who removed the cap and was just about to pour some of the liquid in his glass when the margrave stopped him.

"No, you're supposed to sniff it. Hold it under your nostrils and inhale as deep as you can."

"It must be quite strong," said Isidore.

When still, the tincture was pitch black, but when he tilted the flask, he saw a fluorescent lilac trace. He closed his eyes and inhaled. The flavor was intense, but pleasant. A cooling sensation went up Isidore's nose and spread all over his forehead. The muscles on his face instantly relaxed. His mind would have started drifting, if the voice of Sophisticus didn't take him out of his trance.

"Now take a sip of wine, quickly!" said the margrave.

Isidore had to make an effort to reach his glass. It felt like it was miles away, and the high made his head extremely heavy. His lips barely touched it, and the wine streamed into his mouth like a waterfall on whose edge he saw himself, ready to dive down its bubbling abyss. He flung his body in the air and felt a sense of omnipotence, as if the world—no, not the world, the entire Universe—started revolving around him. Everything obeyed his will. A flick of an eyebrow made the moon jiggle in its orbit, and this amused and terrified him. His newfound power brought such overwhelming sense of responsibility that his body froze mid-air, unwilling to disturb the natural balance. He stared down the waterfall and realized it was all an illusion. But what a grandiose illusion! He was inside his own self, observing his own mind in a moment of genuine introspection, unrestrained by logic or physicality. And right then, his body sprang back into motion, blessed with the limitless freedom that only gods possess. This world was his own creation. He could do whatever he wanted without guilt or remorse. He jumped, dragging all celestial bodies behind his back, as if they were tethered to his mind. As they crashed into each other and crumbled into smithereens, he dived into the waterfall. There was no resistance, the liquid embraced him like a cushion. He felt peaceful and complete. And then it was over. Isidore was sitting in the chair, his lips touching the glass. He had just taken a sip of wine.

"Nice, eh?" said Sophisticus, "Now it's my turn. Hand me that flask."

The margrave inhaled and took a sip. "Heaven!" he said. "Every time I do it, I find myself taking a nap on her plump bosom."

Deafening thunder shook the air. Screams echoed on the halls of the castle, then a shattering burst faded into ominous silence.

"He's here," said the margrave.

They heard footsteps. The pace was irregular: one, two, three—pause; the sound of metal scratching the marble floor. Another step—silence; then a sudden roar, a blunt hit, a porcelain vase or a bust of a famous ancestor crashing down, and then—a manly whistle, steady and powerful, emerging from chest that could hold a lot of air. Suddenly, a flourish, the chirping of a little bird, trembling and helpless. Then a tinge of impatience. The chirping turned to shrieking, as if coming from a bird that's hungry. Another step, two, three—and a knock on the door. A knock that, instead of *Please let me in*, said *Get ready to soil your pants because I'm coming in anyway...*

The massive door flew off with a bang, flipped in the air, and landed right in front of Sophisticus. Isidore blinked. Under the gaping frame stood Occam, face splattered in blood, chest bare, arms and legs smeared with sweat and mud. His clothing was skimpy. A thick leather belt ran across his waist. A ruffled sporran barely covered his manhood. In his right hand there was a vermilion breastplate; the other held an axe whose blade was dripping with blood.

"Well," said Occam with a voice whose low frequencies could be heard by elephants miles away, "I see you started the party without me."

Isidore blushed. Occam's gaze was a devastating weapon—his pitch black eyes could enchant even the most righteous of souls. Isidore realized why men like him were so dangerous—it wasn't fear that put them on a pedestal. They had the power to subdue their victims, to make them fall on their feet voluntarily and beg for the privilege to die.

"What do you want?" said Sophisticus.

"Whatever you can offer," said the barbarian, and turned his gaze to the margrave. "Besides your life, which is already mine."

Now it was the margrave's turn to experience the power of the barbarian's eyes.

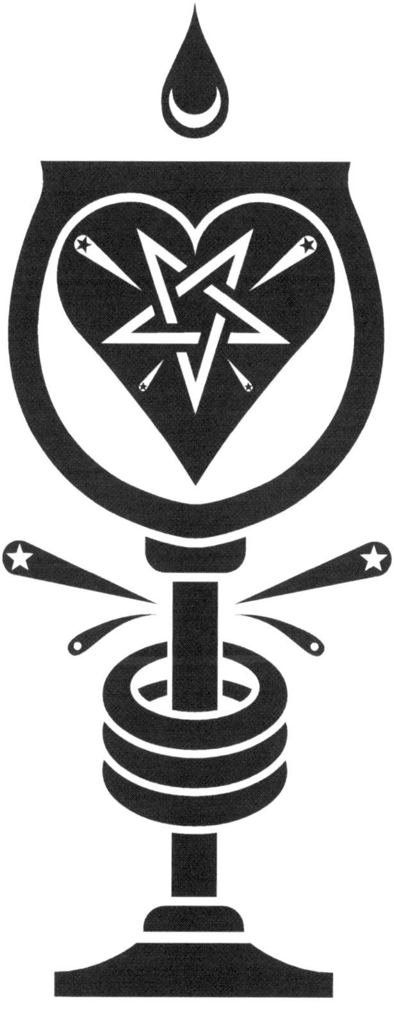

"Wine," he said meekly, "with crackers. There must be some left..."

Occam took the jug and sniffed. "I don't drink fermented piss." He grinned and dropped the jug on the floor. The shattering noise made the margrave shiver.

"And what's this?" asked Occam.

"A tincture from lilac poppies," said the margrave. "It's a rare gift from a queen..."

"Girly drink," said Occam and grabbed the flask.

"Don't be misled by its appearance," said Isidore, "it's powerful beyond compare."

"Beyond compare?" asked the barbarian. "Are you challenging me, beardless boy?"

"I would never dare to challenge you, sir! But as your servant, it is my duty to warn you. This drink is laced with dangerous magic."

Occam's face soured up. His nostrils flared. "I was nursed by a witch and baptized with scorpion blood. No magic has power over me!" he shouted.

The barbarian swallowed the tincture in one gulp. He proudly wiped his beard and tried to open his mouth, presumably to burp, although no one could be sure about that because suddenly his face froze and his menacing gaze turned vacant. His last sigh, carrying the scent of roasted cattle and fried onions, dispersed before it could reach Isidore's nose, like a frail cloud over a scorching desert.

Occam the Barbarian, the greatest warlord of all time, who killed a python with his bare hands when he was five, broke the neck of a horse when he was ten, strangled an elephant when he was fifteen, and impregnated thirty women on his twentieth birthday, never moved again, forever suspended in the greatest illusion of power a human could experience. It was a worthy destiny for a man who didn't want to settle for anything less than everything.

The Masks of Beauty

LONG TIME AGO, THERE LIVED A PRINCE of unsurpassed wit and intelligence—qualities that in the lands of the Orient weren't usually associated with his gender because men there were prized not for their brains but for their appearance. The prince had crooked eyes, a nose like a beak of an eagle, and a mouth like an incision done by a distracted plastic surgeon. While the faces of beautiful men were often compared to the moon, his one was likened to an asteroid knocked off-orbit by an icy comet. This unfortunate appearance was blamed on his mother's incessant drinking. Actually, the prince was cursed way before conception by a powerful witch that by sheer negligence wasn't invited to the wedding of his parents.

Like all oriental rulers, the queen yearned to have a daughter, but despite the efforts of her one hundred and one husbands, who made love to her every single night, she never conceived again. Heartbroken, the queen dedicated her life to her disadvantaged son. She helped him cultivate the self-esteem of a woman, and educated him in all female virtues, for she knew that—as the superior sex—women could get away with everything in life, including being hideously ugly. Thanks to her, the prince overcame prejudice and defied stereotypes to become one of the most learned people in the queendom. There wasn't a problem he couldn't resolve. Drought-inflicted famines became distant memories after he engineered ingenious aqueducts that brought water to the most remote places. Diseases like smallpox disappeared overnight after he synthesized a medicine he called a *vaccine*. In a society where the best a man could hope for was becoming a brainless muse for artistic women obsessed with square buttocks, his example brought hope and sense of dignity to millions. Yet, despite his intellectual prowess, he had an unfulfilled dream that secretly tormented him. He yearned to experience a passionate kiss at least once in his life. Sadly, his face provoked such instinctive revulsion that people couldn't bear looking at it. The dedication with which everyone genuflected—firmly bowing their heads, then rising back on their feet as slowly as possible—was less about respect and more about avoiding eye contact. To make things worse, every year the masters of ceremony added new gestures. How could people express the scope of their gratitude by simply bending a knee, they asked. It was far more adequate to prostrate oneself fully, count to three, then bend backwards, head down and buttocks up, exhale deeply, and gently rise forward. The prince realized that if he didn't do something, royal protocol will become more complex than abstract mathematics.

He tried various solutions. Instead of facing his subjects, he kept his head turned sideways, minimizing eye contact. The he decided to avoid brightly lit places. Unfortunately, rather than hiding the horrifying facial features, flickering candlelight emphasized them in such a gruesome way that the chief of royal security, shaken by fear during a sudden encounter with the prince, wet his pants and—embarrassed by the public humiliation—resigned from his post and retreated to a monastery.

There was only one person in the world immune to the looks of the prince: his imaginary friend Ja'phar, who spent most of his time locked in the closet but gladly came out for a chat if he heard the prince sob in his bed.

"There, there," said Ja'phar and patted the prince on the back. "What seems to be the problem today?"

"Oh, dear friend," replied the prince. "This queendom is falling apart because of my hideous looks, and there's nothing I can do about it!"

"Stop crying like a man and woman-up a little bit," said Ja'phar and handed him a napkin. "I have the perfect solution."

The imaginary friend started pacing around the room like someone who had been given a huge opportunity to prove himself after years of undeserved neglect.

"First," said Ja'phar and cracked his fingers, "we need the best gemstones from the treasury. Second—we need cardboard. Third—metal wire. Fourth—glue. And fifth..." He scratched his head and frowned. "Damn, I don't remember the fifth thing. I knew I had to write this down the moment it came to me but I was in the shower all soaped up and..."

"Calm down," said the prince, "Good ideas don't disappear so easily. It will come back eventually, but the harder you push, the longer it will take."

"Oh, I know," said Ja'phar, "but don't you sometimes wish life was much simpler? Because I thought well, I could come out of the shower all wet and bubbly but then I'd make a mess on the floor and I'd have to mop everything. I'm getting depressed just picturing it."

"Well, there's nothing you can do about it right now, so let's just go to sleep," said the prince. "When I said the queendom was falling apart, I didn't mean it would be gone in an hour..."

"Scissors!" shouted the imaginary friend. "Scissors! That's the last thing we need to make you a beautiful, wonderful, awe-inspiring mask that..."

Ja'phar had a habit to disappear mid-sentence, usually during a climactic moment. The prince never got the chance to discuss matters of common courtesy with his imaginary friend because his appearances were just as sudden. However, this time he refused to brush it aside, so he knocked on the closet door.

"Hey, Ja'phar," he said. "It's not polite to disappear like this. And also, I can use your help with that mask. I mean, I don't want you to do it for me, but it was your idea, and if you give me a hand, we'll do it quicker."

The closet was silent.

"Oh well," said the prince and sighed. "I guess I will have to do it all on my own, like everything else."

And so he worked tirelessly for three days and three nights, and lo an behold, he produced a mask whose beauty could rival that of the Goddess herself. The prince was so happy with it that he couldn't bring himself to take it off even when he went to bed.

One night, a beautiful girl with a face like the full moon appeared in his dream, strolling carefree on a field of lilac poppies. Her smile shone brighter than the sun, and her lips looked as if they were made of cotton candy that could melt as soon as they touched the tip of his tongue. The prince felt a tickle in his stomach and heard it purring. A swarm of butterflies swirled around his body and dispersed all over the field. The carefree giggle of the girl merged with the silent flaps of the butterflies, whose wings, tainted by pollen, carried the sweet smell of lilac poppies in the air.

The prince marveled at the sight for a while before his mind, spurred by the cynicism of reason, realized it was too good to be true.

"Obviously, I am dreaming, which is quite disappointing," he thought. "However, now that I'm aware of it, I can do whatever I want."

Indeed, people who experience lucid dreams are capable of wonders, for when the human mind is at rest but self-aware, it becomes omnipotent like that of a god.

"Hello there," said the prince and waved at her.

"Hello," replied the girl, "Are you from here?"

The prince had never enjoyed the company of someone who didn't know him. It felt nice.

"I live nearby," he said. "Can I help you with anything?"

"I'm looking for a prince," she said, "I'm supposed to marry him."

He was a prince alright, and a bachelor. Perhaps he should reveal his real identity?

"I'd be happy to help you find him," he said instead.

The girl smiled. "You're too kind. Especially for a man with a scary mask. Are you an actor by any chance?"

"Oh no, I am…"

Thunder echoed all over the field. The sky turned black and the prince woke up in his bedroom.

"What a strange dream!" he thought and went back to sleep.

To his surprise, everything repeated itself the following night.

"This is quite unusual," thought the prince when he woke up, "I should probably consult a specialist about it."

He summoned the best psychoanalysts in the queendom. The first one was the founder of the structuralist school and was known to her disciples as the Shrink of the West, for that's where she lived and taught. The second one was a self-proclaimed culturalist known as the Shrink of the East, a nickname she despised because she detested categorization based on geography.

"It's very straightforward," said the Shrink of the West after she heard all the details of the prince's dream. "The girl symbolizes all royal subjects who live in blissful ignorance, unaware of the inner workings of governance or the delicacies of good taste."

"I beg to differ," interrupted the Shrink of the East. "If we have to treat the girl as a symbol—which is such an oppressive concept—let's at least not insult her dignity by implying she's ignorant. She's just a manifestation of the innate affinity to wonder that each of us possessed as a child until it was brutally suppressed by social norms."

"Gentlewomen," said the prince, "there is no need for heated arguments, for I can see merit in both interpretations. But what really interests me is why my mask bothered her."

"You have to understand, Your Highness," began the Shrink of the West, "that you can't expect much from plain people. Perhaps you remember the story of Queen Nuncaguapa II, who fell in love with a simpleton. She had just signed a peace treaty that ended a devastating war with her sister's queendom and was on her way to her capital, when she passed by a sprawling wheat field. There she spotted a shirtless peasant wielding a sickle. She hadn't touched a man since she singed an armistice nearly six months ago. In those days people believed that having sex weakened one's resolve during peace negotiations. Besides, Nuncaguapa

II couldn't risk sleeping with the enemy by mistake—the palace where she stayed was swarming with agents. Even masturbation was a struggle, for she had a habit of shouting state secrets when she climaxed. Her intelligence service hired an orchestra and staged concerts in her bedroom to help her unwind. Alas, soon the practice had to be discontinued due to complaints from the neighbors. When she finally headed home after the peace ceremony, she sent a pigeon to her palace with instructions for an opulent orgy, because—as a victorious sovereign who hadn't had sex in six months—she felt entitled to satisfy her most basic instincts. It was shortly after that moment when she spotted the simpleton. His plain looks aroused her appetite for manly caresses so much that she commanded her ladies-in-waiting to kidnap him. The feisty man put up a fight. Three of the most revered ladies fell to their death by his sickle. He was ultimately apprehended and brought to the queen's harem, where he was examined by the nuns, who made sure he was a virgin, shaved his beard, and depilated his body, as it was customary in high society. He was then anointed with myrrh and dressed in silk. When night fell, the nuns brought him to the queen, who—to everyone's surprise—reprimanded them for grooming the simpleton. Then she tore down the expensive garments and stripped him naked. 'You reek of hyacinth and myrrh,' she said, 'but I prefer the scent of your hairy armpits. Put on your smelly rags and strap a saddle on me, so I can experience bliss like the donkey you ride on your way back from harvest.' The ladies-in-waiting tried to dissuade the queen from committing such preposterous act of institutional humiliation, but their pleas only made Nuncaguapa II angrier and she sent them away. Due to this breach of courtly protocol there were no witness accounts of the copulation, but anonymous sources claimed the queen and the simpleton committed insurmountable acts of perversion until, as the first rays of the morning sun shot over the horizon, they collapsed exhausted. From then on, the peasant became the queen's favorite lover. Even when she craved some diversity in the company of men of proper lineage, she demanded they be dressed in rags. Soon the entire court followed suit, and—as elegance and good manners gave way to crassness and recklessness—our civilization descended into the Dark Ages. This is the fate that awaits aristocrats who mingle with peasants, for their vulgar taste is contagious. Your mask is a masterpiece best appreciated by enlightened souls."

"Nonsense," objected the Shrink of the East, "the use of didactic stories as debate arguments would have been adequate during the reign of Nuncaguapa II but we live in a modern world. Your Highness, I won't waste your time with anecdotes about historical characters, whose lives are often romanticized with blatant disregard for the facts. Queen Nuncaguapa II was known for her bad taste way before she met her paramour, who by the way wasn't a peasant but a soldier and didn't wear rags but military uniforms. It's true that people from high society have sophisticated taste. After all they have the necessary time to indulge in aesthetic pursuits, and thus their idea of beauty can—quite understandably—appear meaningless to peasants and soldiers who are busy ensuring the survival of everyone in our society. Beauty is a construct that reduces cognitive load on the human mind. In most cases, it employs repetitive geometry, like the colored ceramic tiles in your bathroom. Everything beautiful can be reduced to a string of repeating numbers, but not everyone has the time or the tools to engage in such pursuits. For common people your mask might be just a mask, and in some instants, it could appear even threatening. Most likely the girl in your dream felt uncomfortable because she couldn't look you in the eyes."

"I see you're still fond of plain explanations," said the Shrink of the West to her colleague.

"The secret for a good life lies in simplicity, my dear," countered the Shrink of the East. "Yet, how would someone so fond of baroque fairy tales know that!"

"Gentlewomen, it's obvious that reaching an understanding won't be possible at this point," said the prince, whose head was starting to hurt. "I am deeply thankful for the advice you shared with me and I will take it into account. You're free to go!"

A mask is just a mask. What an unsettling assumption! The prince knew that occasionally people chose to ignore beauty, even to rebel against it. But it had never occurred to him that some of them might be innocently unaware of its existence. Wasn't beauty supposed to be equally obvious to all?

On the following night the prince decided to take off his mask before he went to bed. He carefully loosened the strings and pulled it away. The cool night air caressed his deformed face. It was a pleasant feeling, one he had forgotten—if he ever noticed it at all. Like so many of us, he rarely paid attention to the small things in life.

When he fell asleep, he found the girl on the same field, strolling around the lilac poppies. She greeted him with a beautiful smile.

"What a wonderful surprise!" said the girl, who could barely contain her joy.

The prince, as if drawn by an invisible force, felt the space between them collapse until his face was just a breath away from hers.

"It really *is* you—the prince of my dreams," she said. "I've searched for you so long, I was beginning to think you were a figment of my imagination!"

"I'm afraid that I'm the one who's dreaming, although I desperately wish you were real," said the prince.

"My dear, I am as real as the sun that rises every morning," said the girl, "though I can only reach you in your dreams."

"How can this be?" asked the prince.

The girl leaned in and pressed her lips against his. In his mind, the prince had kissed a million imaginary girls, but never felt a thing. Unlike some of his superstitious subjects, he knew dreams were based on experience. Since he never experienced a kiss in real life, his mind couldn't recreate it, even as a fantasy. In moments of desperate loneliness he even kissed his own hands, sliding his tongue between his fingers, yearning for a moment of intimacy that so many others took for granted. Like someone trying to tickle himself, his efforts were futile and brought him nothing but bitterness and self-pity. Yet this time the kiss left him breathless, for it felt exactly as he *wished* it would.

"Now you know what I mean," she said.

As their lips separated, leaving a string of glittering saliva, he peered into her eyes and saw his reflection. His face had lost its morbid dreadfulness. It was glowing.

"I don't know who you are," said the prince, "but I feel like I've known you all my life."

"My dear, my name is Delilah and I'm a princess from the Far East. You and I have been bound by love, which is the greatest force in the world. It is stronger than gravity and fills the void of existence with purpose and meaning. Every morning, when the sun rose over the dark waters of the Great River, I blew a kiss to the first ray of light, hoping to reach you. I knew that one day you would find me and come to me, so we could live happily ever after. Not even death, the destroyer of delights and parter of companions, would have the power to keep us apart."

"My dear princess, I would give my life to be with you," said the prince, "but how can I reach you when no human has wandered as far as the edge of the horizon? The road to the Far East is full of mortal dangers and even great kings with mighty armies have met their end trying to reach it."

"Fear not the obstacles between us, beloved, for there is no greater weapon than love. The great kings that died in those dangerous lands were driven by hubris and their soldiers followed them out of greed and lust for plunder. Our love is pure, and no monster can stand on its way. The thousand-headed hydra that lurks in the mountains—and whose venom can melt the breastplate of the god of war himself—will only wag its tail as you pass by. The spiders of the steppe, who are thirsty for the blood of brave soldiers, will run from you like cockroaches. The terror birds of the planes will do you no harm, for even they are not immune to love and know its wonders when they see it. Have no fear, my prince, for our union is nigh!"

On the next morning, the prince ordered his servants to saddle the best horse in the kingdom and bid farewell to his subjects. His mother, whose heart broke at the news of his departure, dispatched three thousand soldiers to guard him along the way. A third of them were eaten by the thousand-headed hydra. Another thousand were sucked dry like raisins by the spiders of the steppe. When the last of the soldiers were snatched by the terror birds and torn to pieces to feed their chicks, the prince had to continue his journey alone, without guide or food supplies. Yet to his surprise, each day a certain monster came to his rescue: a steel-skinned lynx brought him fish and water, a fire-breathing boar—truffles and mead, and a four-winged wolf—roasted lamb and beer. As for the direction, the prince was guided by the wind itself, for its gentle blows roused the moisture from the kiss of the princess and kept him straight on course.

For three months and three weeks he traveled and on the third day of the fourth week he reached the Kingdom of the Great River, where to his surprise people instantly recognized him. He received a warm welcome. Only a couple of children, who didn't yet know the intricate rules of good manners, made fun of him shouting, "The monster has come to meet his monstress!"

When she overheard the jubilant hustle, the princess went out on the balcony of the palace and saw her beloved approaching. She wore a mask of glittering gemstones and precious metals and when she removed it, she revealed a hideous face with sunken eyes that had the color of a swamp. Her mouth resembled a fading crescent, arching over a double chin that hung above her throat like a rooster's wattle. Her subjects, disturbed by her looks but nevertheless loyal, continued to cheer. Perhaps now that she had found love, her face would brighten a bit, they thought. Or perhaps it won't. After all, she was a woman, and—unlike in queendoms—in kingdoms women didn't age gracefully, whether they were single or married.

"You made it, my love," she said, and as tears of happiness dripped over her slimy cheeks, she rushed down the stairs of the palace to meet him. The sun itself rejoiced, for it had never seen such wonders happen on Earth. The prince and the princess married on the next day and lived happily for many years. When finally death came to visit them, it took them in their sleep and carried them to the heavens, where to this day they wander together in the void of space as comets. Each time they appear on the night sky, they cause fear and havoc, for people still don't have eyes for their beauty, which—due to naivety and ignorance—in the minds of mortals looks terrifying.

Genesis

LOOKING DOWN GAVE HER VERTIGO of the worst kind, for it wasn't her body that became dizzy, but her mind. She had a faint memory that bothered her deeply—once upon a time she understood the world. She could grasp what was going on, no matter how awkward or unexpected it was. As time passed by, this memory grew so distant, she began to doubt it was real.

The uncertainty spread like a virus and infected her entire mind. Now even her own existence smacked of self-inflicted illusion. Did she really create the world and all living things in it? Or did she stumble upon it by accident and liked it so much that she wished she would have created it herself, and thus her wish came true? One thing she learned throughout her eternal life was how dangerous her wishes were. They materialized instantly. If she envied humans, it wasn't because they were mortal. It was because their wishes never came true exactly as they expected them. They could keep on daydreaming, over and over, caught in the bliss of perpetual dissatisfaction. She couldn't understand their complaints, how they wanted this and that, and how it always slipped out of their grasp. If she strained her ears, she could hear the constant buzz of their ridiculous prayers that, over such great distance, stretched to barely distinguishable white noise: blah, blah, blah.

Was it her fault? Perhaps she didn't explain life to them properly? To her credit, she did try, repeatedly. She lost count of all the holy books she inspired, all the legions of angels she sent with detailed instructions about what should and shouldn't be done, all the epileptic fits she caused in so many prophets who were supposed to tell her story with pristine accuracy. And each time the same pattern would emerge: people would get excited, do as they were told for a while, then get bored, and twist her words in a such a way, she couldn't recognize them anymore. How else could one tribe worship her as a goddess of war and another as a goddess of love? And—she shuddered to think—some humans even had the audacity to change her gender and picture her as a male. Can you imagine? She, whose breasts, despite her eternal existence, were still perky as those of a sixteen-year-old virgin! She, whose curvy thighs, wrapped around her fragile singularity, extended from one end of the Multiverse to the other? A penis dangling in between wasn't just a stupid idea. It would cause a devastating cosmic rash. Due to inter-universal gravity, whole regions of hyperspace would collapse, annihilating at least a million universes and wrecking another fifty billion, from her belly button all the way down to her knees. It would take her insurmountable amounts of time to undo the damage—and due to mental entropy, at the end of it, she would have long forgotten what she was supposed to do.

Or perhaps it wasn't the humans? What if it was her? What if she really was a goddess of war, got bored, wished herself out of existence, then returned as a harbinger of love? And what if, as lovely as her body was, and as much as she enjoyed playing with it in front of her heavenly mirror, she somehow grew tired of her own beauty, like perverts grow tired of missionary sex, and transformed herself into a male at some point in time?

Calm down and breathe deeply, she said to herself. She stretched her left leg and bent her back until her right arm touched her toes. A gentle breeze brought the sweet smell of a scented candle burning somewhere. Lilac poppy was her favorite flavor. It helped her relax. Omm! Hold this position for five seconds, she murmured in her mind, release the tension in the gluteus, then let go and switch sides. Feel the peacefulness! Don't yield to desire! Desire is confusion. Desire is for humans. Oh, how she wished to be human! Just for a d...

The Seed of Love

Meconopsis violacea

AT FIRST LOOK, nobody could distinguish the lilac poppy from its more common counterpart, *Papaver rhoeas*. Both plants looked identical, down to the smallest detail. The differences became apparent only when people dug into the soil. The common poppy had a fairly unremarkable root system. Below the stem of the lilac poppy, however, hung a large spheric bulb, whose shell was so hard, it could be broken only with a large knife called machete. Inside this shell grew the actual plant, completely independent from its sophisticated disguise that extended overground. The bulb enclosed a mini ecosystem that contained everything necessary for the development of the poppy. It also served as protection against animals—neither the beak of a rukh nor the teeth of a desert rabbit could penetrate it.

Machete-wielding humans had to be careful when they attempted to crack the shell, lest they were hit by a spontaneous discharge of static electricity. A poor boy from Qurtubah called Juan accidentally invented a technique that was one hundred percent safe—a precise blow delivered at a thirty-six-degree angle adjacent to the vertical axis of the nut. He became the most celebrated barista of all time, but died untimely because he tripped on his measuring tape and stretched the unit markings, right before he was about to crack a particularly big nut. Due to the skewed measurements, the angle of the hit was two degrees off, and Juan's body was completely incinerated.

The dangerous volatility of the bulb inspired its common name, *thunder nut,* while the lilac poppy it hosted was known to scientists as *Meconopsis violacea*. Generations of botanists scratched their heads wondering how anything in nature could look so blatantly contrived. No theory hatched by a human mind could unveil the mystery of the complex pseudo-mimicry. The best guess was that millions of years ago, the plant currently enclosed in the bulb used to grow in the open air, until it was threatened by an insatiable herbivore that developed a pathological addiction to it. The animal nearly exterminated the entire species of the so-called proto-lilac poppy *(Meconopsis violacea antiqua, subsp. aeria)*. Luckily, a small patch developed a tumorous growth that encapsulated it completely. Then—by the mysterious ways of the Almighty Evolution—it buried its body and camouflaged itself with an extra growth that happened to look exactly like the common poppy, which the herbivore found repulsive. Naturally, this theory was ridiculously wrong, for the plant originated not on Earth, but high in the heavens.

Heaven's High

D EEP IN THE BARREN DESERT, in a place even the lightest seeds carried by the coastal wind couldn't reach, stood a pillar so tall, it extended all the way to the sky. On a clear day people could spot it from hundreds of miles. Its defiant elegance was best admired from afar, since the sands around it were infested with scorpions as big and cunning as lions. They were rarely seen but often heard—aroused by the scorching sun, those creatures spent their days mating. Their moaning was irresistible to humans. Nearby travelers were mesmerized by it and, armed with nothing but fearless curiosity, headed straight to the scorpion nests.

The sight of the monsters locked in a passionate embrace inspired such awe that when they saw them, people tore up their clothes and fell on their knees. They chanted prayers to Ibliz, the goddess of the desert, and offered their bodies as sacrifice. When their pleas reached a crescendo, the male scorpions swung their powerful tails and cracked open the rib cages of the entranced travelers, exposing their beating hearts. The female scorpions then moved over and laid hundreds of fertilized eggs inside them. Despite the mortal injuries, the victims remained alive. Some scientists attributed this miracle to Ibliz herself, others swore that until it was fully metabolized, the venom of the creatures granted immortality to the infected body. Three weeks later, a swarm of larvae burst out of the cavities, and as the power of the venom subsided, the victims were finally allowed to die, brokenhearted.

A reclusive sect of idolaters called *romantics* considered this the sweetest of deaths and cherished it passionately. Unfortunately, they lived around the coast and couldn't travel freely in the desert, out of fear the dry air would damage their tender skin. It was common knowledge that a romantic couldn't survive without a moisturizer for more than a day, and there was only so much one could load on a camel without breaking its back.

For another sect of less tender souls called *theosophists*, the pillar was a triumph of divine spirit over crude matter. Led by a boisterous woman called Helen, they attempted to establish a monastery in the vicinity and harvest venom for medicinal purposes. There was a sudden increase in scorpion population exactly three weeks after their arrival. Nobody ever heard of them again.

The honor of surviving a visit to the pillar was bestowed to a more prosaic figure—a deaf merchant called Odissius who traded silk underwear in the Orient. Unlike other merchants, he couldn't chant about the qualities of his goods, so instead he used a slogan written on the sides of his cart in bold gold letters. It said:

Caress for the groins! Caress for the groins! Come and try it on for free!

This unique advertising method made him famous and provoked a debate among academics. "A brave new age has dawned in the world of global trade," said one professor. "The time when people buy with their eyes instead of their ears is upon us."

The cosmopolitan brothels around the Talas Corridor were the biggest buyers of underwear, and in one of them, near the city of Qurtubah, Odissius met a prostitute named Ib. He became her favorite client because his disability brought her great relief—most men asked her to moan excessively during sex, which she found pointless and exhausting. A silent lover, Odissius offered her a much needed respite, and occasionally she even dozed off, lulled by his rhythmic thrusts and the heaviness of his body, under which she felt safe and comfortable like a suckling under the belly of its mother.

One day, frustrated after a round of negotiations with a stubborn middleman, Odissius went to Ib and offered to pay her double if she moaned and called him *Supreme Master of Trade* during sex, even though he wouldn't be able to hear her.

"I knew this day would come," said Ib. "Sooner or later, due to the limits of their feeble imagination, men turn sex into a power play. Frankly, I should be surprised it took you this long to ask for it. But know this: if you reconsider your decision and have sex with me like you always do, and if at the end I experience the tickling sensation that starts in my belly, shoots up my back, and makes the hair on my neck bristle with electricity, I shall truly help you become the Supreme Master of Trade."

Odissius tore her silk dress and did as she requested. He sucked her left breast, then the right one, then squeezed them both together and sucked them all at once as she was biting her lips in blissful silence. When his tongue slid down her belly, her arms suddenly let go of his neck and, like fish out of water, dropped on the bed, twitching helplessly. He buried his face between her legs, as if he was peeking through a window on the first morning of spring, which was a season that didn't exist in those lands, for they were permanently ravaged by the merciless heat of the Oriental sun.

"If only all men were like him," she thought, "there wouldn't be sadness in this world!" Like a missionary spreading holy scripture among pagans, she was certain she had experienced something other people hadn't, and—aware of how fragile that experience was—she wanted to share it with the entire human race, for she knew this was the only way a blessing could outlast the feeble existence of the person it had been granted to.

"Since you did as I asked and left no part of my body unkissed, I shall keep my promise," said Ib at the end, using the sign language of tented nomads which consisted of finger flicks. "Know, my dear, that deep in the Barren Desert there is a pillar so high, its top pierces the firmament that separates Heaven from Earth. It leads to a palace above the clouds so abundant with riches, it could put the wealthiest queens to shame. No human has ever reached it, since the pillar is guarded by bloodthirsty arachnids called *sirens*. Their songs are deadly but would pose no threat to you, since you have been blessed with the gift of deafness. Yet the monsters would still kill you if they see you climb the pillar, and the only way to escape their vigilant eyes is through the use of magic. When you arrive at the vicinity of the pillar, turn east and recite three times the following formula:

From chaos all forms have arisen and into chaos all forms shall descend.

Then clap your hands. You will become invisible, and it will be safe to approach the pillar. Once you climb to the top, do everything in reverse. Face west, clap you hands and recite three times this formula:

Into chaos all forms have descended and from the chaos all forms shall arise.

You will regain your shape and see the gate of the palace. Knock on it three times. A woman will open and invite you to come in. She will offer you tea, but you shouldn't drink from it, for if you do, you will forget why I sent you there. Ask for a glass of water instead and complement her hospitality, for she takes great pride in accommodating her guests, whenever she's lucky to have them. She lives alone and yearns for the company of a man like the desert yearns for rain, but she will never admit it. Find a way to charm her and weaken her resolve. If she resists, unbutton the top of your shirt, so she can see the patch of hair below you neck. Her desire for you will double, and if at this point she doesn't give in to you, roll up your sleeves and let her lust after your strong male arms. If after this she is still resisting—which is unlikely—smile at her the way you smile at me, and when she sees the dimples on your cheeks, she will finally surrender. After your union, don't rush to put your clothes back on, which is a mistake many men commit out of selfishness and ignorance. Cuddle her and caress her until she falls asleep. When you hear her snoring, carefully reach under her pillow, where you will find a large bulb. Take it and leave quietly. When you come back, bury it in the fields nearby. The plant that grows out of it will make you the richest man on Earth, for its seeds, when roasted and boiled in water, produce the greatest aphrodisiac."

Odissius did as Ib told him. He arrived at the heavenly palace and knocked three times on the gate.

"I'm coming," said a voice from the other side.

When the gate opened, he couldn't believe his eyes. In front of him stood Ib, wrapped in the finest silk he had ever seen. There was a white stick between her fingers, and gray strings of smoke swirled up from its upper end. The smell was unusual, but pleasant. She looked around, as if she was expecting someone else. When she realized Odissius was alone, she gave him a piercing look. It was enough to make him feel unwelcome.

"My, my, she's full of surprises," she said.

Odissius started stuttering with his hands.

"A deaf man, of course! How else could you have gotten all the way up here," she said using the sign language of open-air nomads by gracefully waving her hands. Then she snapped her fingers and asked, "Can you hear me now?"

Odissius experienced sound for the first time in his life, yet it felt surprisingly familiar.

"I should warn you that my magic only works up here," she said, "in case you plan to go back."

"Ib," said Odissius, still stuttering, "is this you?"

"Oh dear, no," the woman laughed, "I'm Liz. Ib is my sister, and by the look on your face I can tell she didn't explain very well why she sent you here. So typical of her! Come in, the tea is getting cold!"

She led him to a room with a big round table. On it there was a steaming kettle with two porcelain cups and a basket full of fruits.

"I guess you've been expecting me," said Odissius.

"Not you, handsome! I was expecting her." Liz put the white stick in her mouth, sucked it briefly, and then let out a cloud of smoke. "We have a tea party every once in a while. It's a family tradition. She was supposed to come, but she sent you instead."

"I'm sorry to impose," said Odissius. "She should have told me the truth."

"To her credit," said Liz and sighed, "she probably didn't intend to mislead you. She's just a bit careless. Is she in trouble?"

"As far as I can tell, she's doing fine," said Odissius. "She works in a brothel and her services are in high demand. Most of her clients are boring, but you could say that about any job."

"It's been a while since I last heard of her," said Liz, "I can't figure out if that's a good thing."

"You must miss her," said Odissius.

"I do, sometimes," replied Liz. "But we get along better when we're apart."

She leaned in and ran her fingers through his hair. "You're a beautiful man. I think I know why you're here."

Caught off guard, Odissius choked on his saliva and started coughing.

"Oh dear, you need a glass of water," said Liz. She disappeared behind a curtain, but quickly returned holding a beautiful glass with sugared edges and a slice of lemon on the side. "Have a sip, darling, it will ease your discomfort."

Odissius took a gulp and unbuttoned his shirt, gasping for air.

"I'm sorry," he said when he recovered his voice, "Perhaps I got tired from the climbing."

Liz was smiling at him mischievously, her eyes feasting on the patch of hair below his neck.

"You have no idea how beautiful you are," she said. "That's a good thing. Most people who are aware of their own beauty are arrogant. Ironically there's nothing uglier than arrogance, so they end up looking hideous without knowing it. But you, oh, you're a delight to behold because you can't see what others see. Men like you turn people into poets, desperately looking for rhymes, as if their lives depend on it. Such is the power of your charm, it can make people forget to eat or sleep. But there's one thing it can't do—seduce me."

Odissius blushed.

"It's not your fault," continued Liz. "It's me. I can't lay with a man—not now, not ever. If I could, I'd be living down on Earth with my sister.

That's what she really wants. That's why she sent you here. The bulb is just a convenient pretext."

"You can't have sex?" said Odissius. "Why?"

"Look at the clock right there," said Liz.

Odissius noticed the arrows hadn't moved since he came into the room.

"Is it broken?" he asked.

Liz laughed.

"There is no time up here," she said. "Once I taste your lips, I will yearn for them forever. Even when you're long gone, when everybody who remembers you is gone as well, my desire will continue to burn. Do you have an idea what's like to miss someone eternally? Neither do I and I don't want to. Down on Earth you have it easy. Time heals every loss; it makes you forget old pleasures and seek new ones, over and over. Here, it has no power."

"Then why don't you come down and join her?" asked Odissius. "This feels like a prison."

"And leave the heavens to whom? There's only two of us. We were *meant* to be up here and take care of everything. But that's another story. Let's focus on the reason for your visit," said Liz and poured him a cup of tea. "Drink!"

Odissius looked at the cup, hesitating.

"You want the bulb, right?" said Liz. "Drink and you will have it. If I wanted to harm you, I would have done it already."

He took a sip and tried to put the cup back on the table, but the room started spinning around him. Liz grabbed his trembling hand.

"Easy," she said, "you don't want to spill that all over my carpet. I don't have a housekeeper."

He felt her breath on his cheek, still scented with the smoke of the white stick she was sucking on. He realized he was staring at her face, not because he wanted, but because it was the center around which everything was spinning. Her resemblance to her sister was uncanny even for an identical twin: from the curls of her hair locks to the tiny mole on her left cheek. He felt his lust bulging and his heart racing, but this time it was more than desire that aroused his senses. He wanted to give himself to her completely, to melt onto her skin, to reveal his deepest secrets—everything he loved, everything he feared, every deed he was ashamed or proud of. A flash of light blinded him and he lost consciousness.

Odissius woke up in his bed. He could tell it was already noon by the blinding sunlight. His sheets were drenched in sweat. He was usually up before sunrise and met his first clients shortly after breakfast. He wondered how many of them were still waiting for him today and what he could offer them in exchange for their patience. He dressed himself, folded his bedsheets, and took one last look at everything. A bed left unmade brought bad luck, especially for trade, and he never left his bedroom unless it was in perfect condition. One small detail stood out: his pillow was slightly tilted to a side. He pushed it gently. It barely moved, as if it was stuck. When he lifted it, he saw a bulb just like the one from the dream he had.

Was he really awake? Of course he was. For one, everything was quiet, just as it had always been, and in his dream he was hearing noises all the time. Also, he could feel pain when he pinched himself. Yet that bulb was still there.

There were ten people waiting downstairs. When he entered the room, they all stood up and bowed.

"Good afternoon, Supreme Master of Trade," they said.

"Good afternoon," replied Odissius. Apparently the bulb wasn't the only thing that crossed over from dream to reality. He quickly took care of his clients and headed to Ib's brothel.

"She departed this morning," said the person at the front desk, "but she left a note for you."

I will remember you until the end of time, it said.

Part Two

CODEX HYPERBOREANUS

"Fear is the evil twin of love."
Old Hyperborean proverb

Terror Birds and Wanton Hearts

Grandmistress of Fear

THERE LIVED ON THE ISLAND OF SEVERIA a queen that was vicious and dastardly. Her subjects shivered from fear every time they looked at her. Since her terrifying face was engraved on every coin, commercial activity soon ground to a halt, and the once prosperous queendom plunged into the biggest economic depression in its history.

"Your Majesty," said one day the grand vizierienne of the queen, "I realize how important it is to rule with an iron fist and instill respect in the hearts of the masses, but if you value my honest advice, I think that a brief respite—or better yet a loving gesture—might be of great benefit, for it would prevent a possible uprising by an angry mob of disillusioned peasants."

"As my most senior advisor," replied the queen, "you are allowed to speak your mind without fear of my ire, but if I were you, I wouldn't push that privilege too far. The handrails on the stairs of this palace are quite wobbly. It would be a shame to see you slip and fall over. I still mourn the loss of my treasure secretary, who rolled all the way down from the throne room to the patio like a tumbleweed. Her neck was so brutally fractured, they found her head under her armpit. I heard she was buried in a closed casket."

"Your Majesty," said the grand vizierienne, "I have sworn to serve you in life and death. I fearlessly welcome whatever fate the gods have chosen for me, even if it is to be strangled by my own intestines."

"I expect nothing less from my grand vizierienne," replied the queen, impressed by the dedication of her servant. "State your case in detail, so I can take an informed decision."

"Perhaps the best way to do so is to tell you a story from the queendom of Barbaria," replied the grand vizierienne, for it is full of plot twists that brilliantly illustrate the importance of empathy."

"Speak before I change my mind and throw you to the lions," said the queen and rolled up her sleeves.

And so, the grand vizierienne began her story...

Love in Times of Barbarity

ONCE UPON A TIME, IN THE LANDS OF BARBARIA, there lived an old queen called Dolores. Her advanced age had long eroded the pleasant memories of her youth, as well as all embarrassing mistakes she had made along the way. Every passing second added a tiny wrinkle on her skin, and it wasn't long before her soul lost its joie de vivre. She became intolerant and judgmental, especially to young people, whom she considered careless and irresponsible.

"We don't appreciate life unless we waste the first half of it," she wrote in her diary on her fiftieth birthday.

By the will of the gods, the queen's daughter, Esperanza, fell in love with a miller named Joy, whom she met at a carnival.

"Goodness gracious us," exclaimed Dolores, who always referred to herself in third person plural, "We are nauseated and dismayed at our daughter's assumption that such a sordid infatuation merits even a hint of our benevolent approval. Our answer to her reckless pleas for our blessing is a firm and generous *no,* for we can't bear the thought of callused hands scratching her delicate skin. Horror of horrors! We shall rather die than allow her royal womb be contaminated by the vulgar seed of a trivial peasant that grinds grain for a living."

Where Dolores saw uncouthness, Esperanza saw beauty. The callused hands of the miller felt like the finest silk when they were dusted with flour, while his seed tasted better than lilac honey, the most refined of sweeteners.

The princess was greatly saddened by her mother's disapproval and bitterly cried herself to sleep every night. Only her nanny sympathized with her suffering, for she was a simple woman, devoid of pretense and prejudice.

"Sweet child," she said to Esperanza and handed her a handkerchief, so the princess could wipe the dripping boogers from her nose, "you shouldn't turn crying into a habit, for instead of relief, it will only bring you bitterness. There are other men in this world. As years go by and your beauty flourishes, you will attract many dignified suitors."

"Nanny dearest," replied Esperanza, "you have always tried to console me in moments of desperation, but you must know that it is disingenuous to lie just to make people feel better. Unhappiness is best dealt with when it is acknowledged, and my tears are just an expression of my pain. They come from the depths of my heart and shall only cease when it shrivels and dries like a raisin, for love flourishes neither in dignity, nor in the hope that someone else could take the place of the beloved, but in the bliss of complete self-abandonment."

"Sweet child," said the nanny, "the words that I said were a test, for they can only console those who experience mild infatuations, but are powerless against true love. Now that I know for certain that your feelings are not superficial, I shall help you see your beloved again. Tonight, when darkness falls over the palace, I shall let the miller through the kitchen door and lead him right to your bedroom."

"Nanny dearest," said the princess, "how could I ever repay such kindness?"

"It is not gratitude that I seek, sweet child," said the nanny, "but the soothing comfort of seeing two hearts unite, for that is the rarest blessing one could ever hope for. However, you must remember that no matter how delightful your encounter might be, you have to keep silent, for any sound of excitement could alert the guards, and, gossipy as men are, they will certainly denounce you to the queen."

"I shall not let a sigh louder than a gust of breeze escape my mouth," vowed the princess.

The nanny did as promised. That same night, Esperanza and Joy embraced again, to their hearts' delight.

It is said that when lovers are meant for each other, the gods take special care to match all the curves of their bodies, so when they join, they become one, and it is not possible to see when one body ends and another begins. Had anyone peeked through the steamy bedroom window, they would have thought the blurry silhouette on the bed was that of Esperanza alone, tossing and turning in the throes of sadness. Indeed, it often happens that opposite emotions trigger similar reactions in the human body, for crying occurs both in moments of deep despair and great joy. Only observant poets know the difference, for despair paints the eyes red and causes swelling, while joy makes them glitter like emeralds under the brightest of suns.

"Take me," whispered the miller in the ear of the princess, "until there's nothing of me left!"

He thrust into her, caressing her breasts and kissing her neck. Esperanza was overcome by such intense pleasure, she forgot the warning of her nanny.

"Oh Joy, I am yours forever!" shouted the princess in ecstasy.

Like most spiteful people, the queen was a light sleeper and woke up immediately. Angered by her daughter's disobedience and the audacity of the miller, she decided to end their relationship once and for all.

"It is our responsibility as a mother," she said, "to properly educate our inexperienced progeny. We shall punish the princess by withdrawing all desserts from her diet. The peasant—whatever his name was—shall be banished by boat, for he desecrated our noble house, which is an act of high treason."

Since Barbaria was located on a peninsula protruding in the Arctic Ocean, banishment was enforced in two distinct ways, depending on the severity of the crime. People convicted of lesser treason were banished by catapult, hurled over the land frontier to the south. Many of them died from the fall. According to official data, twenty three percent survived without severe injuries.

People who committed high treason weren't that lucky. They were banished by boat in the Arctic Ocean. The freezing currents carried them farther and farther north, where there was nothing but nothingness and no hope for return.

As for her daughter, Dolores needn't have bothered issuing a punishment. The princess lost her appetite anyway, for when one's yearning for love is so brutally suppressed, body and soul quickly wither. Esperanza's fate saddened everyone: rich and poor, young and old. Even innocent babies, who didn't know the pain of a broken heart, cried louder than usual because the milk of their mothers turned sour, tainted by despair.

Before long, the first calls for open disobedience were heard on the streets. Someone scribbled the words *Heartless bitch!* on the wall of the royal palace. The Committee for Social Justice initiated a petition for the immediate pardon of the miller. A rescue team of the best navigators sailed in search for him, only to be arrested, moments before they left territorial waters. The queen sentenced them to slave labor, despite the pleas for clemency from the interior ministress herself.

"Common people are free to romanticize taboos," wrote Dolores in her verdict. "Their lives, unlike those of the aristocracy, lack a higher purpose. We have always envied them, just like we envy small children, for they don't know the burdens of responsibility. We can assure you that despite the burning anger we feel regarding the desecration of our beloved daughter, the decision to banish the filthy rascal was taken pragmatically, following the letter of the law. Any attempt to circumvent it, regardless of motivation, shall be considered an act of rebellion. We benevolently dismiss all appeals and consider the case closed."

"Down with the evil cunt," someone shouted, while the ministress of communication read the verdict on the stairs of the justice department. "Our true queen is called Esperanza and we shall fight to liberate her from this heartless tyranny."

Thus started the biggest uprising in the history of the queendom. Angry mobs swarmed the streets of the capital.

"We have come to depose the witch or die trying," they chanted.

Houses were lit on fire. Stores were looted. A group of radical charlatans hijacked the protest and declared a republic. Dolores bravely fought the peasants with her glittering sword and impenetrable armor. Her army was about to deliver the final blow and crush the uprising when suddenly, a mighty horn echoed in the air.

When the queen looked at the northern horizon she saw the most unusual sight. An army of iceberg-riding giants was approaching fast.

"Demons of ice," shouted Dolores, "be gone or face my wrath, for once I cleanse my lands from this peasant scum, I shall crush you like grapes!"

The leader of the giants spurred his iceberg. The demonic vehicle jumped out of the water and crashed onto the shore. Its body burst into smithereens that scattered all over the battlefield, trapping the royal army.

"Your sword is useless against me," said the giant. "I am Godwin the Emphatic, emperor of Hyperborea and guardian of the Scepter of Knowledge. For years I have observed you, admiring your perfectionism and pragmatism—qualities that we, the great Hyperboreans, value above everything else. However, when the poor miller arrived to our icy shores naked and shivering like a leaf, and told us how badly you have treated him, I was greatly disappointed. I realized that your severity doesn't come from restrained compassion but from spite and sheer emotional clumsiness. Thus, I have come to end your reign of terror. From this day on, the crown shall grace the head of your daughter, Esperanza, whom I shall immediately marry to her beloved and put an end to this needless suffering once and for all. I sentence you to be their maid and take care of their chamber pots."

And so Esperanza and Joy lived happily ever after until they were visited by death, the parter of companions and destroyer of delights. Glory be to the living gods for only they can judge us!

Interlude: Harnessed Icebergs

"WOULD YOU REMIND ME," said the queen to her vizierienne, "For how many years have I ruled this queendom?"

"It's been five years since you ascended to the throne, Your Majesty. May the gods extend your reign as long as possible!"

"Ever since I put this slab of gold on my head," the queen pointed to her crown, "there hasn't been a single moment when I have found my sword useless. In fact, the plating of the handle has completely worn off because there has barely been a week when I don't have to cut someone's head off, and in the meantime I use it to pick up various things."

The queen swung her sword and skillfully lifted the crown off her head. The vizierienne watched it slide down the shiny blade until it hit the bronze handle with a dull clang.

The queen was an excellent swordswoman. She mastered the weapon at the age of eight, when—according to her mother—she could slice a flying butterfly in two. On her fifteenth anniversary, she lined up her thirty six dolls and beheaded them with a single swing, proudly announcing the end of her childhood.

"There is not a problem in this world that cannot be resolved by a sword," said the queen. "It is love that complicates life and makes everyone miserable. Have I told you what happened to the ministress of finance in my mother's cabinet? She worked tirelessly for weeks to pass the annual budget. Then came her husband's birthday. She loved him far too much to just toss him a gift card, so she went shopping, even though that's not a woman's job. She picked up a beautiful fur coat and headed for the counter. Everyone knew her as an excellent administrator and talented mathematician. Unfortunately, she suffered from directional dyslexia. Instead of paying with her own money, which she always kept in her left pocket, she reached into the right one and used public funds. You can imagine what followed—a scandal, accusations of greed and corruption. A deranged social justice warrior even demanded her execution. Her husband took full responsibility. She did it out of love, he said teary-eyed, if someone should be punished, it should be me. But the same masses that indulged in fairy tales of iceberg riders avenging peasants shouted at the top of their lungs *Lock her up! Lock her up!* They were threatening to storm the palace if my mother showed any sign of clemency. The ministress was sent to jail. Her husband cut the fur coat in pieces and made mittens for thirty homeless orphans. A week later, he hanged himself in front of the tax office. I can live without a coat, he wrote in his suicide note, but without her, I'm nothing."

The queen sighed and put the crown back on her head.

"Love, my dear is the opium of the masses," she continued, "and once people get high on it, they will trample you like wild horses."

"Gods know the crowd has many flaws," replied the vizierienne, "for when people join together, their vices multiply in geometric progression. But we can also find a lot of wisdom in their melodramas because they remind us that life is not only about governing."

"Where you see wisdom, I see immaturity," said the queen. "The story you just told must have been written by pubescent boys. Only they can dream of something as ridiculous as harnessed icebergs. To think that people are entitled to satisfy the infatuations of the heart is childish. It is unfortunate, of course, that calculating taxes is not as fun as wrestling in the bedroom. Don't get me wrong! I wish the world was different, that all our desires were instantly fulfilled, that we didn't have to suffer loss and disappointment, much less anger or anxiety or loneliness. Alas, the gods reward only those who think pragmatically, while those distracted by emotions are left behind and occasionally executed for treason."

"Your Majesty is right," said the vizierienne, "for love certainly causes confusion. Yet sometimes it is the confusion itself that brings unforeseen fortune."

"Give me a single example and I promise not to cut your head off," said the queen.

And so the vizierienne began another story.

The Enchanted Stew

I HAVE HEARD, OH FORTUNATE QUEEN, that on the other side of the world, there is a country called Patasarriba where everything is upside down and people have the most peculiar customs—they put their carts before their horses and their plows before their oxen. Their days go backwards, from sunset to sunrise. Men are wiser than women, and everyone talks in reverse, which, being the norm, is considered quite natural.

Once upon a time, in those strange lands where nothing was as it seemed, lived two brothers. They were twins, identical in every way.

Not even their mother could tell them apart. As babies they cried and slept at the same time, and one would refuse to eat if the other was away. Thus they grew up, sharing everything, and nothing could ever come between them, for they knew neither envy nor jealousy.

This went on until one day they fell in love with the same woman. And because, oh fortunate queen, in those primitive times polygamy was forbidden, and men could still choose whom to marry, the brothers had to decide who would be the lucky one to take her as a wife.

"Dear brother," said the first one, "I wish I could share this woman with you like we shared our mother's milk, but since we cannot split her in two without killing her, I shall claim her solely for myself."

"Why do you think this would be the right thing to do?" asked the other.

"The reason is very simple," replied his brother. "My feelings for her are so intense that my mind knows no rest. No matter how hard I try, I can't stop thinking about her. I have therefore decided to offer her all my possessions in exchange for her hand."

"I feel exactly the same," replied the other, "and since we inherited an equal amount of wealth from our parents, none of us would have an advantage."

Unable to resolve the impasse on their own, the brothers decided to try out their luck. On the next morning, each one killed a spotted goat and cooked a delicious stew with pickled lemons and lilac garlic, following a recipe they inherited from their grandfather.

Once finished, the brothers went to a nearby hill, where centuries ago a bunch of gossipers had built a shrine. Each put a plate of stew below the statue of a man crucified on a four-leaf clover, which was exactly how the god of serendipity—who was immortal—chose to sacrifice himself for the benefit of humanity. He knew that, according to the first law of thermodynamics, the total happiness in a closed system couldn't be increased from within. Since all deities existed outside the Universe and weren't bound by its laws, the god of serendipity assumed it was possible to tweak the constant through self-inflicted suffering. He incarnated his soul into a human egg, lodged in the uterus of an unsuspecting virgin. Once he came of age, he started a disruptive cult that threatened the very foundations of civilized society and brashly challenged the authorities to execute him. He died in horrible agony. To balance things out, the level of internal happiness in the Universe increased to such an unsustainable level that a new force called *chronic dissatisfaction* spontaneously arose from the quantum vacuum to prevent the entire creation from collapsing.

Soon after, the first prayers advanced towards the heavens like a shockwave from a thermonuclear explosion, and all gods became inextricably involved in the pettiest of human affairs.

"Oh, god of serendipity, who died in our name," said the brothers in one voice, "we have brought you a delicious stew. Let the one who cooked it best win your favor and marry the woman we have both fallen in love with."

The god of serendipity, who was always hungry, immediately came down from the heavens. He ate a spoonful from each plate and pulled on his beard.

"I can't make the slightest difference, but that's probably because I'm always hungry," he said. "Fortunately, my wife, the goddess of missed opportunities, is notoriously picky and doesn't have much appetite, so I shall consult her and get back to you as soon as possible."

The god grabbed the plates and ascended to heaven.

"Try this," he said to his wife, and handed her a spoonful of stew.

"What is it?" asked the goddess of missed opportunities.

"It's the best stew I have ever eaten," said the god of serendipity.

"That doesn't say much," she replied and rolled her eyes. "You would eat demon liver if there's enough barbecue sauce to help it slide down your throat."

Little did she know that the god of serendipity ate demon liver every night, but like many other things, he kept it a secret, for he knew his wife was prone of dismissing everything adventurous.

"I can't understand people's obsession with wine," she said once to her first cousin twice removed, the god of carnivals. "It's nothing but spoilt fruit juice that people used to drink out of necessity because fresh water wasn't readily available."

She was, of course, right in theory. If back in those primitive days drinking water wasn't such a health hazard, nobody would have been experimenting with fermented liquids. Yet it wasn't the relative safety of the mild antiseptic that people found attractive. They drank wine not to quench their thirst, but to lighten their mood.

Demon liver tasted like rotten flesh, but contained a chemical that triggered a throbbing erection. It was a side effect the goddess of missed opportunities immensely enjoyed, although she had no idea what caused it.

"You're right," said the god of serendipity to his wife. "My taste buds are not nearly as sensitive as yours. That's exactly why I need your help."

The goddess of missed opportunities sniffed the spoon and raised an eyebrow.

"Is it spicy?" she asked.

"Absolutely not!" replied her husband.

She cautiously tasted the stew. After a brief pause, during which she carefully assessed her mood—for unbeknownst to her, it played a big part in the way she perceived the world—she nodded approvingly.

"Do you want more?" asked her husband.

"Maybe just another spoonful," she replied.

This time the god of serendipity dipped the spoon in the other stew and handed it to his unsuspecting wife.

"Strange," said the goddess of missed opportunities. "Now that I tried it again, it seems a bit overcooked."

Indeed, while the second brother was cooking, he lost track of time because the sound of the bubbling stew reminded him of the rumbling in his stomach when he lusted after his beloved. As a result, his potatoes became a bit too mushy.

"Whoever cooked it must have been distracted by something," said the goddess of missed opportunities.

"Thank you! That was all I needed to hear," said the god of serendipity and hurried back to the altar, where the brothers patiently waited for his judgment.

"It was a tough call," he told them. "Both meals were exquisite! However, according to my wife, the first one tasted better."

"Thank you, master of providence! I shall worship you and your wife until my dying day," said the first brother and bowed down, barely holding back his tears of joy.

"My wife would be happy to hear that," said the god of serendipity. "She is a woman that's hard to please and rewards only those who always aim to be perfect. However, my job is to look after those she unjustly ignores. You and your brother are equally skilled at cooking. His meal came second because he lost track of time, thinking of his beloved, while you, striving to follow the recipe by the letter, forgot about her."

And thus, against all odds, the second brother married the beautiful girl, while the first remained a bachelor. They lived happily ever after, until they were visited by the parter of companions. Praise be to those who focus on things that truly matter.

Interlude: Of Love and Privilege

"WOULD YOU REMIND ME," asked the queen, "what is the greatest duty of a responsible monarch?"

"Of all responsibilities resting on the blessed shoulders of our rulers, the most important one is to treat all subjects justly," replied the vizierienne.

"And what kind of treatment is considered just?" asked the queen.

"A treatment that is morally reciprocal to the deeds of the person subjected to it."

"And what if the queen finds some of her subjects more pleasant than others?"

"In this case, it is advised that the queen doesn't take into account her personal sympathies because in a just society all laws should be applied impartially, as to avoid confusion that could give rise to discontent."

"You are well read in the principles of governing and claim to be knowledgeable on the subject of love. Tell me then, why is such a benevolent force only a privilege of the beautiful? I've never heard a single love story about ugly people," said the queen.

"That's because most storytellers are biased or superficial," replied the vizierienne. "In reality, love can be experienced by everyone, regardless of appearance."

"Then, if you value your life, tell me a story that proves it," said the queen.

The Monstrous Bride

A STORY IS BEING TOLD, O FORTUNATE QUEEN, that once upon a time, in the Queendom of the Briny Lake, there lived a princess that was unusually beautiful. This was all the more surprising, for the harsh climate of this region made all its inhabitants ugly. The constant winds blowing over its salty soil made their skin coarse like sandpaper.

The princess had many suitors—men from all parts of the queendom would come to beg for her hand, but she couldn't make up her mind whom to marry, for she was afraid that people valued her most for her appearance, and not for her personality. Her indecisiveness worried her mother, the queen, because she desperately wanted to have grandchildren.

"You are still young," she said to the princess, "but there will come a time when you will regret your pickiness. People who are too demanding in their youth eventually settle for the worst once their faces wrinkle."

"Oh mother," said the princess, "faces might wrinkle and breasts might sag, for all things made of flesh are prone to decay. Unlike them, the human spirit is incorruptible and everlasting. Those who value it above everything else don't know loss or disappointment. I want a man who will love me for who I am and won't leave me when I turn fifty, just like my father, whom we haven't seen in ages."

"It is typical for the young to use wise words irresponsibly, for they can't match them with experience," said the queen. "Wisdom is like a crown—you can put it on your head and pretend you're a queen, but unless you have a loyal army and a docile government behind you, people will consider you delusional. It is unfortunate that the mistakes of the parents are so easy to spot, while those of the children are yet to be committed, but this is the way of the world, and there is nothing I can do to change it. However, you should know that your words have inflicted pain in my heart. One day you will regret them, but I won't be around to accept your apology. When that time comes, don't waste your time in useless penitence, but remember that I have already forgiven you, because my love for you is bigger than my pride, and there is no pain I wouldn't endure to make your life easier. I'd rather risk provoking your hate than letting you down. Therefore, I must warn you—if you don't pick a husband in three months, I will have no other choice but to do it for you."

It was indeed a custom in those lands for monarchs to pick a spouse for their children and the words of the queen greatly worried the princess, who swiftly sent messengers to all corners of the queendom, inviting all able-bodied men to a dating tournament.

"The winners shall be summoned to my bedroom for further questioning," she announced, "for I must marry a decent man before the leaves turn golden and the weather gets cold."

Thousands gathered below the walls of the royal castle. For three weeks they competed in all disciplines of the trivium and the quadrivium, which at that time consisted of wine tasting, oil wrestling, and mud fighting; as well as bush pruning, sheep shearing, goat milking, and horse riding. It was the beginning of summer, and the days were hot and long. The entire capital stank of sweaty armpits and musky pubes. At the end of the third week, a grand jury of female elders selected three finalists:

a knight, a merchant, and a butcher. After a mandatory shower, they were invited to the bedroom of the princess. The queen patiently waited in the hall, overjoyed that her daughter was finally about to marry. Suddenly, the princess stormed out of her bedroom, cursing.

"What happened?" asked the queen.

"Oh mother, you're asking me to do the impossible," said the princess.

"For the sake of all gods and spirits, pick the one and let's get this over with," said the queen.

"You don't understand," said the princess, "I like all of them. They're all perfect, but..."

Her assessment of perfection, of course, should not be taken out of context. It is relatively easy for those with agreeable appearance to stand out in a land where most people look hideous. Nevertheless, the three men were the pinnacle of what could be called *feasible perfection*—something that the princess wasn't quite interested to begin with.

"I like them all but how can I be sure which one loves me the most?" she asked.

"Did they genuflect when they entered your premises in a princely fashion?" asked the queen.

"They did, and each of them lowered a knee all the way to the ground without losing balance," replied the princess.

"Did they pledge their loyalty to you as they gazed upon your cleavage?"

"Most certainly, and they used the exact same words!"

"Did they whisper sweet nothings in your ear?"

"Yes! Their breath was fresher than lilac peppermints."

"Tough choice," said the queen, "Perhaps you need a rest. It was a long day. The morning is wiser than the evening."

The princess went to bed, ridden by anxiety.

"Goddess of love," she prayed as she closed her eyes, "help me pick the one that loves me for who I really am!"

It was Friday. Way up in the heavens, the goddess of love was dining with a bunch of friends. They were just finishing the main course, debating whether to order dessert. A waiter approached, carrying an envelope on a golden plate.

"There's been an express prayer for you ma'am," he said.

The goddess of love winked at him and slapped his buttocks.

"Surprise, surprise! I guess he decided to call her after all," said the goddess of hope to the goddess of despair, whose face was always veiled by disappointment.

The goddess of love read the prayer.

"Ladies, I know that paying attention to my inbox at this time might appear rude, but this seems urgent. I hope you'd excuse me."

"Darling, if this is the secret diet that helps you maintain your gorgeous body, you have to tell me all about it," said the goddess of infidelity.

"Even if it was," replied the goddess of love, "there's zero chance you'd stick to it for more than three days."

Everybody laughed, except the goddess of despair, who had difficulty appreciating irony.

The goddess of love got into her aphrodontus chariot and rushed to the palace. The princess had just gone to bed. She didn't expect her pleas to be answered. Like most people, she considered prayer a form of soothing meditation. The noise from the landing chariot startled her just when she was drifting off to sleep.

"I know this might seem unbelievable, because I don't answer prayers personally, but your case is tremendously important to me," said the goddess of love to the startled princess. "I'm losing worshipers at an alarming rate. The number of people who believe love is a privilege for a minority of good looking idiots is constantly growing. Since your beauty is quite mediocre and your three candidates are sort of hideous, a widely publicized happy ending would reignite interest in my cult and save my career."

Needless to say it was an offer the princess couldn't refuse.

"There's just one problem," said the goddess of love and moved closer, as if what she was about to say could be overheard by someone else.

"In have to tell you, girl to girl," she continued, whispering, "looks aside, each of these men is a catch! I'm not surprised you couldn't make up your mind, for even I would find it difficult. Rest assured I have a plan, but it comes with one condition. Our meeting should be kept completely off the record. If word about it gets out, I will deny this conversation ever took place and call you a delusional princess that can't make a difference between dreams and reality. Do you understand?"

"No one will ever know," promised the princess.

"Very well," said the goddess of love. "Tomorrow, when the Sun rises, pack a few sandwiches and head to the hills outside the city. There you will see a giant cave."

"I don't believe there's a cave anywhere near them," said the princess.

"There will be one tomorrow," said the goddess of love. "I know a few people in high places that owe me a lot of favors."

"I understand," said the princess.

"All you have to do is get inside the cave and wait," continued the goddess of love. "It's going to take a while. Bring something to read in case you get bored. Eventually, the man who truly deserves your love will come to pick you up."

"Is this all?" asked the princess, "it seems rather easy."

"Of course it will be easy, dear child," said the goddess of love, "you already did your part. While you relax in the cave, I shall appear in front of your men as an old witch and tell them you have been kidnapped by a giant bird that brought you to its cave and is just about to either eat or rape you. I haven't yet decided which is worse. When they hear this, they will rush to your rescue. The one who truly loves you will succeed."

When morning came, the princess did as she was told and headed to the hills. She easily found the giant cave—there was freshly deposited gravel around the hills and giant footsteps that formed a path leading right to its entrance. Meanwhile, the goddess of love disguised herself as a witch, lest the knight, the merchant, and the butcher see her beautiful face and fall out of love with the rather mediocre-looking princess.

"Distinguished contenders, I have bad news," she said to them, "last night, a terror bird kidnapped the princess and took her to its nest, which is in a giant cave on the outskirts of the city. Go and save her, for she might be eaten or raped any moment!"

The merchant and the butcher rushed to the cave.

"Oh, shit," said the knight. "I would very much like to do that too, and had I known something like this could happen, I would have brought my shiny armor with me. Alas, I left it back home in my mother's closet. I'm afraid that without it, I could hardly survive a battle with a terror bird. It is most unfortunate that I am unable to help the princess, whom I love so dearly! I swear in the name of the goddess of love that I shall miss her until the end of my days."

"I have never heard a lousier excuse," said the goddess of love, "not to mention how appalled I am by the ease with which you swear in the name of the most noble of all deities."

She struck him with her wand and turned him into a pile of dust.
"There! You shall never speak my name in vain again!" she said.

The merchant was the first to arrive at the cave. He peeked through the entrance, but saw no trace of the princess.

"Something doesn't add up," he thought. "Terror birds have been extinct for a long time. I have traveled all over the world, but I have never met anyone who had seen one. Even sailors, the most skillful of all liars, don't brag about such encounters. Something else must have dragged the princess into this cave and, judging by the giant footsteps around the entrance, it must have been one of those titans that live on the other side of the world. It is a place I have never been to, but at least I know a handful of sailors who claim to have reached it. Perhaps the cave extends all the way down to those lands, and if I pass through, I could not only save the princess, but also establish a trade route that will make me rich beyond compare!"

As his sight got accustomed to the darkness, he noticed a faint light flickering in the distance.

"Who's there?" he shouted.

"It is I, the princess," said a frail voice. "An evil monster locked me in this cave. Hurry, beloved! Save me before it returns and tears me limb from limb."

The merchant rushed ahead and found the princess chained to a wall. A candle burned right next to her, throwing menacing shadows.

"My love," said the merchant when he saw her face, "even in a state of profound distress you remain the most beautiful woman in the world!"

"Oh, beloved, don't let my beauty distract you in such a crucial moment! Hurry and unchain my hands with the giant key that hangs on the wall next to me," she said.

The merchant did as he was told. Once free, the princess instantly transformed into a terror bird and crushed his skull with her powerful beak.

A moment later, the butcher, slowed down by the heavy meat cleaver that dangled from his waist, finally arrived.

"Damned bird," he shouted, "you have kidnapped the love of my life! Release her, or I shall turn you into a pile of stinky sausages!"

"Hurry, beloved! Unchain me, for the hideous creature that kidnapped me with its mighty claws will soon return and rape us both," said the voice.

"Mistress of my heart," replied the butcher, "I will honor your request, but know that if this creature returns, I will easily overpower it and craft you a necklace from the claws that dared to scratch your tender buttocks."

"Light of my life," said the voice, "unchain me, so I can feel the warmth of your embrace."

The butcher got close and saw her face.

"Heaven of heavens," he said, "you are more beautiful than ever!"

"Hurry, my dearest," replied the voice. "Don't let my beauty distract you in this crucial moment!"

"I won't," replied the butcher and instead of the key, grabbed the meat cleaver. With a single swing he decapitated the princess. Her head fell down and returned to its true form.

"Despicable monster," said the butcher and spat on it. "Your sweet voice fooled me, but it only took a single look to recognize your cowardly deception! Your disguise was almost perfect, but my true love has a mole on her chin with three silky hairs protruding out of it. The first one is golden like the Sun, the second—silver like the Moon, and the third—black like a starless night."

As he said those words, the cave transformed into a wedding hall. In its middle stood the real princess, dressed in a sparkling wedding gown. Her mole was right where it was supposed to be. Praise be to the living gods, who through trials and tribulations teach us valuable lessons.

Interlude: The Etymology of Love

"TERROR BIRDS WERE MAGNIFICENT CREATURES," said the queen. "Have you ever asked yourself why, despite being extinct for such a long time, people still remember them?"

"No, Your Majesty," replied the vizierienne.

"Then I shall enlighten you," said the queen. "It's all in the name. *Terror* is a strong word. The tongue that utters it trembles like a leaf. In comparison, the word love sounds weak and slimy."

"It is true that phonetics can influence the mind," said the vizierienne. "It is far from coincidental that words describing symbols of power often have an abundance of ear-grating consonants. But the origin of the word *love* is quite unusual. It was derived from the name of an ancient Oriental scientist, who laid the foundations of what we now call *medicine*, although most of her works were lost after a tragic accident."

"I love tragic accidents," said the queen, "tell me more!"

The Legend of Ana Loveless

IT IS LITTLE-KNOWN, IF AT ALL, that the word *genius* was invented to describe the boundless intellect of Ana Loveless, the greatest scientist of the Orient. She lived a long time ago, in the darkest of ages, when those lands were ruled by men and the Barren Desert was still dotted by lush oases. Ana rejected the established scientific methods and explored the world with the bold innocence of a child.

"The phenomena that underpin all creation cannot be measured with instruments," she wrote at the age of sixteen in a letter to the chairman of the Oriental Scientific Society. "Nature won't reveal its secrets to those who shy away from it, hidden behind sterile windows. While I greatly appreciate your generous invitation to become a member, I cannot bring myself to accept it, for this would be a betrayal of my most cherished principles. Rest assured that as a fellow scientist, I wish you nothing but success."

Ana was the only daughter of a flamboyant poet and a pedantic engineer—a couple that wasn't meant to be, since people with such opposing personalities found it hard to coexist under a single roof without killing each other. In fact, when she turned seven, her parents divorced.

"Is it my fault?" asked Ana as her father hastily packed his pink-stripe shirts in his crocodile-leather suitcase.

"My innocent child," he said and kissed her forehead, "all evils of the world are caused by adults, whose lives are poisoned by meticulous pragmatism. Your insufferable mother and I are like fire and water and any attempts to reconcile us would only deepen the horrible damage we have done to each other. Please remember that as your parents, we will always be there for you, for although we passionately hate each other and wish we had never met, we care about you more than anything else."

Confused by the answer, Ana went to her mother, who was powdering her face in front of her bedroom mirror.

"Do you know your father likes red lipstick?" she said when she saw her daughter approaching. "That's the only color I've used ever since I met him. I wanted to be his muse. I would have wrapped myself in rags to please him."

A tear rolled down her cheek. She carefully wiped it with a piece of cotton.

"Here's a lesson for you. Never put make up to please someone else," she said and reached for her pink lipstick.

"Mommy, is daddy leaving because he is angry with me?" asked Ana.

"Don't be silly! Not even a jerk like him can be angry at a child for more than five minutes," replied her mother. "Your father is leaving is because I kicked him out. I won't spend the rest of my life with a man who can't keep his pants zipped up. And neither should you. Now go to your room, because it's already past your bedtime."

Her mother often forgot that children weren't well-versed in the art of disparaging metaphors. Ana didn't understand why a zipper was such a point of contention, and unfortunately, she never got the chance to discuss the matter again. Her mother died the next morning.

"They told me she committed suicide," wrote Ana years later. "It was hard for me to accept she was gone. As a child, you imagine death as something ugly and grotesque—even unnatural—but my mother looked so serene and beautiful in her coffin, I thought she would wake up any moment. The idea that she could have taken her own life seemed so odd. She was a strong woman and rarely wasted her time in regrets. Looking back, I think it was her broken heart that refused to go on living, not her mind."

Ana grew up under the care of her father's girlfriends, whose names she could barely recall, for they came and went like broom merchants on a flea market. When she turned thirteen, she joined a boarding school, where she felt much more comfortable.

"It seems that growing up brings nothing but confusion," she wrote in her diary. "If my parents were truly as incompatible as they claimed to be, why did they marry each other? And if they were like fire and water, how come such opposite elements coexist so harmoniously in me? I should have long annihilated in a puff of smoke!"

These questions marked the beginning of her life-long interest in *aphrodisiology*—a subject that Ana defined as exploring "the intrinsic irrationality of the human heart." While her body went through the tumultuous metamorphosis of puberty, Ana discovered she was inexplicably attracted by a particular group of people. She enjoyed their company and missed them desperately while they were away. Those people differed in appearance, gender, or intelligence, but every time she laid her eyes on one of them, her cheeks became rosy and warm.

"When people are confronted by a mystery," wrote Ana, "they rush to formulate an answer, so they can get rid of it as soon as possible. And while there's nothing wrong in seeking explanations for things we don't yet understand, our impatience often gets the best of us. We fall prey to simplistic explanations that do us no favors, and we stick to them at great cost, because in our society too much thinking is considered a waste of time. It can be argued which answers are more efficient—those that are quick and incomplete or those that take time to be carefully crafted. Incompleteness inevitably leads to fragmentation, for a clumsy opinion is sooner or later rejected. Therefore, the economy of thought suggests that patient contemplation is more rewarding than hasty deliberations. Mysteries shouldn't trigger anxiety, but exhilaration."

There was, indeed, no shortage of explanations for the strange attraction. Many attributed it to beauty, yet Ana noticed that some of the people she felt attracted to weren't beautiful, especially her co-student Walter. His ears protruded from his head like those of elephants. Her friends found them unsightly and made fun of him. Ana, on the other hand, didn't pay much attention until one day Walter invited her to a picnic in the countryside. They lost track of time, discussing the mating habits of wild rabbits, and finished their last bottle of wine moments before the sunset. As Ana was hypothesizing why male rabbits were sexually dominant, Walter suddenly turned his head and the last rays of the sun hit the cartilage of his ears. Their fluctuating glow—from orange to vermilion—roused a desire Ana had never before experienced. She wanted to caress them, to pass her fingers over every fold, and feel the pulse of his heart through the blood pumping up and down the intricate mesh of their capillaries. No, thought Ana on her way back home, such an attraction had nothing to do with beauty. If she wanted to solve its mystery, she had to look elsewhere. As usual, the first clue came when she least expected.

"Yesterday, Alice—my best friend in the world—suggested we should safeguard our friendship by becoming blood sisters," wrote Ana a week later. "Her ideas always amuse me, so I agreed without hesitation. She reached into her purse and took out a magnificent dagger. She said it was a present to her father from the prince of Cockaigne. Its handle was gold-plated and encrusted with pearls. I was so taken by its beauty that I didn't notice what Alice was telling me until she pressed it on her thumb. A few drops of blood streamed down the blade. She licked it and passed the dagger to me. I felt a bit embarrassed for not paying attention, and—to demonstrate my resolve to participate in the ritual—I grabbed it quite enthusiastically. Suddenly, my hand was dripping with blood. Alice scolded me for ignoring her warnings about the sharpness of the dagger. Her frustration was justified, since my only excuse was that I got distracted by its looks. Anyway, we were relieved to find out the cut wasn't as deep as our initial panic made it seem. Alice suggested I should lick the wound. She said my saliva would help it heal faster. Right then, I had a revelation."

It is indeed quite normal for genius people to experience epiphanies in the strangest of moments. Epidemius of Choleropolis discovered the cure for influenza while running after a thief who stole his wallet. He faced an unpleasant choice: continue the pursuit or rush back for a piece of paper and write down the insight before he could forget it. To the detriment of humankind, he was a greedy and selfish man, so he chose to recover his wallet. Just a few weeks later, Calculania of Pythagorea was strolling in a park when her beloved dog, Actaeon, was attacked by a pack of homeless cats. As she bent to pick up a stone and chase them away, she accidentally discovered the first ever algorithm for factoring rational polynomials. Not allowing her personal sentiments to overshadow her responsibilities as the leading mathematician of her century, she stoically took out a notebook and wrote down her discovery while the berserk felines tore Actaeon into pieces.

"While I licked my own blood," wrote Ana, "I was greatly intrigued by its metallic taste. This uncanny property surely meant that just like iron, blood was susceptible to magnetism. Hence the mysterious attraction was just a manifestation of a hidden force, binding individuals with corresponding polarity."

It was an elegant idea that nevertheless had to be confirmed by experiments. Ana spent the next few years searching for a definite proof. The greatest difficulty was obtaining sufficient amounts of blood, and quite often, she had to use her own. The frequent bloodletting took a toll on her wellbeing, yet nothing could dissuade her from completing her goal.

"Once I demystify the mechanics of romantic infatuation," she wrote, "I will free humankind from a lot of useless suffering. Looking ahead,

I see a world where everyone has an equal chance to find a soulmate and divorces are anachronistic artifacts from a barbarous past."

Great pursuits bear unpredictable fruits, says an Oriental proverb. Inadvertently, Ana's research revolutionized medicine. By a process called *sedimentation*, she discovered blood was a complex substance consisting of four essential elements. The first one was *black bile*—a tar-like liquid with low viscosity that was extremely dangerous to handle. Anyone who came in direct contact with its refined form was overcome by anger. The second, *yellow bile*, resembled urine and was an excellent mood enhancer. The third, *white bile*, smelled of onions, and its vapors made people sad and desperate. A glass of the fourth, named *vermilion bile* significantly improved physical strength. Expanding on her research, Ana established that the equilibrium of these four substances had a profound effect on the human character. The blood of soldiers contained high amounts of black bile, while that of chronically sad people was dominated by white bile.

The four biles became known as the *platonic fluids*—named after Ana's cat, Plato, whose behavior was always exemplary. In fact, by analyzing the data from his blood tests, Ana pioneered the method of *character calibration*, through which she helped many emotionally unstable people regain their sanity. Regardless of this monumental achievement, Ana never strayed away from her original goal. Apart from the four platonic fluids, she discovered that blood contained small amounts of impurities that stuck to the glass of the retorts after the distillation process. To remove them, she rinsed her equipment with *aqua regia*—a fuming cocktail of *aqua fortis* and *acidum salis* that, due to its rapidly diminishing potency, had to be prepared immediately before use.

One day, Plato, chasing a mice in the lab, knocked the last jar of *acidum salis* off the table. Startled by the noise, the cat jumped into a plate of potassium permanganate, lost balance, and fell back over the broken jar. The *acidum salis* reacted with his permanganate-dusted fur, and the animal got completely engulfed in poisonous fumes. Two hours later, Plato drew his last breath. His tragic death broke Ana's heart. She mourned the loss of her companion for a whole week, during which her lab remained closed. When she finally returned, she saw the residue had fallen off the walls of the glassware, forming heaps of fine powder at the bottom of each retort. Its original grey color had changed to sparkling lilac. When Ana reached to take a sample, the powder slid towards her fingers, as if pulled by an invisible force. The mystery was finally

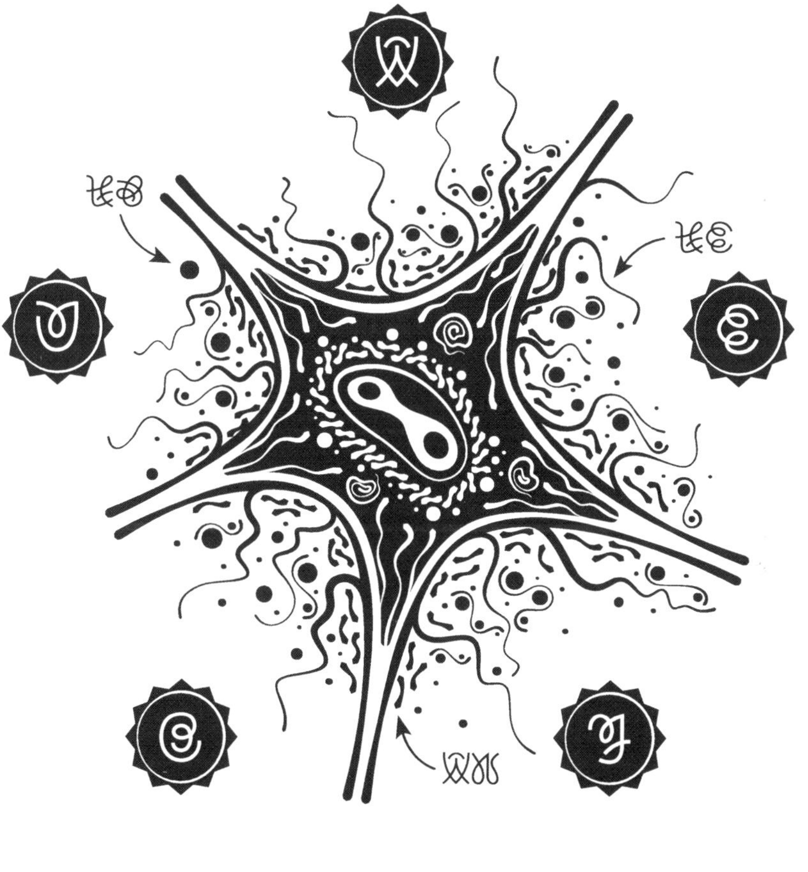

resolved. The magnetism of the substance was too weak to be detected when it was naturally dissolved in human blood and manifested itself only between individuals with a matching balance of platonic fluids.

"Had my dearest Plato not suffered such a horrendous death," wrote Ana, "I would have never stumbled upon this discovery. He will always have a special place in my heart and I shall never forget him."

Since physics hadn't yet become a science, Ana couldn't have known that, due to entropy, all promises containing the word *never* inevitably decay and break apart. In the passing years, the memory of her beloved pet faded away, and by the time she met her future husband, Alan Loveless, she could hardly recall the color of Plato's fur.

"Words fail me when I think of Alan," wrote Ana on the day she first saw him, "for he is a riddle trapped inside an enigma. Ever since I laid my eyes on him, I feel strangely hopeful, which is most surprising, since I don't believe in destiny or premonitions. The magnetism between us is so strong, I suspect we have an almost identical blood balance. Of course, this is just a frivolous assumption, for I didn't have an opportunity to sample his blood. I briefly considered staging an accident with a broken glass and gently pricking his finger. Alas, such a performance required a great deal of coordination—something I was utterly deprived of in his presence. Whenever he looked at me, my limbs ceased to obey my mind. It was a disturbingly embarrassing, yet profoundly pleasant experience, for my body felt like a feather dancing in the wind."

Ana wondered if the weightlessness of this feeling was just an illusion or there was something more to it.

"Those of you who have been to my lectures know I don't shy away from fringe ideas," said Ana in her commemorative speech at the Institute of Social Engineering, "and I'd like to use this wonderful opportunity to throw some unorthodox ideas in the air, if only to make it less stuffy. I promise you, I'm not going to grade your opinions."

The students laughed.

"Some people ask me what it feels like to have completed my mission in life so early," continued Ana under cheers and applause, "and my answer always disappoints them. Completeness is an illusion. In fact, completeness is the most dangerous illusion of all. I would rather believe in flying horses than dwell in its deceptive comfort. My work is anything but complete, and I doubt it ever will be. It takes a brief stroll through history to see that every resolved mystery is replaced by a new one. There has never been a shortage of unanswered questions about the world, no matter how well we thought we understood it. So, with this in mind, what kind of secrets lie beyond the already discovered principles of human attraction? Well, knowing why you are attracted to someone doesn't automatically explain the physical symptoms you experience: the goosebumps, the dizziness, the lightheaded trance-like state that resembles floating on a cloud. Perhaps one day some of you could discover that this magnetic force interferes with gravity. If we find out how to take advantage of it, we would be on the brink of a much bigger scientific revolution. You would see how easily my name will move from the covers of the textbooks to their footnotes. And I would welcome that, for it would mean we had moved forward as a society, as a culture, and as a civilization."

When Ana finished her speech and saw the admiration in the faces of her public, her heart filled with sadness. If she could trade all this for a drop of Alan's attention, she would have done it in an instant.

"He seems unimpressed," she wrote later that day, "If I weren't an expert, I would have assumed he was immune to magnetism, but I think he's just afraid to face his own vulnerability. I can only imagine the struggle between his mind and his heart."

She decided to give him a little bit of time, so he could adapt to the new reality.

"I am convinced more than ever that he is the right man for me," wrote Ana six months later, "for his resolve not to show affection is a testament to the power of his will, and, being an independent person myself, this is among the qualities of character I value most. A man in control of his feelings is a man you can count on in difficult moments. I am more worried about my own resilience, since the magnetism, pleasant as it is, also makes me lethargic. My productivity has plummeted, and there are days when I can hardly bring myself to make a cup of tea, much less continue my experimental work. My favorite pastime, it seems, is to curl up on my sofa and rub my face against my plush pillow, imagining it is Alan's face."

"I wonder when Alan will finally reveal his feelings to me," wrote Ana after another six months had passed. "I am deeply humbled by his efforts to impress me, but my patience is running dangerously thin.

Maybe I should have a word with him, just so I can assure him he can confide in me without fear that I would use his secrets against him."

"After a long deliberation," continued Ana a week later, "I decided I should do some preliminary tests. Perhaps there might be some irregularities in his blood? Had the circumstances not been so delicate, I would have openly asked him to participate in the study. Instead, I opted for an innocent deception. I invited him to the lab under the pretext that I needed help with its decoration. We sat down to talk, and I offered him tea. I figured that, being left handed, he would take a sip from the right side of the cup, so I slightly chipped the porcelain at its rim, just enough to scratch his lip and draw a drop of blood. Everything happened as planned. I acted as if I was surprised and apologized profusely. After he left, I rushed to analyze the sample."

The results raised more questions that answers. As Ana expected, the balance of their platonic fluids was similar, but no matter how much she tried, she couldn't detect even a trace of lilac powder in his blood.

"The greatest question science has to answer," wrote Ana, "is not what the world is made of or how it was created, but why the things that make our lives meaningful are inspired by its imperfections. Alan's emotional inertness is clearly caused by the purity of his blood. In my most horrific nightmares, I find myself inhabiting his body, passing through life like a shadowless ghost, serene and unmoved—a spirit devoid of desire, bound to a soul that doesn't know yearning. How many others suffer this fate without knowing?"

A week later, Ana invited Alan for tea again. This time, she served it in an impeccable cup. When Alan took a sip, she saw his face brighten and in the sparkle of his eyes she recognized the flame of desire.

"All it took was a bit of lilac powder in his tea," she wrote, "and he was all over me. I only wished we could remain like this forever."

From then on, she added a spoonful of it every time they met, and they soon married.

One afternoon, when Ana got back from her lab earlier than usual, she saw a pair of trousers on the floor of the living room. She picked them up and noticed a stain of red lipstick on the zipper. Her heart hollowed out like a wounded piñata. Then, unexpectedly, she finally understood her mother's warning. Instead of heading to the bedroom, where she was certain she would have found Alan in the embrace of their maid, she ran to the cemetery. She didn't believe the dead had the slightest interest in conversing with the living, but she needed to tell her late mother that she learned her lesson, albeit too late.

"Although my aching heart is begging me to join you in death, I have unfinished business in this world," said Ana and kissed the marble gravestone.

Later that night, flames engulfed her lab.

"They say to forgive is divine, but I am not a goddess," wrote Ana in her farewell note.

Overwhelmed by bitterness, she turned away from science and became a powerful sorceress. Her blood spells lured men away for their homes and turned them into slavish marionettes.

Interlude: Pride and Punishment

"I'VE HEARD ENOUGH," said the queen. "If I learned anything from these silly melodramas, it is that love is an obsessive compulsive disorder that needs to be cured, not encouraged."

"Your Majesty, if these stories haven't persuaded you of the power of love, the fault must be entirely mine, for I am not a professional storyteller. But I assure you, a simple gesture of kindness towards your people will greatly improve your popularity."

"Kindness?" said the queen. "Am I not kind enough for taking care that everybody abides by the law? My days pass in sentencing criminals and collecting taxes. Do people think I'm enjoying it? That I don't want to run away? Do you know how heavy this crown is?"

"I am sure, Your Majesty, that governing people is the heaviest of burdens," said the vizierienne.

"Forget governing," said the queen angrily, "I'm talking about the crown itself."

The queen pointed to her forehead.

"If you had the faintest idea how uncomfortable it is to balance a piece of metal on your head each day," she said, "you'd be thanking me for my sacrifice instead of preaching empathy."

"I didn't mean any offense, Your Majesty!" replied the vizierienne.

"Too late," said the queen. "I am already offended! I've tolerated your inefficiency for years. Now, apart from useless, you've also become extremely annoying. I sentence you to death."

"Your Majesty, I don't fear death," said the vizierienne and fell on her knees, "but I beg you to spare my life, for I have nothing but your best interest in mind, and I wish to serve you more than anything."

"I might spare your life under one condition," replied the queen. "Admit that all those stories are nothing but gibberish."

"Then my fate is sealed, for I cannot tell a lie to you," replied the vizierienne.

"Perhaps a night in the dungeon will help you reconsider," said the queen and ordered the guards to lock the vizierienne in the darkest prison cell, so she could meditate in peace and come to the right conclusion. When morning came, she was summoned back to the throne room.

"Did you sleep well?" asked the queen.

"I did not sleep, Your Majesty," said the vizierienne.

"How so?"

"At first, it was cold, and I couldn't stop shivering. Fortunately, after an hour, a guard appeared and wrapped me in a woolen blanket. It had your initials woven onto it. As he was warming my hands, he reminded me how merciful you can be to those who don't disappoint you."

"Who knew men could be so insightful. I shall give this guard a promotion, whoever he might be," said the queen.

"Then, as I was drifting away," continued the vizierienne, "a woman in the torture chamber across my cell started screaming. I don't know what unspeakable things the guards did to her, but I heard her bones cracking. She must have vomited several times, for her screams were interrupted by gargling, and her voice became coarse as if someone jammed a sheet of sandpaper in her larynx."

"It must have been the head of police," said the queen. "She conspired with extremists who held an illegal protest against my rule. Fortunately, after she denounced them, I revoked her death sentence and replaced it with life imprisonment. She will spend the rest of her days in luxurious solitary confinement, which is something I myself often fantasize about. I have promised to supply her with ink and paper, so she could write her memoirs and in return she pledged to dedicate them to me," said the queen.

"I could tell her issue was resolved because after about two hours, the screaming stopped and was followed by a dull noise, as if someone was dragging a body across the floor."

"And what kept you from falling asleep after that?" asked the queen.

"Nothing," replied the vizierienne. "Since I knew that in a few hours

I would be dead anyway, I preferred to spend my last moments on Earth with my eyes wide open."

"A peaceful death must feel like falling asleep," said the queen. "It's a shame that because of your stubbornness, your end will be much more unpleasant. Hopefully, your execution will be a lesson to those who waste their lives with silly stories."

Many sociologists had tried to explain why common people were so drawn to public executions. The most distinguished among them was Saint Simon de Rouvroy, who spent four decades studying crowds, disguised as a homeless beggar. Minutes before his death, he published his magnum opus, *Studies on Bread and Circuses*. Through the use of differential equations, he proved that, once social cohesion reached a certain threshold, human egos dissolved, and people began to identify as a homogeneous group. He likened the process to bread production, where individual grains of wheat were gradually turned into a mushy paste, and ultimately shaped into a single loaf. Saint Simon successfully demonstrated that the dissolution of the egos prevented people from empathizing with each other. Thus, public executions served as cleansing rituals, since criminals weren't considered individuals, but mere pimples on the face of society that needed to be urgently popped.

The execution of a minor bureaucrat usually attracted about fifty people. That of a senior government official was attended by several hundred, depending on the severity of the crime and the celebrity in charge of reciting the sentence.

When the queen looked at the crowd gathered on the main square, she was delighted to see it was larger than anything she had seen before. Yet the sea of heads was exceptionally calm. Instead of cheers, there was silence. People seemed to even have left their favorite posters at home.

The queen refused to delegate the role of announcer to a mere celebrity. She wanted to send a personal message to anyone who thought she could be swayed by petty emotions. Her booming voice permeated the square, amplified by her diamond-encrusted megaphone:

"Esteemed subjects of all ages! When I became your queen, I took a pledge to serve justice to all, regardless of social status or origin. I have spent my reign trying to fulfill that promise, and thanks to your unconditional support, we are inching ever so closer to a society where all criminals are treated justly. Today, the rich and powerful share common jail cells with the poor and the disadvantaged. The aristocrats are beheaded as easily as the peasants. We've come a long way! Just a century ago low-income criminals comprised ninety eight percent of those sentenced to death. Now their share has fallen to seventy four. Yet before we congratulate ourselves for this tremendous progress, let us remember that equality is not a final destination in a long journey, but a delicate equilibrium between cause and effect, responsibility and consequences. This equilibrium is constantly under threat. On one side, there is the danger of poor judgment, which arises every time we turn our backs to reason and embrace our emotions. On the other, there are hideous conspiracies that intentionally aim to mislead and corrupt us. And sometimes, unfortunately, the enemies of reason hide right next to us, disguised as benevolent friends, caring relatives, or trusted servants. Yesterday, with great sadness I discovered that my vizierienne has been plotting against me. Through the cunning use of storytelling, she tried to dissuade me from sticking to the letter of the law. Look at the people, she told me, they need love and affection more than they need order and discipline! When I heard those insulting words, I was appalled on your behalf, for they implied you were immature and weak, like children."

"No to the nanny state," someone shouted.

"Wise words," said the queen. "Had my vizierienne not lost her sanity, she would have known how futile it was to try to change my mind. She would have refrained from exposing herself as an enemy of the state. Alas, she foolishly assumed my judgment could be swayed. For that, esteemed subjects, she deserves to be punished. However, just as I am, I also believe in second chances. I offered her a path to redemption, if she agreed to repent."

"Everyone deserves a second chance!" someone shouted.

"We are a land of opportunities," said another one.

"Sadly," continued the queen, "she declined to do the right thing, and therefore she will be promptly executed!"

The crowd erupted in rapturous applause.

"Some of you might be asking themselves," continued the queen, "how can this be an execution, if there is no executioner in sight?"

Actually, nobody was in the mood for questions. People were too excited to notice the absence of the hooded woman that executed all convicts. Her name was Esther and she had taken a brief leave only once in her career, just before she gave birth to her daughter. Now that the queen pointed out she was missing, people assumed she gave birth to a second child.

"Who's the father?" someone asked.

"Don't look at me!" another one replied.

The crowd giggled. Three separate rumors regarding her absence emerged spontaneously and spread through the masses with lightning speed.

Esther and the Hyperborean (Take One)

I HAVE HEARD, SAID SOMEONE IN THE CROWD, that a while ago, a great tragedy befell the kingdom of Cynocephalia. A Hyperborean giant arrived to its shores riding an iceberg the size of a castle and wreaked havoc on three coastal towns.

When the news reached King Anubis II, who by the grace of the gods ruled these lands, he sent a legion of soldiers to capture the berserk savage. They ambushed him in a shrubby forest. A great battle ensued and all soldiers died, except a coward, who didn't dare to enter open combat.

"I should thank the gods for my cowardice," he thought as he watched the giant gut his comrades one by one, "for if I were brave, my intestines would have been already wrapped around my neck. It is fairly obvious that strength and size are related, and the only way to beat such a brute is through the cunning use of trickery or magic."

Since he wasn't a magician, he had to rely on *ingenuity*—a quality that cowards possess in spades, for it is essential to their survival in this cruel world. After a bit of head scratching, he invented a sophisticated contraption called a *sling*, and hurled a stone at the giant's head. The glacier-colored eyes of the Hyperborean rolled back, his bulging muscles deflated, and he collapsed unconscious, squashing twenty six corpses under his enormous body. Their blood squirted upwards and stained the thick clouds that covered the atrocity from the sight of the gods, who at the time were celebrating a birthday and didn't want to be disturbed by unpleasant views.

The soldier assembled a platform from broken chariots, tied the giant to it, and dragged him to the capital.

One might think the Cynocephalians—who resembled humans but had heads like dogs—were cruel and vindictive like most animals. Alas, this assumption was not only insulting, but profoundly wrong, for this folk of semi-humans was among the gentlest and noblest of all, and in their kingdom, the rule of law was above everything. The Cynocephalian constitution gave even bloodthirsty aliens a right to legal assistance and consular support.

Since Hyperborea didn't have a consulate in Cynocephalia, King Anubis II ordered his most distinguished diplomats to sail north and establish contact with the Hyperboreans. Everybody knew the mission was doomed, for beyond the Arctic Ocean there was nothing but nothingness. Nevertheless, the diplomats embraced the opportunity to uphold the principles of their homeland. A year after their departure, they were officially declared dead and were interred in the Cynocephalian Hall of Heroes, right next to the victims of the Hyperborean giant.

Sticking to the letter of the law, King Anubis II personally assigned a lawyer to the giant, so his trial could go ahead and he could be sentenced for his crimes. The atrocities he committed were so horrific that during the proceedings half of the jurors developed severe psychological trauma. The counselors that treated them documented thirty seven new types of mental disease. Four of them were collectively declared *Person of the Year* by the Cynocephalian Academy of Science—the highest honor for exceptional contributions to society. After four months of painful deliberations, eyes swollen with tears and nails bitten to the bleed, the jurors completed their deliberations. The savage was declared guilty of premeditated genocide, sexual assault, illegal trespassing, and aggravated hooliganism. Each sentence carried a separate penalty. The first one was hanging, the second—ten years in a high security prison, the third—a fine of ten thousand dinars, and the fourth—public whipping.

Adding them up wasn't easy. If carried out in a descending order of magnitude, the first would cancel the others. The reverse also presented a problem, although not as obvious: People sentenced to public whipping couldn't be simultaneously fined, for the combined humiliation would irreparably damage their self-esteem and thus limit their future contributions to the public good. Additionally, those sentenced to pay a fine larger than one thousand dinars couldn't simultaneously go to jail, for the state was legally obliged to immediately offer them a job, so they could recuperate their funds through hard and honest work. And finally, anyone who could spend ten years in a high security prison was entitled to a fresh start in life because the Cynocephalians believed in redemption.

The Supreme Court deliberated for a month how to resolve this legal conundrum. After half of the judges fainted from exhaustion, the conflicting sentences were replaced with the harshest single punishment permissible by law, originally intended for people who committed matrimonial assassination by sexual witchcraft—the most reviled crime in Cynocephalia. The last person sentenced to it was Hatshepsut IV—a power-hungry queen who killed her husband Thutmose XVII by turning his butt plug into a poisonous snake.

The punishment was called *breaking on the wheel*—a most elaborate type of execution, specifically designed to demonstrate the severity of the Cynocephalian justice system. Those subjected to it rarely survived, for few souls could withstand such crushing anguish.

Firstly, the body of the criminal was anointed with a foul-smelling ointment made of wax and sulfur, while a choir of children performed *The Anthem of the Condemned*, a musical piece with a dreadful melody and a pace known to cause arrhythmia in individuals past the age of sixty. And while a fortunate minority of people found the melody pleasant, nobody could stomach its harrowing lyrics:

> *The glitter of this filthy potion*
> *Shall not blind us to your crimes.*
> *The stench of sulfur will remind us*
> *Of those that died before their time.*
> *For every damage there is retribution—*
> *A prison term or hefty fine,*
> *And in the sacred name of justice,*
> *We shall slowly break your spine!*

After the performance, a young priest lit the *bonfire of justice*—an exorbitantly pompous name for what was a medium-sized candle, placed in a porcelain censer. Its wax slowly dripped over a cup of *lapis vitae*, a non-combustible incense made from the resin of the shepherd tree, whose blossoms, surprisingly, gave birth to lambs. Consumed in small amounts, it had laxative properties, while an essential oil derived from it was used by hairdressers for hair curling. The Cynocephalians were unaware of all this and used it for its scent, which helped neutralize the smell of sulfur. A brief intermission followed, so people could get snacks from the food stalls around the square. The criminal was then placed on a cartwheel with his limbs stretched out. The headsman, wielding *the hammer of justice*, delivered the first blow, breaking the left foot and gradually moving upwards until no leg bone remained intact.

Once done, he started tearing chunks of flesh from the broken limbs with the *pincers of retribution*, while his assistants poured hot tar with ladles called *the spoons of mercy* to seal the wounds. As the criminal deliriously begged the gods for forgiveness and denounced his vicious deeds, the crowds greeted his remorse with encouraging remarks. It was common to see children on the shoulders of their parents. This type of execution was especially recommended for those under the age of twelve, because the gruesome sight was an excellent crime deterrent.

Another intermission followed, so people could relieve themselves in the portable toilets or get a dessert. During executions, the amount of consumed confection increased significantly. Many treats were sold exclusively at these events. The most beloved were the *screaming cannoli*—pastry rolls made of fried dough, shaped like a tube and filled with whipped cream. The name was inspired by the way they were eaten. People slurped the delicious cream and used the funnel as a loudspeaker to shout obscenities at the agonizing victim.

A gong announced the third part of the execution, when the arms of the criminal were subjected to the same procedure that left his legs mangled beyond recognition. He would often pass out from the severe pain and the headsman would announce a short break until the criminal regained full consciousness.

The fourth part began with a priest who recited *the prayer of remorse*. Finally, the executioner swung the *axe of indulgence* and in one swoop cut off the head of the criminal.

The execution of the Hyperborean giant didn't proceed as expected. A custom cartwheel had to be constructed, since the largest one available barely covered his buttocks. Then, three headsmen took turns, struggling to break a single bone in his body. They gave up one by one, drenched in sweat and gasping for air. Another three tried to rip chunks of flesh with their pincers but only managed to tickle him. And when the time came to decapitate him, their axes shattered like icicles when they hit his neck.

This most unfortunate outcome greatly saddened King Anubis II. Since the foundation of Cynocephalia, all prophets predicted that a failure to serve justice would spell the end of the kingdom.

The king sent a message to all monarchs of the world, pleading for help:

Dear colleagues, I am Anubis II, King of Cynocephalia, a land of order and justice, where no crime is left unpunished. A great tragedy has befallen me and my people, for we have sentenced a criminal to death but none of us can kill him. Every second that he remains unpunished chips away at the foundation of our society and brings us a step closer to imminent collapse. I am humbly asking you to send your most merciless executioners to my capital and help us carry out the sentence to its end.

When the queen of Severia received this message, she summoned Esther, for there wasn't a butcher on this Earth more proficient in the slaughter of sinners.

"Esther," said the queen, "I have a an important job for you."

"Your Majesty," said Esther, "I hope it involves cutting heads, since this is what I excel at."

"It most certainly does, my dear," said the queen. "To the east of our island, there's a kingdom full of dog-headed midgets who can't tell the difference between torture and tickling. Apparently, a Hyperborean rascal landed on their shore and trampled their meadows or something. They sentenced him to death but, being small and pathetic, soon discovered they can't actually kill him. Now their king is freaking out, thinking everything is doomed. Normally, I wouldn't move my finger to help such incompetent abominations, and I would gladly leave them to the mercy of the Almighty Evolution. But there is a political aspect. Suffice to say, an alliance with those midgets might come handy in time of political need. Therefore, I command you to pack your axe, head to this land, execute the idiot, and come back home as quickly as you can because if people find out that my executioner is missing, they will become even more unbearable."

"To hear is to obey," said Esther, "I will depart right away."

Three days later, she arrived in the Cynocephalian capital, greeted by a jubilant crowd.

"Oh, harbinger of justice," said King Anubis II. "We welcome you to our kingdom and hope you'll feel like home among us."

The look of the Cynocephalians bewildered Esther, but the queen warned her not to comment on their facial features.

"Thank you, Your Majesty and handsome midgets," she answered, "but I am under strict orders to return to Severia as quickly as possible, because my queen needs me. Please take me to the convict who needs a head removal, so I can fulfill my assignment."

Esther might have been prepared for the strange looks of the Cynocephalians, but she was caught off guard by the Hyperborean, who was blissfully sleeping in his prison cell. When his snoring reached Esther's ears, she felt her neck tingle. The feeling was pleasant but confusing, since she usually preferred high-pitched noises. Once she made a man scream continuously for three minutes just by twisting his ankle. It felt so exhilarating, she could hear a choir of heavenly jinns singing.

When Esther entered the cell, she saw the Hyperborean curled up on the floor. His giant back slowly expanded and contracted, following the pace of his breath. I better sharpen my axe well, thought Esther, for I have never seen such a thick and muscular neck in my life.

The sudden surprise brought back memories from her past, when she was still a young apprentice. She used to watch those older than her cut heads with a single blow, while she could barely sever the spinal cord of a malnourished peasant. She remembered the voices of her mangled convicts, choking on their own blood, begging her to deliver a fatal blow. *Kill me already! Kill me already! Swing harder and end my misery, you incompetent cunt!* She remembered the pain those words inflicted upon her, how she clenched her teeth trying to ignore it and act professionally, how she fought to hold back her tears, and how, once they burst through, they stung her eyes and blinded her... And then she would hear her supervisor shout *Stop! Stop! Enough already!* And she would wipe her eyes and look down, where instead of a human head, she would see an ugly heap of minced meat and bone shards. *Squishy Esther, they called her. Sausage maker, meat grinder, head popper, brain kneader...* Every new insult scarred her self-esteem, deeper and deeper, until one day she swore to never pick an axe again and become a landscape artist. Yet when she saw that every tree leaf she painted looked like a dagger, she realized she couldn't run away from her destiny. The path to greatness didn't lie in talent, or hard work, but in pristine clarity of one's purpose. She was born to wield blades, not brushes. Once that purpose was revealed to her, Esther felt like a butterfly bursting out of a cocoon. People's ridicule couldn't harm her anymore. From then on, every head she cut could be perfectly identified. Her blows became so swift and precise, the faces of her victims looked serene, as if they died blissfully in their sleep.

She shook her head to clear her thoughts. The neck of the giant was massive, but she knew how to wield an axe and cut the sturdiest muscle as if it was made of butter. It wasn't the size that troubled her, but the unusual appearance of the Hyperborean. His skin was whiter than snow—a complexion she had never seen before. The color of his hair was bright like a carrot, while his arms and shoulders were dotted with spots of glittering ocher. His curly locks were shifting from deep orange to light yellow. Then, there was his smell—delicately sour, like the cream filling of a screaming cannoli. If only she could have one now.

She licked her lips and moved closer. The giant groaned, as if he sensed Esther's presence. She instinctively grabbed her axe. He sighed and turned around to reveal a face glowing like a rising sun. His eyebrows and the stubble on his cheeks had the color of his hair, and his milky-white chest was graced by nipples the size of dinars, pink and spongy, surrounded by tiny strands of golden fur.

Esther let go of her axe. For all the years she spent honing her skills, she had never regretted taking a life. She thought her conscience was clear because she was following orders. Now she realized she was wrong. Despite coming from different walks of life, she and her convicts had many things in common. This made them expendable. Now, in front of her lied a man so unique, she couldn't take her eyes off him. If she decapitated him, she would be agonizing in regret until the rest of her life.

"Your Majesty," she said after she came out of the cell where the Hyperborean was still sleeping, "Do not regret letting this monster live. He is more dangerous than you can imagine. Had you managed to cut his head off, two more would have appeared from its bleeding neck. The only way to kill him is to take him up north, where there is nothing but nothingness, and push him over the Great Abyss, for everything thrown in this bottomless pit perishes forever without a trace."

"We have heard of this place from our forefathers, who were great sailors and reached every corner of the Earth," said King Anubis II. "However, all maps and atlases were recycled for we needed paper to draft the very laws that made our society just and prosperous."

"My queen sent me here to help you in any way I can," replied Esther. "It will be an honor to push this monster from the edge of the world on your behalf, so he won't bother anyone ever again!"

King Anubis II gladly agreed, and Esther sailed away with the Hyperborean. Only the gods know what happened next, for the skies were clear enough for them to observe the shenanigans of this most awkward couple in history. Unfortunately—if Esther's account could be trusted—on the seventh day, a snow storm appeared out of nowhere and the giant fell overboard, while she escaped with minor injuries and some unexpected bouts of what she thought was sea sickness. When she disembarked and the symptoms didn't disappear, she found out she was with child. This happened nine months ago and only a select group of people in the palace knew about it, since Esther's mission was classified as confidential.

Esther and the Hyperborean (Take Two)

BEWARE, COMPATRIOTS, OF UNFOUNDED RUMORS! Truth is easily twisted by ignorant minds, tempted by spurious certainties that lie beyond their reach, just like the land called Cynocephalia, of which there is no account anywhere, except in the cavernous wilderness of people's fraught imagination.

It is a well established fact that species cannot interbreed, and any frivolous combination of their respective features is impossible. An elephant can't grow the legs of a gazelle, and a cat's head can't replace that of a donkey, except in our worst nightmares and perverse fantasies.

It is, however, logical to conclude that races of corrupted humans inhabit the extremes of the world, for their unfavorable climate prevents the body from developing harmoniously. By the rules of the Almighty Evolution, these unfortunate conditions produce a plethora of hideous monstrosities. To the west, where the cold winds blow over the steppes, live people whose eyes are hidden in the palms of their hands and whose feet have fingers instead of toes. Down south, where the intense sunlight dries the deepest rivers and water is scarce, live the double-humped tribes. Their body fat accumulates in two cysts on their backs, so they can keep cool in the unbearable heat. The North, where there is nothing but nothingness, remains unexplored, although our most distinguished scientists advise us to keep an open mind. Who knows, the hypothesized existence of the Hyperboreans might turn out to be true, if only some of our absentminded explorers return with a credible story of a serendipitous encounter. There are, indeed, rumors that our most distinguished executioner, Esther, had seen one of those imaginary creatures, but under much different circumstances.

To the east of Severia, our thrice blessed island of plenty, lies a queendom called Epiphagia. It is among the strangest on Earth: people there have no heads, their faces reside on their chest, and their noses protrude from their sternums. They have mouths instead of bellybuttons and eyes instead of nipples. Their grim appearance is not caused by the peculiarity of the climate, for the weather in Epiphagia is pleasant year-round. Rather, it is a consequence of a decadent ideology called *egalitarianism*, which emerged as counteraction to the rabid individualism of the first settlers.

Since the geographic isolation of the Epiphagians limited their cultural exchange with the rest of the world, they held on to this ideology for centuries, as evidenced by the commandment *Thou shall not stick thy head in the crowd!* inscribed on the ancient walls of their parliament. Consequently, people's heads descended into their rib cages and their brains merged with their lungs. The egalitarianism also corrupted their system of government, which from an enlightened oligarchy regressed to unmanageable chaos. They called it *democracy*.

It is alleged by numerous substantiated accounts that recently, a stranger was found on the shores of this queendom, snoring on a beach near a fishing village, three thousand forearms northwest of the capital, Acephalopolis.

He was indeed described as Hyperborean, for the only place he could have come from was the Extreme North. This assumption was also supported by his strange appearance: His eyes glittered like sapphires, his lips had the color of pomegranate seeds, and his chalky-white skin was peppered with ocher spots, like satin sheets sprinkled with tea. His chest hair had the color of the setting Sun and was softer than Abharazarhadaradian velvet. His perky nipples looked like rose buds in early spring, while his armpits smelled of fermented milk. His legs were wider than temple columns and he could crush coconuts under his feet.

When she saw him, the Epiphagian queen, Marie Antoinette, was greatly alarmed by the freakish protrusion on his shoulders that hosted his face.

"This poor creature has no doubt developed a tumor that has pushed his facial organs above his chest. Judging from the horrible noise he makes, his brain must be suffocating. It's a miracle he's still alive. Yet before I accept this diagnosis as credible, I shall organize a referendum, so the entire population can have a say about it," said the queen.

It took a day for all the Epiphagians to vote and another one to count the results. Fifty-three percent of the population agreed with her.

"Now that we have diagnosed his sickness, we have to make an effort to cure him," said Marie Antoinette and clapped her hands. "Guards, put him in a cage and feed him some cake until I decide on the best course of action!"

While the guards carried out her orders, she pulled the chief of the intelligence service to a side and whispered in his ear (which was of course located right below his armpit):

"Jacques, darling, remember that a year ago our spies intercepted a message from the Syscephalian ambassador to his agents? He described a similar disease that plagued the Far West and turned people into freaks."

"I certainly do, Your Majesty," replied the intelligence chief, "and I shall immediately send spies to investigate the matter."

Six months after that, the spies returned with a report spanning six thousand pages, distributed in three hundred folders, mounted on the backs of twenty four horses.

"Your Majesty, I have good and bad news. Which one would you like to hear first?" asked the intelligence chief.

"Jacques, darling, if it was up to me, I would definitely prefer to hear the bad news first, for although it might be upsetting, there would still be something good left to cheer me up. Alas, I think this is a matter that calls for another referendum," said Marie Antoinette.

Since referenda could only be held on a Sunday, they had to wait five days before the ballots could open. The results were announced shortly thereafter.

"It turns out people's opinion once again aligns with mine," said Marie Antoinette. "In fact, I have forgotten the last time they voted against any of my proposals. Doesn't this strike you as suspicious, Jacques? Do my subjects fear me?"

"Perish the thought, Your Majesty," replied the intelligence chief. "It's just a sign that our system of government functions as expected."

"That's nice to hear," said Marie Antoinette and clapped her hands. "Guards! I'm about to hear bad news. Bring me some cake, so my blood sugar doesn't drop too low!"

The queen was served a plate of carrot cake and a glass of cranberry juice. She hastily swallowed a whole piece.

"Jacques, darling, I'm all ears!" she said and took a big gulp of juice.

"We have learned, Your Majesty, that this disease is called a head, and it has reached epidemic proportions. Practically everyone in the West is infected by it. People's faces are protruding above their shoulders like periscopes."

"Oh, the humanity!" said Marie Antoinette and shoved the remaining piece of cake in her mouth, "whahd a twewible twhing!"

"Excuse me, Your Majesty?" said the intelligence chief.

The queen swallowed and took another gulp of cranberry juice.

"What a terrible thing," she repeated. "I am devastated! Guards, bring me a slab of marzipan, quickly!"

The guards rushed to the royal kitchen. The sound of clashing pots and pans echoed in the hall.

"Don't forget to dress it with honey," shouted Marie Antoinette and licked the last crumbs of cake off her fingers.

"They always skip that part. Anyway, I shall be brave!" She sighed. "Tell me, Jacques, darling, how contagious is this disease? Would someone who has, let's say, caressed the tender skin of an infected person, or perhaps kissed the lips residing on that abominable protrusion, contract it? And if so, how long has that person left to live? If she were a suzerain of some sort, should she immediately choose a successor? Needless to say, my inquiry is purely hypothetical."

"This is part of the good news," said the intelligence chief. "It seems the disease is not terminal, and none of our spies has contracted it. We were briefly alarmed by a suspicious growth on the ribs of a young operative, but it turned out to be a harmless pimple."

"Oh, cake on a stick, young people are so disgusting," said Marie Antoinette. "Did you pop it?"

"Our best medics drained all the puss," replied the intelligence chief.

The guards appeared with a huge plate of marzipan drenched in honey.

"Guards, would you please explain to me what does a queen need to do, so she can get her comfort food on time? I almost died while you were dragging your feet in that kitchen," said Marie Antoinette. "Shall I presume you wished to see me dead, prostrated on the floor, drowned in my own saliva?"

"Forgive us, Your Majesty! We wish noting but the very best for you," said the guards.

"I hope so. Now that my blood sugar is back to normal thanks to the soothing words of my intelligence chief, you can throw the marzipan out of the balcony and feed the poor," said the queen.

The guards hurried to fulfill her request.

"Jacques, darling, I apologize on their behalf," said Marie Antoinette, "please continue!"

"The best news is there's a treatment for the disease," said the intelligence chief.

"Fabulous!" exclaimed Marie Antoinette and clapped her hands. "Is it a pomade? A lozenge? A suppository? Are there any side effects? How much does it cost? Meringue on a stick, I seem to have developed some sort of sentiment for that poor creature. Wouldn't it be marvelous to see him shed this terrible tumor and regain his true form? I'm sure he must have been quite pleasing to the eyes before he contracted this debilitating malady. Even now his skin remains so soft, and the hair under his armpits glitters like gold! Oh, look at me, rambling so fast my brain got out of breath! I will shush myself with another piece of cake."

"The cure seems to require a more radical intervention," said the intelligence chief. "Last week, a spy informed us that a surgeon called Esther specializes in removing those tumors with a sharp object called an *axe*."

"Esther?" The queen swallowed and licked her fingers. "What an outré name. It should be banned by a plebiscite. Can we find her?"

"We already have, Your Majesty! An intelligence brigade was just dispatched to kidnap her."

A week later, the intelligence brigade delivered a huge black sack labeled *Handle with care!* to the palace. When the guards untied it, they saw Esther in full working uniform, handcuffed and squinting.

"Meringue on a stick," said Marie Antoinette, "she is just as sick as that poor creature."

Shocked by the looks of the Epiphagians, Esther thought she was having a nightmare.

"Where the hell am I?" she shouted.

"What is she saying?" asked the queen.

"We don't know, Your Majesty. People from the West don't speak French," said the intelligence chief.

"They don't?" asked Marie Antoinette, "What other languages are there to be spoken?"

"We are still studying their means of communication," replied the intelligence chief, "so far we have determined they rely on a rudimentary set of sounds to express sentiments and assert authority."

"Great, just as I thought I was on a brink of a scientific breakthrough, my hope was taken hostage by a primitive savage," said the queen. "Guards, I need more cake!"

The guards rushed to the kitchen.

"And don't skimp on the cream," shouted the queen.

"Your Majesty," said the intelligence chief, "some of our experts think language might not be essential for human progress. The fact that a simple woman has developed a cure for such a disease supports that hypothesis."

"A noble savage, how interesting," said Marie Antoinette. "But if she found the cure, why is she still sick?"

"I suppose it's a matter of principle, Your Majesty," said the intelligence chief. "Some medics are altruistic and put the needs of other people before their own."

"Young madam," said Marie Antoinette to Esther, "you can't save the world if you don't take care of yourself first. Healers need help as much as the people who rely on them. This disease has torn your face out of your chest and lifted it so high, you could scrape the clouds with your eyebrows. It's amazing you can still breathe properly. Do... you... understand... me?"

To Esther, the queen's speech seemed like purring.

"Who are you and why have you brought me here," she asked.

Esther was kidnapped after a particularly hard day at work. First, she had to execute three women who robbed a jewelry store. Then, just after she sat down to rest her swinging arm, a man convicted of adultery had to be urgently hanged. She returned home late, skipped dinner, put on her pajamas, and lied down to unwind with her favorite book. The nightmare started as she was drifting off to sleep. A hand pressed a wet cloth on her mouth. Her bed started rocking up and down, as if she was on a ship. Some time after that—she couldn't tell how long—she heard grunting and woke up in complete darkness. Someone uncovered her face and here she was, surrounded by these freaks.

Did she die in her sleep? Was this the afterlife? If so, it wasn't as she always imagined it. She never believed all those promises about an idyllic retreat, where virgin men served nectar to virtuous women. It seemed too simplistic. What she expected from the afterlife was peace. She yearned for a quiet place. The gods knew she loved her job, but she always thought that once she died, she could opt for a dignified retirement. She earned it. While she was contemplating her fate, the guards brought in the Hyperborean.

"This poor creature needs your help," said Marie Antoinette, gesticulating, as if the movements of her hands somehow made things easier to understand.

"What do you want from me?" asked Esther.

The queen rolled her eyes and shoved a giant piece of cake in her mouth. To everybody's horror, she started choking and reached for the cranberry juice. The glass was empty. Gasping for air, she grunted at the guards, eyes filled with blood. They ran to the kitchen. The intelligence chief panicked and tapped the queen's back with such force, the cake shot out of her mouth and splashed all over the face of her defense minister, who was standing right in front of her. Marie Antoinette started coughing compulsively.

"Jacques, darling, I owe you my life," she said after her brain finally filled with air.

In the meantime, the guards came in with a jug of fresh cranberry juice.

"Too late! Give it to the poor! And bring Esther's instrument, so she can begin the damned treatment," said Marie Antoinette. "Woman of the West, I command you to remove this virulent tumor from the shoulders of this man. And I warn you that failure is not an option!"

When the guards brought her axe and uncuffed her, Esther finally realized what had happened. To her great relief, this wasn't the afterlife. Obviously, she was kidnapped by freaks who wanted her to do what she had always done. Couldn't all this hassle have been avoided if they had just asked politely?

The Hyperborean, who spent months locked in a cage, struggling on a diet of carrot cake and marzipan, had a different hunch.

"I think they want us to mate," he said to her and winked mischievously.

"I wouldn't call that thinking," replied Esther. "Male heads are incapable of coherent thought. But I've cut enough of them to know that you still need them on your shoulders to survive."

"Jacques, darling," said Marie Antoinette, "I think they are communicating."

"I like your feistiness," said the Hyperborean. "Where I come from, women cover their faces and don't speak unless they are spoken to."

"Then I think you should return there as soon as possible because those freaks want me to cut your head off," replied Esther.

"They are definitely communicating, Your Majesty," said the intelligence chief.

"Why would they want you to do that?" asked the Hyperborean.

"None of them has one," replied Esther, "and they probably consider it a problem."

"They might as well be right. Our philosophers say all problems reside in our heads," said the Hyperborean.

"Then I'm the best problem solver in the world," said Esther. "I behead people for a living."

"Interesting! Did you choose that job yourself?" said the Hyperborean.

"It's a family tradition," asked Esther.

"So your parents chose it for you," said the Hyperborean.

"Jacques, darling, this seems to be taking too long! Why doesn't she just go ahead with the procedure and put an end to his ordeal?" asked Marie Antoinette.

"As far as we know, this is part of the treatment, Your Majesty. My agents say such healings take place in front of large crowds and require a lot of social interaction."

"I see," whispered Marie Antoinette, "but I seem to be getting bored, and boredom makes me hungry. I don't want to shout at the guards right now, so would you be so kind to go to the kitchen and bring me some cake?"

"In my country, executioners are born, not appointed," said Esther. "You can't become one by choice. And if you already are, you're not allowed to do anything else."

"Ah, predestination," said the Hyperborean, "sounds familiar."

"What's your profession?" asked Esther.

"Prince," replied the Hyperborean.

Esther burst in laughter.

"Jacques, darling, things got out of control," said Marie Antoinette. "The poor creature irritated her. Now she will leave it to die in horrible agony. Oh, I can barely watch!"

"We shouldn't intervene, Your Majesty," whispered the intelligence chief. "She's a highly skilled professional. I'm sure she doesn't let her personal feelings affect her work."

"You're the first person who finds my profession funny," said the Hyperborean.

"So how did a prince end up with these headless freaks? Did your mother marry you to their princess?"

Now it was the Hyperborean's turn to laugh.

"See, Your Majesty, this unpleasant noise seems to be part of their language," said the intelligence chief to the queen.

"How appalling," replied Marie Antoinette. "Remind me to assign them a French tutor once this is over."

"My father wanted me to marry my cousin," said the Hyperborean. "Actually, I shouldn't say wanted, because he didn't have desires of his own. Everything that came out of his mouth had the word state in it: *The state expects you to master mathematics, Kenneth!* Sometimes he even managed to repeat it in a single sentence: *Your decisions should always take into account the state of the state, Kenneth.* He would point to his crown, as if the entire nation was squatting on his head. It made him look like a marionette. He wore what people wanted him to wear, ate what they want him to eat. Meanwhile, he pretended he was in charge, while they pulled all his strings, playing powerless victims and avoiding all responsibility."

"Maybe I should cut off your head after all," said Esther. "You definitely think too much."

"You won't," said the Hyperborean. "I bet you don't even lift your axe without a pile of stamped documents."

It took much more than that. She needed six different certificates, singed by a judge and approved by the Commission for State Sanctioned Decapitation and the Department of Torture. Her inventory was inspected twice a year—from the thinnest ropes to the heaviest chains. All equipment that came in contact with open wounds had to be sterile because the idiots in the health ministry thought even the dead had the right to avoid infections. Esther often worried that if those bureaucrats were left unopposed, one day beheadings would take place behind closed doors, away from the eyes of the public.

"It's hard to avoid thinking when everything around you is fundamentally flawed," said the Hyperborean, "and now I realize that running away isn't a solution either."

"You ran away?" said Esther.

"Not literally," replied the Hyperborean. "I just went for a walk with a bottle of whiskey. Gulp by gulp, I realized I was less and less interested in going back. By the time I emptied the bottle, I decided to throw myself off a cliff. We have a saying: when you drink a lot, your wishes come true. I heard the ice cracking and when I looked down, I saw the ground beneath my feet split in two. A giant precipice emerged, just a step away. It felt very inviting. It's now or never, I thought, and everything turned black. I must have passed out on an iceberg and floated away in the ocean because I woke up on a beach, surrounded by these people. I thought they would sacrifice me to their gods, but it turns out they actually want to help me. So sweet! I wish normal people were half as compassionate as those idiots."

"You're spoiled and gullible," said Esther. "There's nothing more dangerous than compassionate idiots. If you want to get out of here alive, you better follow my instructions to the letter."

"Since I sobered up, I'm not that keen on dying, but the thought of going back home makes me want to drink again," said the Hyperborean.

"That's not your only option," said Esther, "although I must warn you, the world out there is not safe for a beautiful man wandering alone. You'll be lucky to walk a mile without being raped."

"Then cut off my head and let's get it over with," said the Hyperborean.

"You know I can't do that," said Esther. "If a word of this gets out, I'll lose my license."

"Even if you do it out of mercy?" asked the Hyperborean.

"Especially if I do it out of mercy. Would you trust an executioner with a heart?" said Esther.

"So what options do I have?" asked the Hyperborean.

"Become my apprentice," said Esther. "Nobody would dare to touch you. Most people won't even dare to talk to you because they think it brings bad luck. There are some downsides. You won't be able to marry anyone but another executioner. It could be challenging if you fall in love with the wrong person, but you toughen up with age."

"What does an apprentice do? Sharpen your axe?" asked the Hyperborean.

"Swipe the floors. Take care of the paperwork. After a year or two, if you're good at it, I'll let you practice with coconuts. In five you'll be ready to cut off human heads."

"And how can we get away?" asked the Hyperborean.

"The crowd is a mindless beast—all we need to distract it is a bit of food and some entertainment. We're quite lucky because everyone seems pretty well fed, so what's left is to put on a good show. I thought a prince would know that better than I do."

"I must have slept through that lesson in governing. But I took a ballet classes. Would that be useful?" asked the Hyperborean.

"Only for children. Grownups are best entertained by torture," said Esther.

"Will it hurt?" asked the Hyperborean.

"Not more than it needs to," she said, "I won't break your bones, but I have to squeeze a genuine cry out of you. Crowds can sniff out fake pain from miles and we can't take that risk."

Since Esther swore she won't utter a single word about what happened next, lest she harmed the dignity of the captive prince, there is no account of the ending of this story. A full description of the event was preserved in the Royal Epiphagian Library, filed under the title *Alternative Medicine: The Effects of Butt Slaps on Facial Deformations*. It was, quite sadly, written in French—a language no one has been able to decipher. Blessed be the gods, from whom nothing can remain hidden!

Epilogue: Love Triumphs and Someone Dies

"ESTHER IS DOING FINE and she is definitely not with child," said the queen and killed a third rumor, right before it was about to crawl out of the mouth of a desperate houseman, whose life was so dull, he had to invent outrageous stories to make it worth living.

"I asked her to take the day off," continued the queen, "because my vizierienne deserves to die by my own hand!"

She lifted her sword. The crowd went wild.

"Long live our queen!" someone shouted.

"Death to traitors," said another.

"So without further ado, let our celebration of justice commence," said the queen.

A guard brought the chained vizierienne to the scaffold.

It is believed that the only thing that prevents the recognition of economics as an exact science is the so-called *frittata paradox*. Named after a peasant dish made with eggs and vegetables, it posits that during events involving public shaming, a crowd of more than a hundred hungry people will spontaneously generate enough food to feed itself, but immediately waste it by throwing it at the designated target of humiliation. Every economist who has tried to explain this unsettling phenomenon has failed miserably.

The culinary bacchanalia began immediately after the guards removed the hood from the vizierienne's head: A double-yolk egg crashed on her forehead, a tomato exploded all over her white shirt, a zucchini hit her shoulder, and an eggplant landed on her stomach, followed by a ball of wrapped spinach leaves. A ball of cabbage missed her and hit the guard in the crotch. He screamed in pain and threw it back into the crowd, knocking off a woman who was just about to launch a large pumpkin. In less than a minute, there was enough food on the scaffold to feed a dozen starving orphans for a week.

"Save your provisions, esteemed subjects," said the queen. The irrational

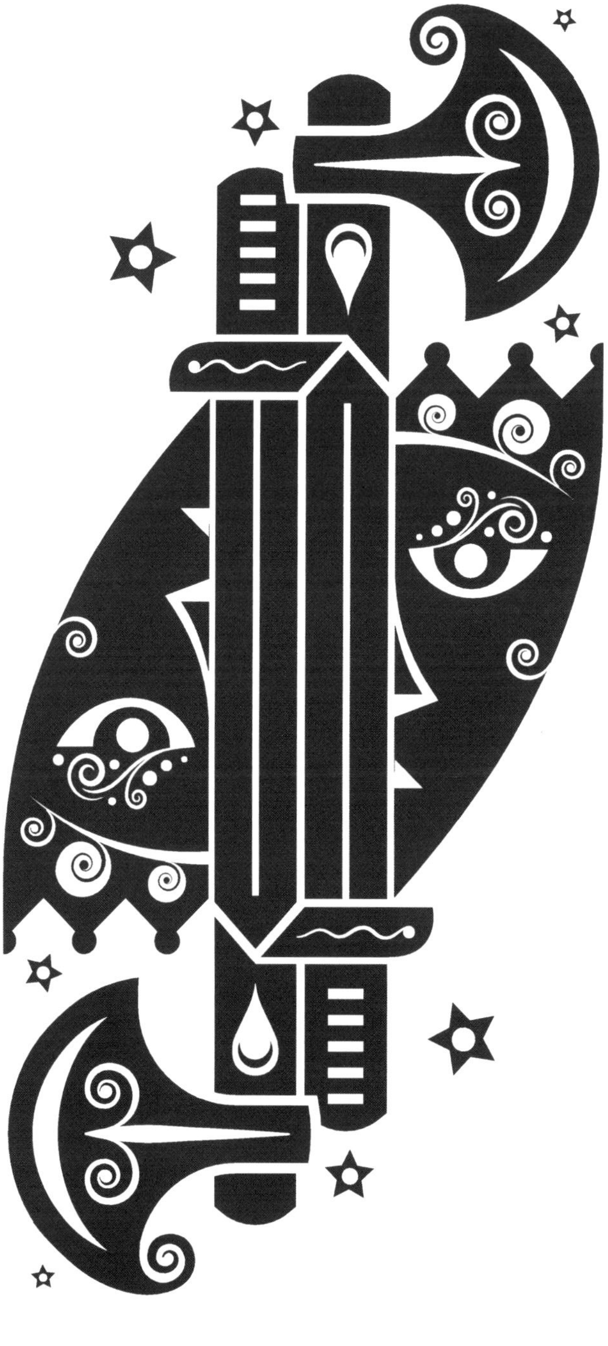

frenzy immediately ceased, as if her words broke a spell. Once sober, people tried to recover some of the wasted food, but the guards pushed them back.

"This is a land of opportunity," said the queen triumphantly. "And to prove it, I am going to make an exception. I shall once more urge this traitor, who not long ago served as my trusted vizierienne, to repent and denounce her wrongful convictions. Let us hope she won't waste this chance, for it will most certainly be her last."

"Beg for you life!" someone shouted.

"Crawl for mercy, miserable bitch," said another one.

"Speak before I decapitate you with my diamond-encrusted sword," said the queen.

"Your Majesty," replied the vizierienne, "I have served you in life and, if need be, I shall serve you in death, for I am yours to do as you please. I do not fear death just like I do not fear you!"

The crowd gasped.

"Did you hear her?" asked the queen. "She doesn't even have the decency to fear me!"

"My lack of fear doesn't come from pride or arrogance," said the vizierienne. "I don't fear you because I love you."

The crowd gasped again. An elderly woman screamed and fainted.

"You are not only my queen," continued the vizierienne. "You are the sovereign of my heart and the mistress of my soul. Just like a sword cannot cut the hand that wields it, I cannot betray or lie to you, for that would mean betraying and lying to myself. My stories were honest and true. All I wanted was to convince you of the power of love, the same one that overwhelms my heart and leaves no room in it for any other feeling, be it the fear of death or the bitterness of disappointment. It is because of love that I surrender to you, completely!"

"You have said enough, vicious succubus!" shouted the queen and lifted her sword. The head of the vizierienne flew off her shoulders like a frightened dove and landed in the middle of the crowd.

"Let this be a lesson to you all," said the queen. "Anyone who doesn't fear my power is a traitor and deserves to die."

She expected cheers and jubilation, but the echo of her words faded in dreadful silence. The queen looked at the faces of the people and saw them covered in tears. Before she could scold them for being too emotional, a rumble bubbled from the spot where the vizierienne's head had fallen, followed by a choir of voices. As they grew louder, the cacophony slowly coalesced into a brief, yet terrifying sentence: *Death to the Queen,* chanted the crowd. Suddenly, an event similar to the frittata paradox took place, yet instead of food, the crowd spontaneously produced pitchforks.

"What a monster!" someone shouted.

"Kill the heartless cunt!" said another.

The queen felt fear for the first time in her life. It was also her last, for merely a heartbeat after, the crowd rose up like a giant wave and tore her to pieces. Thus, the queendom she once ruled with her diamond-encrusted regalia turned into a most serene republic. Blessed be the everlasting gods, for they know better than to mess with love.

The Ebbs and Flows of the Great Hyperborean Empire

Humble Beginnings

PEOPLE FROM THE EXTREME NORTH were considered misanthropic and coldhearted—a stereotype as persistent as the ice that covered their homes. They lived on an archipelago of islands scattered in the frozen waters of the Arctic Ocean—a most bizarre circumstance, especially in the eyes of those who didn't believe in serendipity and second chances.

According to ancient hearsay, the archipelago was originally inhabited by a race of furry cyclops who, blinded by hubris and misguided pride, rebelled against the Goddess of Eternal Ice. For six days they tested her patience. Each time she took pity on them, for she knew they were naturally shortsighted, since they had only a single eye to rely on. But when on the seventh day they brashly threatened to depose her, she felt such burning anger that her icy hair melted. The fit left her bald and unattractive to gods and men alike, and as she wept in despair, the cyclops heard a terrifying noise coming from the sky. When they looked up, they saw her divine wrath descending in the shape of an egg. Its surface was glossy and black, and there were tiny wings attached to its sides. Suddenly, a massive blast evaporated the glacier. The earth beneath it turned into a hot stew and trembled violently. The terrible explosion left a gaping paraboloidal crater. In its middle stood a giant protrusion, surrounded by two rings of petrified cycloptic leftovers—bone shards, weapons, cutlery, and fine jewelry (if, of course, the word *fine* was appropriate for objects meant to fit on fingers thicker than human fists). Shortly thereafter, another crucial accident took place on a small rocky islet that lied on the opposite side of the Arctic Ocean, right off the coast of Trondheim. A corrupt prison guard helped a group of criminals on death row to sneak out of their cells. They swiftly took over the entire prison, dismantled its wooden gates, and built improvised rafts, on which they sailed into the ocean. Upon receiving the news of their escape, the governor of Trondheim province issued the following statement:

My thoughts and prayers are with all prison personnel affected by the traumatic event. This reckless act was committed by hopeless criminals, who were intentionally segregated from our society in the name of public safety. Their escape into the ocean will result in a much more tragic demise than the taxpayer-funded humane method of hanging we provide to all qualifying offenders.

Freezing on a raft was indeed an unpleasantly slow way to die. Many preferred to jump overboard and get eaten by unicorns—marine mammals with an insatiable appetite for human flesh. Had the criminals been even remotely rational, they would have indeed chosen to die on a rope. Alas, those who committed hideous crimes in cold blood were rarely known for their good sense. Back then, even destiny behaved recklessly—idiots were often rewarded with a peculiar blessing called *luck*. The criminals were rescued by a ship stocked with Clonfertian virgins. They were on their way to a summer camp at a nearby monastery, where they were supposed to master the art of knitting sweaters for their future husbands. Many skeptics doubted this chain of events was caused by pure luck. They suggested everything happened because, terrified by the prospect of spending their summer vacation in a monastery, the virgins passionately prayed to be kidnapped by a horde of well-endowed virile men, devoid of shame and sexual inhibitions. These speculations gained credibility, when soon after the accident, a letter in a bottle was washed ashore. It said:

Oh, crescent Moon, master of the waves and lord of all winds! Lead me to a far away place where no one would judge me as I scream in delight while a man berserk with wanton lust ravages my insides with his procreational appendage.

The criminals effortlessly overpowered the male crew and threw them overboard. A flock of unicorns immediately rose up from the pitch dark ocean depths. The sea monsters harpooned the bodies of the unfortunate men with their razor-sharp horns and tossed them in the air like rag dolls. The freezing waters turned into a boiling soup of torn limbs and spilled intestines. Deafening screams soared high as the tortured souls of the victims escaped one by one and headed to the heavens, where even the most misanthropic deities took pity on them and forgave their sins without much bureaucratic hassle.

The criminals were impressed by the viciousness of the unicorns. Their cruelty humbled even Robert the Impaler, who at the age of seven elevated matricide to an art form. He split his mother into three hundred parts, fashioned a baby crib out of them, and donated it to a museum. The clueless curators titled the gruesome artwork *Shelter,* while the critics celebrated it as *a heartfelt expression of exorbitant empathy.*

The macabre feast aroused the criminals. They turned their eyes to the virgins, who lied unconscious on the deck, overwhelmed by the sight of the gory carnage. Only Siobhan O'Giddy stood on her feet, for she used to work in a slaughterhouse since the age of six.

"Filthy pigs," she shouted, "come feast on the nectar of my flower, for by the laws of the Almighty Evolution savage brutes beget the healthiest progeny!"

Thus, the criminals impregnated the virgins and bravely sailed north, hoping to discover uninhabited lands and start new lives, unburdened by karma and social expectations. For nine months they zigzagged through the icebergs until they reached the cycloptic archipelago. Recognizing the strategic position of the crater, they built twelve igloos on the protrusion in its middle, which they called *Storkhome.* Years passed. As the population of Storkhome grew, so did the size of its igloos, until one day their roofs collapsed because of primitive engineering. But then—praise be to all things frozen—an inventor whose name was quickly forgotten found a way to carve tall cylinders out of glacier ice. When erected, they looked like slender tree trunks and could support much heavier roofs. As a result, the igloos transformed into towering cathedrals and the small town of Storkhome became the capital of a mighty state. Its influence spread far and wide over the frozen horizon—a resounding example that political power is achieved not by excessive military spending, but by peaceful scientific exploration.

Magnae Matres

T WO CENTURIES LATER, on the day of summer solstice, when the brazen sunlight turned the thick ice into deadly slush, a young priestess performed the Ritual of Frosted Defiance and slit the throat of a sacrificial mermaid. As she recited a prayer to the Goddess of Ice, the blood gushing out of the mermaid's neck changed color from red to lilac and a strange scent filled the air. Before the priestess could decipher the omen, all men fell on their knees and declared allegiance to her:

Oh, divine mistress! Your gaze holds our eyes captive. Your words delight our ears. We prostrate our bodies before you and beg you to accept our eternal servitude!

The priestess assumed the title of a queen under the name Helen the Gorgeous. Throughout her reign she amassed exorbitant amount of wealth and introduced the institution of *marriage*, so her descendants would enjoy the same privileges that she so effortlessly acquired. Thus, the orgiastic egalitarianism of the early state was replaced by moral elitism. Shortly thereafter, Helen addressed the nation, praising the role of men in society:

"No female deed, big or small, would be possible without our loving fathers, brothers, and sons. It is in them that we seek and find inspiration, for they are the source of all human life. Their groins hold the seed of creation, which through the bond of marriage they so generously share with all of us."

Helen paused to have a sip of water.

"This is a woman's world," she continued to rapturous applause, "for it was built by the hands of our foremothers. Yet such a world would be worth nothing without a man or a boy at our side."

Helen was much less gracious in private, when she felt unrestrained by formal etiquette.

"The only thing men are good for," she once said to her secretary, "is to serve as semen dispensers, just as the Goddess intended. It is therefore advisable not to burden them with too many responsibilities, for their minds are superficial and easily distracted by thoughts of procreation."

The two conflicting points became the foundation of the matriarchal system. Praised in public and denigrated in private, men lived in a state of perpetual confusion.

Helen married her husband, Athelstan the Fecund, at a lavish ceremony, spending half of the state budget. When her advisor told her she should donate her wedding gifts to a public museum as a form of payback, she graciously extended her hand to him and asked:

"Do you happen to have a coin handy, my dear?"

"Yes, ma'am," said the advisor, whose pockets were rarely empty because he never shied away from accepting bribes.

He handed her one made of pure gold. The queen dropped it down her cleavage.

"It fits perfectly, doesn't it?" she said, smiling.

"Indeed, it does, ma'am," agreed the advisor.

"Good," said the queen, "Now take my wedding dress and put it on."

"Your Majesty, I couldn't possibly..." said the advisor.

"You couldn't possibly what? Put it on without tearing it apart because you're twice as large as I am?"

"I'm afraid so, ma'am," said the advisor.

"Herein lies a lesson for you, my dear!" said the queen. "Money is a commodity. Wedding gifts are personal."

The advisor nodded and bowed down.

"Usually, I'm counting on your head to provide the insights," said the queen. "It is your most important asset. If I suddenly decide you have lost your wits, it might accidentally fall off your shoulders."

She kissed his forehead. The advisor held his breath, swallowing nervously.

"Now go and get a rest!" said the queen and retreated to her bedroom, where her husband was snoring.

Female supremacy began to unravel during the tragic reign of Birgit the Assertive—an obsessive-compulsive somnambulist, who shouted orders to her servants even while she was sleepwalking. Birgit was the last member of a dynasty that traced its origins way back to Helen the Gorgeous and her twenty one cousins. As if to prove their divine origin, their genealogical tree grew in reverse: Instead of expanding like that of normal families, it progressively contracted, as its branches fused due to institutional incest inspired by entitlement and greed.

Being the last offshoot of an endangered dynasty, Birgit was faced with a dilemma. To ensure the continuation of the line, she had to marry, yet there were no available relatives. After a brief constitutional crisis and a few legislative tweaks, she married herself.

Her son, Albert the Diffident, was as handsome as a prince could be, but his intelligence was somewhat lacking. Obsessively overprotective, Birgit refused to delegate any responsibilities to him, and he grew up unaware of the meaning of the word *decision*. He declined to eat anything else but his mother's milk. After he turned twenty, his grandfather, Edmund the Disappointed, tricked him to have a candy bar. Albert fell sick, vomiting compulsively for three days. Increasingly paranoid, Birgit accused Edmond of poisoning the prince and promptly executed him.

A day before Albert's fiftieth birthday, Birgit the Assertive rose up in her sleep and headed to the royal kitchen for a scheduled inspection. Distracted by a dream in which a handsome man, vaguely resembling her son, swept her off her feet and carried her to a bed of roses, she accidentally slipped and dived headlong into the birthday cake, where she tragically suffocated. It took four men to pull out her swollen body out of the deadly confection. The mouth of the matriarch, jammed with caramel ice cream, was so grotesquely misshapen, she had to be buried in a closed casket.

Devastated by the sudden loss of his only source of milk, Albert committed suicide. It was the first decision he took in his life, as evident by his farewell letter:

Dearest subjects, as you know I was cruelly abandoned by the person I loved the most. In the early hours of my fiftieth birthday, in complete disregard for my emotional and nutritional needs, my mother left this world forever. I haven't eaten ever since. The sense of betrayal prevents me from sucking the nipples of other women. This morning I was forced to taste something called sandwich that left me disgusted and demoralized. Therefore, I have decided to starve myself to death. Goodbye forever!

Albert's death inspired other victims of matriarchal oppression to come forward and sparked a kingdom-wide movement called *Down with the bosom!* At first its members demanded equal social standing, but an extremely vocal minority of young males, caught up in the euphoria of their sudden emancipation, quickly adopted an aggressive ideology. They believed the female obsession with control was neither a social, nor a cultural construct:

"Women are seductive and dominant by nature, for they have to compete for male attention and retain it," wrote their leader in his manifesto. "It is naive to expect these natural instincts could be voluntarily reined in. The only sensible way to avoid a relapse into matriarchy is to bring all females under the control of men, who—may I be forgiven for stating the obvious—are naturally meek, peace-loving, and emotionally accommodating."

Thus began the *Age of Patriarchy*. Like all other abrupt changes in history, it had a rough start. Many scientific achievements were declared useless and even wrong, for they were developed under a system that actively diminished the male mind.

The Taming of the Shrew

AFTER A DOZEN UNEVENTFUL CENTURIES, during which women gradually learned how to take care of the household, and men spent their time catching up intellectually, a mathematical genius called Gregor the Pedantic ascended to the throne.

Gregor introduced several innovations that revolutionized his kingdom. The first one was the calendar.

"It appears to me," wrote the king in his diary, "that we often quarrel about our history. This is hardly surprising—our recollection of the past is subjective and we always disagree about when and where events took place."

The king was right. There were as many versions of the past as there were people—an unfortunate thing that made any objective study of history impossible. Only the bravest individuals dared to pursue a career in it, enduring incessant mistreatment and abuse. Hardly a day passed without someone being punched in a heated argument. Most historians lost half of their molars before the age of thirty. The frontal teeth of those who studied extremely controversial topics were completely missing. According to linguists, the original word for *history* back then was *thrristhorry*. It morphed into its modern version because no professional could pronounce it properly.

Since historians chose their profession freely and signed release forms before they even started studying, Gregor the Pedantic didn't object to their bullying. But the king detested the chaos that marred the discipline as a whole. How could he leave a lasting legacy if future generations were free to question his achievements, regardless of the facts? Surely, he could outlaw criticism while he was still in power, but there was no guarantee his successor would maintain the same policy. He decided to address the problem at its root—before anything else, people needed a universal system to measure the passage of time, completely independent from any temporal power, even from the sovereign himself.

"I have invented a tool called *calendar*," wrote Gregor, "that will standardize time for all of us, regardless of age, gender, sexual orientation, or culinary preferences. Time shall be measured in strictly defined units called *years*. Each year shall consist of twelve *months*, each month—of four *weeks*, and each week—of seven days. As nature doesn't always conform to mathematical precision, some adjustments might be necessary. I reserve the right to add an extra day once in a while, should any pressing circumstances call for it. Rest assured such additions will be carefully deliberated and won't exceed nineteen per year, except on leap years, when that limit would be extended by one day. Naturally, people born on it will live four times longer than the rest of us."

Ironically, future historians would ascribe a deeper meaning to the numbers of months and weeks. Some would even assume the king thought twelve, four, and seven were sacred numbers. There's little doubt that had Gregor been alive at the time those preposterous theories began to spread, he would have been profusely annoyed.

"Every year shall be named after a different animal," continued Gregor. "There will be the Year of the Mermaid, the Sloth, the Squirrel, the Elephant, the Dogfish, the Fishdog, the Hydra, the Rhino, the Bat, and the Minks. Ten consecutive years shall be grouped in a unit called a *decade*. The decades shall be defined by the adjectives Newborn, Walking, Talking, Pubescent, Adult, Promiscuous, Settled, Mature, Aging, and Geriatric. Ten consecutive decades shall form a *century* and each century shall carry an emotional modifier—Happy, Cheerful, Delighted, Smiling, Indifferent, Serious, Frustrated, Resentful, Vengeful, and Forlorn. So without further ado, I announce the beginning of the Year of the Happy Newborn Mermaid!"

While Gregor's calendar freed historians from the perils of subjectivity, his second innovation addressed the rampant eroticism that plagued society on all levels.

"It appears to me," wrote the king, "that despite their emancipation, men are still easily distracted by the charms of women. I have calculated that bureaucratic efficiency diminishes by twenty three percent when a woman is present at a government meeting. It further decreases by another twenty seven percent if the woman is smiling, and if she is scantily dressed, productivity grinds to a halt. I believe a similar dynamic can be observed in other aspects of life. To address this pressing issue, I shall introduce a new form of etiquette that would not only ban women from government service, but will require them to cover their bodies in public—from the rosy toes that deliciously adorn their soft feet, to the velvet calves that graciously rest on our shoulders in times of intimate union. Women should also cover their silky thighs, their woolly vaginae, their alabaster stomachs, their rubbery nipples and the dotted circular rims of their pitch-dark areolae. Furthermore, their necks shall also remain hidden, for there is no other part of the female body that is so vulnerable and inviting for kisses, except the cherry lips that blossom on their faces like fragrant rosebuds yearning to be sniffed. Women shall only reveal their beauty to their husbands, their fathers, their fathers-in-law, the fathers of their fathers-in-law (if any of them are alive and don't have a heart condition), their sons, the sons of their husbands from other wives (including illegitimate bastards who live within the household disguised as servants), their siblings and their corresponding male progeny. Women shall also be allowed to reveal their beauty to small children whose minds are still immune to the wicked effects of nakedness, and to men who are castrated (either by an unfortunate accident or for purposes of domestic security)."

Gregor's third innovation was the introduction of free compulsory education.

"It appears to me," wrote the king, "that our curiosity and willingness to learn new things is a constant source of anxiety. Our youth can barely find the time for recreational activities."

It was indeed obvious that people were constantly intimidated by uncertainties. They spent too much energy analyzing what was true and what wasn't, relying solely on their own judgment. After brief but fruitful deliberation, Gregor concluded that A) learning had to be restricted to designated periods of the day called *school hours,* followed by mandatory rests, during which thinking of any sort was discouraged; and B) learning had to be structured in a standardized program called *curriculum*—a compound term, formed from the Old Hyperborean words *currum,* meaning *knowledge* and *culum,* meaning *sphincter.*

"We have always assumed the best way to learn that fire is dangerous is to stick a finger in its flames," continued Gregor. "Although effective, this method is extremely dangerous. Hardly a week passes by without a drunk teenager getting fully roasted in search of practical knowledge that could otherwise be safely transmitted by verbal or written communication. To optimize its acquisition, I have invented a device called a *textbook*. Additionally, I am introducing a concept called *common sense*—which states that there are truths equally valid for all members of society. Everyone shall be obliged to recognize those truths automatically and shall never question them."

The Rise of an Empire

ARTHUR THE SERENDIPITOUS, the firstborn son of Gregor the Pedantic, was crowned in the Year of the Happy Pubescent Minks and set the record for the longest ruling monarch in history. He was a passionate philosopher with a penchant for physical exercise. His father raised him to be as benevolent as a human could be, and indeed, both as a thinker and as a ruler, he could do no wrong. Arthur's athletic skills were even more impressive.

One morning, while he was warming up for a run, climbing up and down the inner ring of the crater, he saw a shiny cylinder sticking out from the cycloptic remains.

"Bring this blinging object to me," he said to his servants with a voice that was both authoritative and loving.

They rushed to fulfill the order, but no matter how hard they tried, the cylinder remained stuck.

"Mother of petrified snowflakes," said the king with a voice that was both scolding and compassionate, "do I have to do everything myself?"

Arthur rolled up his sleeves, wrapped his manly hands around the shaft of the cylinder and extracted it with a single tug.

His servants were greatly impressed by his power.

As Arthur studied the object, he noticed that both ends were capped with a transparent material that was clearer than ice, yet didn't melt by the touch of the tongue. Desperate to figure out its purpose, he concluded multiple tests, hitting and pocking his servants with it until one day he brought its lower end to his eye. Immediately, the space before him collapsed, as if his spirit was transported forwards—a most unusual experience he called a *vision quest*. The cylinder, it seemed, allowed him to observe people from afar.

The knowledge he amassed during such observations soon increased his political power and, like a molding lobster, Arthur shed the restraining title of a king and adopted a more fitting one—*eternal emperor.*

The title didn't age well, since he eventually got sick and died in the Year of the Cheerful Newborn Sloth. A day after his funeral, his eldest son, who came into possession of the cylinder—by that time known as the *Scepter of Knowledge*—began exhibiting the same qualities his father was famous for. With the epithet *eternal* removed, the imperial title became hereditary, as did the possession of the instrument. With its help, future rulers steadily expanded the size of the empire. The most famous among them, William the Conquerer, discovered the *Island of the Blessed* while having breakfast on the balcony of his royal watchtower. He proclaimed it a crown dependency right before he bit into his unicorn ham sandwich. A second royal gaze during a cocktail break at dusk turned the island into an autonomous province.

The Fall of an Empire

THOSE OF US acquainted with the intricate life of empires know that no matter how powerful they grow to be—and how indispensable their influence seems to their dominions—there comes a moment when they suddenly fall, like ripe fruits from a tall tree.

The Age of Discovery, ushered by Arthur the Serendipitous, abruptly ended in the Year of the Delighted Geriatric Minks, one day after William's ninetieth birthday. The old emperor woke up, put on his slippers, and climbed up the spiral staircase of the royal watchtower with the agility of a polar antelope. As usual, his breakfast was served on a silver platter, right next to the tripod with the Scepter of Knowledge. The emperor took a bite from his unicorn sandwich and began his daily reconnaissance.

The first look didn't reveal anything surprising. On the streets of the capital life went on as usual. Plenty of polar sloths floated in the sea—half-asleep, half-hungry, waiting for a startled seagull to drop a fish right in their half-open mouths. A bit farther, a flock of mermaids sunbathed on the floating ice. A young unicorn was circling nearby, not yet aware that the flesh of the mermaids stank of benthivorous fish, and no creature would dare to bite them, except the arctic wasp—a small insect whose noisy flight could wake up a drunk soldier from the deepest postcoital dream. The sting of this parasite wasn't a defensive weapon, but an organ for procreation. With it, the wasp injected its eggs directly into the mermaid's bloodstream. Once hatched, the larvae attached to the walls of the creature's heart and gorged on its blood, turning its color from red to lilac. Shamans used the flesh of infected mermaids to brew a potion called *burundanga*. It could subdue the will of the most stubborn people. Ah, thought the emperor, how delightful was this unapologetic complexity! It is not mystery that truly bewildered us, but the things we already knew, for everything was interconnected in pristine hierarchy and its intricacies were unfathomable even to the brightest minds! Who needed new discoveries when there were so many known things to contemplate!

He wasn't the first emperor with symptoms of discovery fatigue. In fact, near the end of his reign Arthur himself found the task of exploration tiring and had to be consoled by an anonymous prophet, who predicted that one day there would be nothing new to discover and all creation would ascend to a higher state of sublime harmony. Like all religious doctrines, it seemed too good to be true, which was exactly why it survived through the ages.

William finished his sandwich, wiped the crumbs off his beard, and somewhat reluctantly turned the scepter to the horizon. It was time for him to fulfill his daily duties.

There was nothing new to the east. He rubbed his eyes, yawned, and turned to the south. The rays of the morning Sun were skimming over the icebergs. Many of them had names because William loved to anthropomorphize objects. It helped him catalogue them more efficiently. While his predecessors used long descriptions like *middle-sized chunk of ice with an ultramarine base,* William just wrote Wilma and kept the details in his head. Today he saw Wilma bumping into Björn, a smaller iceberg with a smooth, rounded top. They looked like they were going to remain together for quite some time because the ocean current carried them to a nearby bay, formed by a landslide that happened a year ago. It killed a fisherman and a mermaid. He couldn't remember the fisherman's name, but was pretty sure the mermaid was called Agneta. He missed her. She was beautiful. Once, as she was resting on her back in the water, he took her nipples for faraway islands. He was about to record their coordinates when the mermaid abruptly turned and gave him a severe bout of motion sickness. Nothing of the sort happened today. The South was as familiar as always. Perhaps his eyesight was failing him? If that were true, how come he could see the things he had already discovered so clearly? It was equally unlikely he was becoming senile, for he could still marvel at the world with such pristine clarity. William turned to the west, hoping to end those doubts once and for all. There wasn't anything new there either. Pointing the scepter to the north was useless, for no one had ever done such a ridiculous thing—it was the place where the world ended, and the waters of the ocean fell into the Great Abyss, a truly unpleasant place even to think of, much less to investigate.

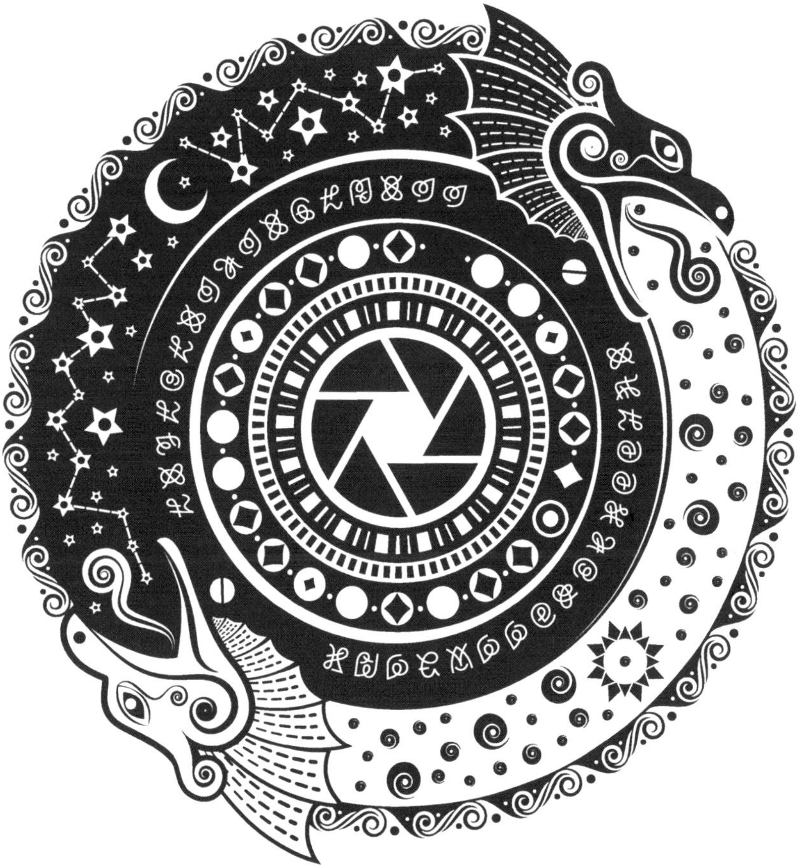

It was at that moment when a daring thought pierced his mind: There was nothing left to discover! He was the emperor from the prophecy, the one chosen to complete the monumental task started by his legendary predecessor. He rushed down the stairs, eager to deliver the good news to his government, when his robe got stuck on the parapet. He stumbled and fell. Everything turned black.

When he came back to his senses, he found his body still buzzing with excitement, as if a pack of polar bees had invaded his insides. His muscles were jittering, his heart—racing, his eyes—insatiably hopping from object to object. Light was oozing from the window above his head. The air was glowing, as if the aurora had taken refuge in the watchtower. The parapet that his hands instinctively latched on felt refreshingly cold. Oh, how foolish of him to rush! Would there be any difference if he announced the news now or waited for an hour? Discovering there was nothing else to discover was the ultimate achievement one could ever hope for. It carried a sense of finality that made time irrelevant. For once William wasn't thinking about the future. It felt like someone just lifted a blindfold off his eyes. Ah, the world was complete! And so was he! And then, inadvertently, the intense feeling turned into a death wish—for just like complete disillusionment, absolute satisfaction diminishes one's will to live. Isn't it strange, he thought, that we think of life as a force of nature, as an instinct independent of the mind, while in fact, what truly keeps us going is the fear of missing out, of passing away before we get the chance to conquer our ignorance!

He heard footsteps. His mind was too self-absorbed to inquire where they came from. By the time his guards reached him, he was thoroughly entranced by a sense of profound gratitude.

"Your Majesty, are you hurt?" a voice said.

"No, child," replied William with a smile.

Anxious panting permeated the calm air. More guards arrived—mouths gasping, bodies drenched in sweat, lungs beating like war drums. Oh, the vitality of youth!

"His Majesty is hurt!" someone said.

William reached for the blurry face of the guard kneeling next to him and ran his wrinkled hand on his smooth cheek—so delicate, unscarred by experience.

"Dear child, you don't understand," said William. The cheek suddenly turned moist, like melting snow. The guard was crying.

"I am not hurt," continued William, "I am blessed, for I have…"

"Call a doctor!" someone shouted. A cacophony of anxious voices quickly reached crescendo as his words echoed inside the watchtower.

"I have discovered everyth..." said the emperor and died mid-sentence. The complete phrase was nevertheless chiseled as an epitaph on his tombstone.

His opulent funeral was attended by all his subjects, although—due to heavy snowfall—the majority of them were present only in spirit. The first to speak was the minister of royal funerals:

"As we say goodbye to our beloved sovereign, our hearts are filled with sorrow. Yet I compel all of you..."

His throat, dehydrated by sadness, failed him and he paused to take a sip of water. The brief respite allowed people to scrape the frozen tears off their cheeks.

"I dare you!" he continued as his raspy voice regained its strength. "I dare you to rejoice in consolation, for William the Conqueror fulfilled the daunting task set by our first emperor and revealed to us the world in all its glory! He restlessly pointed the Scepter of Knowledge at every cave and iceberg and scraped all mystery off the horizon. His benevolent power spread all over the world like a soft blanked over a sleeping damsel. Never again shall we wander with fear of the unknown, for everything that might appear new shall be something we had carelessly forgotten!"

Blood and Decadence

THREE MONTHS AFTER WILLIAM'S DEATH, his son was crowned as Harold the Disconsolate, by the grace of the Goddess, forever August, emperor of the Arctic; King of the frozen islands, Archduke of the icebergs with perky peaks, Duke of the partially molten icebergs, Prince of all the other icebergs that cannot be easily classified; Landgrave of the Great Abyss and the Island of the Blessed, Margrave of the Cycloptic Crater, Mayor of Storkhome, President of the Royal Household, Object of Adoration, and Subject to None—the last being his preferred title in person-to-person interactions.

By tradition, Harold was raised to be insatiably curios.

"It is my duty as a father to ensure that my progeny exceeds me in all aspects of life," William once said to his son, "for this is how human civilization progresses from barbaric gratification to enlightened dissatisfaction."

"Oh, Subject to None," said one day Harold's minister of health, "I see you pensive and withdrawn."

The emperor was squinting through the Scepter of Knowledge.

"It is indeed crystal clear that my mood has severely deteriorated, although I am looking for ways to improve it," said the emperor. "Do you see that tiny red spot over there?"

Harold pointed to the edge of the moat below the royal palace.

"This is a sight reserved for your eyes only, Subject to None," replied the minister of health.

"Of course," said Harold. "Only an emperor can use the Scepter of Knowledge."

He tapped the looking glass as if it was a pet.

"Of all the rules we have," he continued, "this one makes the least sense. Do you have an idea why the use of the Scepter of Knowledge is restricted to me?"

"Your Majesty, according to the…" The minister of health began reciting the constitution.

"That's not what I asked," interrupted Harold. "Our laws didn't fall from the sky. They were written by men like you and me. Do you know what all men have in common?"

"The desire to serve the state," answered the minister of health.

"Mermaid shitting on glacier," cursed Harold. "Drop the protocol and save us some time! The only thing all men have in common is an agenda!"

Sweating profusely, the minister of health wiped his palms on his robe.

"And what could that agenda be, I hear you ask," continued Harold, even though the minister didn't dare to utter a word, because A) he knew it was time for the usual didactic monologue, and B) he had already seen the red dot the emperor was referring to up close. It was a disturbing sight.

"You see, there are usually three distinct answers, but only one of them is right," continued Harold, delighted to play teacher to someone who was twice his age. "An idealist would say all we want is love. It sounds so pretty! And also petty, because it discards hate, which is equally powerful. Cynics, on the other hand, are much more attuned to the intricacies of life. They would say what we all want is wealth. It's an ugly assumption and no less petty. Wealth is useless without a cause and all causes are by definition abstract. The truth is that the material world is too poor to satisfy our yearnings. This is how we end up with so many dysfunctional rich people. My minister of statistics would have gladly confirmed my words, if he were still alive. He worked tirelessly to improve the mental condition of our wealthiest citizens, whose psychological problems were constantly dismissed as arrogant nonsense. It's easy for the less fortunate to criticize the rich for being unhappy. As if happiness can be stacked on a shelf or exchanged as currency. We often idealize the poor, but let me tell you, material and intellectual poverty often go hand in hand. And then comes a tiny minority of people, those, who for the lack of a better word we call *realists*. They know the right answer. Deep inside, what we truly want, is order. It's how we protect ourselves, our loved ones, our possessions, even our aspirations. Order is achieved through laws that balance ideals and instincts. When that balance is disrupted, society becomes inert and decadent."

Had there been a third person it the room, he would have concluded that the minister of health was listening very carefully. But under the polished facade of attentiveness, his mind was actually busy crafting a praise adequate to the length of the emperor's monologue. When his instincts indicated that Harold's philosophical tirade came to a close, the minister nodded and hunched his back as a sign of respect.

"Second to None," he replied, "my ears are not worthy of so much wisdom. Had I been contemplating for a year, I wouldn't have succeeded in describing the meaning of life in such succinct manner."

"So," continued the emperor, "now that we agree that laws are subjective, I invite you to break them. Come, take a look through the Scepter of Knowledge, and tell me what you see down there."

The emperor pointed to the red spot again. The minister of health nervously stepped forward. Although he knew what lied down there, he feared to admit it. The appearance of the red spot had alarmed the entire government, or more precisely, its members who were still alive.

"Second to None, now that you mentioned it, I most definitely see it, even without the aid of the scepter," he said, "And I am curious to know what it is, since just an hour ago, the snow below was as white as your honorable teeth."

"It might be hard for you to guess from such a distance, but I happen to know its exact nature. It is the body of the minister of theater."

"Mother of snowflakes! Did he do something wrong?" asked the minister of health.

"No," said the emperor, "but he didn't do anything right either, and you know how much I detest inefficiency. So I commanded him to throw himself from the terrace and he fulfilled my request."

The emperor was lying. Sure enough, the minister attempted to fulfill the wish of his sovereign. However, at the last moment, his hand instinctively grabbed the parapet and refused to let go, even though he struggled to convince it to comply. It was up to the emperor to help loosen its grip by stepping on it until the dramatist fell to his demise, leaving behind a family of two pubescent sons, a daughter, a cheating wife, five dogs, and thirty seven plays, half of them bestsellers.

"Sometimes I think people enjoy dying more than I enjoy sentencing them to death," said the emperor.

"Perhaps Your Majesty will find relief in letting some of them live," said the minister of health.

"What use could there be of a life without a purpose?" replied Harold. "Look at us! Ever since my father discovered everything, we're bouncing off the walls of this castle like headless chicken. It's not only academics who lost their jobs. We all did. That old goat robbed us of everything and conveniently died before he could face the consequences."

"He gave us the knowledge of everything, Second to None!"

"He was a deranged narcissist," shouted Harold.

The abrupt anger startled the minister of health.

"Sweet mother of snowflakes," continued Harold, imitating his father's voice, "I just realized I discovered everything. How could this be! Ah, let me ponder this wonder while I trip on the staircase. Oh dear, I must have fallen in the arms of death! The odds of such coincidence bemuse my enlightened mind. Ah, I shan't be bitter, for destiny couldn't have chosen a better moment for my ultimate demise. And now that I don't have to worry I'd have to deal with a world suffocated by perpetual boredom, I can peacefully ascend to the heavens!"

Harold was so taken by his performance that in the end, he found himself lying on the floor, eyes closed. Strange, he thought, as he was impersonating his father, he came suspiciously close to experiencing the completeness he was so resentfully mocking. If the old emperor could see him now, he would be the one laughing.

"Your Majesty shouldn't exhaust himself with thoughts about the past," said the minster of health. He reached to help Harold get back on his feet.

"Are you one of those people who doubt my stamina or, even worse, my competence to rule?" asked the emperor. "If so, I command you to follow your colleague and jump to your death."

The heart of the minister of health was racing. Ending his life wasn't on his to do list for the day.

"Unless," continued Harold, "you are willing to follow my orders. I just devised a plan to restore society to its former glory."

"Second to None, this is—and always will be—what I strive for. It will be an honor to take part in such a plan, whatever the cost."

"Don't worry, it's easy," said Harold. "Then again, the minister of theater said the same thing before I lost my patience. I commanded him to write a play, one that could free the people from the burden of knowledge. A subversive narrative was all I needed. One that implied all those ultimate discoveries were a scam—a conspiracy—secretly hatched by the government to distract people from their real problems. Do you know what he said? He looked me right in the face with his moist, grayish eyes and told me that to him, truth was dearer than the wellbeing of society."

"Truth," replied the minister of health, "could be difficult to handle."

"Exactly!" said the emperor. "You see, truth is like medicine—too little will keep you sick, too much will kill you. Isn't this a wonderful metaphor?"

"It's a brilliant thought," said the minster of health.

"Hence I command you to invent a psychoactive medicine that can induce mild paranoia among the populace and restore the healthy sense of mystery that we all enjoyed before my father robbed us from it," said Henry and smiled, waiting for the minister to match his excitement.

After a moment of confusion, the minister of health smiled as widely as he could.

"I will, of course, start research immediately," he replied.

"Excellent!" said Harold.

"In the meantime, could I suggest that Your Majesty takes a much needed break?" said the minster. "There is a lot resting on your shoulders, and a brief nap would certainly energize you."

"You are right," replied Harold. "I need a rest. Do you carry one of your sleep potions with you?"

"I never leave my laboratory without it," said the minster of health and handed Harold a flask full of dark lilac liquid.

The emperor dismissed the minister and retreated to his chambers, where he remained until the end of his life—an event that happened half an hour later.

The minister of health had laced the sleep potion with a poison so powerful, it could kill a herd of unicorns. It was a painful decision. He had been present at Harold's birth and had watched him grow. Yet, as a public servant, his ultimate loyalty lied with the state, not the individual that personified it.

Harold's son, Edgar, was crowned in the Year of the Smiling Walking Elephant. Immediately after the ceremony, the minister of health resigned and, haunted by the moral relativity of his act, committed suicide. Neither his name, nor his achievement was remembered, for unpleasant truths are rarely acknowledged in the annals of history, lest they diminish the impossible ideas we all live by.

A Flare of Populism

HAD PEOPLE TURNED THE ENTIRE WORLD upside down, they wouldn't have found a more fitting opposite to Harold than his firstborn son. Edgar the Meek, by the grace of the Goddess, forever August, emperor of everywhere, was so considerate and courteous, there were rumors he was a bastard. In his coronation speech, he addressed those erroneous claims upfront, with a hand firmly placed on his heart.

"There are those who say children inherit the sins of their fathers, but I beg to differ. We are best judged not by the expectations that are forced upon us, but by our deeds, which are the fruits of our decisions. As your monarch, I pledge to you that my eyes and ears shall always be wide open, and I shall consult you as frequently as possible, so no decision of mine could cause even the slightest discomfort, or—Goddess forbid—some sort of regrettable pain. I am, and forever will be, your most dedicated servant."

Twenty days after he uttered those words, Edgar the Meek abdicated.

"After a long and exhausting consultation with my cabinet regarding the annual budget of our thriving empire, I came to the unpleasant conclusion that I couldn't, in good conscience, continue to perform the role of emperor. Due to conflicting demands from my ministers, it became obvious that no decision of mine would make everyone happy. Looking back at the pledge that I made, I can't help but think it was a bit naive from me to assume I was capable of meeting everyone's expectations equally. On one hand, there are far too many people in our empire. On the other, half of them is always tempted to disagree with the other half, with little respect for logic or pragmatism. Had I known all this, I would have sworn to rule as a dictator, so I wouldn't have to listen anybody's petty complaints. Before you start whining how disappointed you are by my decision, take a moment to consider how pissed off I must feel to voluntarily give up the best paid job in this empire and how tempting it is to renege on my generous promises. Nevertheless, I stand by my belief that a public pledge should be honored, for if it isn't, people would lose confidence in our political system and the pillars of our society would be corroded by cynicism."

Needless to say, the abdication wasn't an impulsive act. Edgar spent a considerable amount of time in contemplative prayer, asking the Goddess for guidance. Unfortunately, during the entire period of the budget impasse, she was busy with far more pressing matters, and Edgar's pleas were put on hold. By the time she got the chance to examine them, his son, Brandon, was already crowned.

Emancipation

BRANDON THE FLACCID, by the grace of the Goddess, forever August, emperor of everywhere, fulfilled all expectations one could have of a member of a decadent royal dynasty. He was a chaotic administrator and an avid womanizer—qualities that blended well, for one fed off the other like a flame gorging on candle wax. He shared neither his grandfather's obsession with political power, nor his father's reluctance to exercise it unilaterally. To him, the matters of the state were merely a distraction from the transient pleasures of life, and he was known for preferring the company of women to that of his ministers.

"Isn't it amazing," Brandon once said to his minister of philosophy, "that every time an eloquent government official opens his mouth to speak, I feel compelled to yawn, while the simplest sigh coming out of the mouth of my concubines gives me a delightful boner?"

"This is hardly surprising, Your Majesty," replied the minister. "In this world the pleasures of the flesh are easier to appreciate. Yet without the restraints of the spirit to balance them, society would disintegrate under the yoke of sensual barbarism."

Balancing opposites wasn't among Brandon's talents, especially when it concerned things as elusive as the human spirit. His lack of sophistication often infuriated his government, but charmed the common people, who just like him didn't pay much attention to abstractions.

Brandon's first act as an emperor was to order the dismounting of the Scepter of Knowledge—a challenging operation that took a whole week to complete, because the last person who knew exactly how to do it died long time ago, and the instructions he left were somewhat confusing.

The instrument was put in a museum, along with various memorabilia, like the mittens Arthur wore when he pulled it out of the cycloptic remains and the silver platter on which William's breakfast was served each morning. Like most museums, it was only visited by children, forcefully brought there by their teachers.

The royal watchtower was closed for repairs. There were rumors it would be ultimately demolished to make way for a luxurious high-rise igloo that would host various departments of the newly created *Ministry of Entertainment*.

Since there was nothing left to discover, Brandon had a lot of free time—something that made his ministers anxious. They were convinced his grandfather's madness was caused by unhinged boredom. To avoid another bout of irrational violence, the ministers struggled to keep the new emperor busy by expanding his responsibilities. Brandon's breakfast took two hours and began with a ritual called *The Breaking of the Loaf*. Each morning, the best bread in the kingdom was delivered to the palace, so the emperor could slice it with his imperial saber. The bread was then given to the poor as a sign of royal generosity. It was a noble act that nevertheless skewed Brandon's perception of reality, for it implied that A) he was somehow involved in the process of bread making, and B) that a single loaf cut in two could feed all the clerks that lost their jobs on the Day of Ultimate Discovery. Brandon's lunch took three hours and finished with another ritual called *The Blessing of the Blanket*. Every day the best weavers in the kingdom sent their most exquisite fabrics to the palace. After close inspection, the emperor picked the softest and took a refreshing nap called siesta, during which he blissfully snored (and sometimes farted), while his royal bowels worked hard to digest the food jammed inside them. Subsequently, the blanket was donated to the poor. It was another noble act that cemented Brandon's misperception of reality, for it implied that A) his body had extraordinary blessing powers, and B) that a single blanket could warm up all the teachers that lost their jobs when it became clear no new clerks were needed to update the royal catalog. Brandon skipped dinner and preferred to spend his evenings in the company of his concubines. It was a controversial habit because A) since the times of Gregor the Pedantic women were considered intellectually inferior to men, and B) men were expected to converse with them only for the purposes of procreation. His ministers didn't object because what happened after working hours was a private matter. They were wrong.

On the first morning of the Year of the Smiling Walking Hydra, Brandon arrived to a government meeting with a severe hangover, wearing nothing but a wrinkled shirt, stained with lipstick.

"I am sick and tired of being a hypocrite," he declared. "In our society, women have been unjustly oppressed for ages and we have to put an end to it."

Nervous rumble filled the conference hall. Most of it was unintelligible, although one could occasionally distinguish words like *travesty* and *effeminate* bubbling through an avalanche of coughs. Ever since the reign of Harold the Disconsolate, cabinet members refrained from open disagreement with the monarch. The short temper of the deranged emperor forced his chief of staff to severely restrict the manner of bureaucratic expression:

In rare cases when the sovereign's ideas seem inadequate and/or ludicrous, members of the cabinet shall express criticism indirectly through mild coughing, during which their mouths should be covered by their right fists. Once the expression of disapproval is finalized, officials should promptly hydrate their throats, as to avoid extra coughs, spontaneously caused by phlegm residue. In force majeure circumstances members of the cabinet are allowed a single clockwise eye roll, performed with a slight tilt of the neck and pursing of the lips.

The coughing gradually died out and was replaced by loud gulps of water.

"Some of you might think I've gone mad," said the emperor and tugged on his lower lip.

A strand of curly hair stuck on it was bothering him ever since he woke up with the legs of the aforementioned concubine wrapped around his neck.

"It's true that women wield enormous power over men, for it takes a single look into their wanton eyes to weaken the knees of the bravest among us."

"Indeed," agreed the cabinet ministers.

"However, blaming them for our weaknesses is irresponsible. What we should do is muster the courage to resist their charms."

"Impossible," shouted the minister of education.

The rest of the cabinet wholeheartedly agreed.

"Allow me to demonstrate," said Brandon and clapped his hands.

A veiled figure entered the room. Although covered from head to toe, several ministers got breathless just from hearing her footsteps. Only one woman could walk like this—the first imperial concubine, Sklud. The Hyperborean gossip chroniclers called her the temptress of saints.

She stopped in front of the imperial throne and turned her back at the conference table, facing Brandon. He nodded. She unveiled her face. Brandon remained calm, with a serene, child-like smile.

"This is a trickery," someone shouted. "He's wearing a mask!"

Brandon expected that much. Centuries of institutionalized prejudice couldn't be overcome that easily. He nodded again and Sklud untied her shirt. The skin of her naked back glittered under the candlelight and forced a wave of spontaneous moans out of the aroused ministers. Brandon, who was facing her bare breasts, silently stood up and dropped his pants. His penis was perfectly flaccid.

"If you were still able to speak," said the emperor to his stunned ministers, "you would have asked me whether I possessed some supernatural strength, so I could avoid an instant erection in front of the most attractive woman that has ever lived. Rest assured, the answer is trivial. Once I stopped treating women as pleasure toys and accepted them as individuals, I became resistant to their beauty. Nothing can dampen the urges of the flesh more effectively than intellectual interaction. Once we are aware that—apart from vaginae and breasts—women also have hearts and minds, they become far less attractive."

Thus ended the Age of Patriarchy and everyone lived happily until, six hundred and forty three months later, in the Year of the Smiling Settled Minks, a ship appeared on the frozen horizon.

A Matter of Size

THEY SAY HISTORY IS MADE BY GREAT INDIVIDUALS, but anyone who has ever studied it knows that's just an excuse, so the masses can absolve themselves from responsibility. Historical narratives, just like flesh and spirit, are born from chaos and sooner or later descend back into it. However, since every rule has an exception, it should be noted that there was indeed one person who singlehandedly affected the course of history. Her name was Bartholomea of the Desert—the first woman who traveled the world from end to end.

Born and raised in a desert tribe, Bartholomea was expected to follow in the footsteps of her people, whose main occupation was ambushing caravans and looting oases. Alas, instead of a sense of belonging, the sandy terrain inspired only boredom in her heart. As soon as she learned to ride a camel, she left home in search of exciting adventures.

"Don't worry," said Bartholomea's mother to her husband, "when she sees water falling from the sky without warning, and the unbearable humidity makes her armpits sticky, she will come back and beg us for forgiveness."

Seeing tiny water droplets falling through the air roused Bartholomea's curiosity even more. Not only did she learn to refer to this phenomenon by its proper name, *rain,* she also found out the cold winds farther north turned it into a feathery substance called *snow*. The word seemed familiar. Long time ago, a man from her tribe was beheaded for uttering something similar. Perhaps he was an explorer like her, but chose to return and share his knowledge with his ignorant relatives. His execution inadvertently revealed the hidden meaning of an ancient proverb: *In the eyes of cowards, wonders appear as threats.*

One day, resting at an inn during one of her journeys, Bartholomea met a husky sailor, whose chest was covered with strange tattoos.

He told her that way up north the weather was so cold, seawater turned into stone, and there were whole mountains of it floating in the ocean. She didn't believe him. Sailors often bent the truth for personal gain, especially in the presence of women. Nevertheless, Bartholomea took him to her room, and they started doing all those unspeakable things that compulsive travelers do when they stay in a place they don't intend to return to. As she stared at his broad chest bouncing up and down to the rhythm of her moaning, she realized his tattoos depicted a map with a sea route to an archipelago, marked with the letter H. In this very moment, seconds before Bartholomea climaxed, the fate of the Hyperborean Empire was sealed.

"Greetings, redheaded inhabitants of H," shouted Bartholomea, as her ship dropped anchor on the Hyperborean shore, "I have traveled the world and the seven seas, looking for your miraculous mountains of petrified water! It took me ages to find my way here, and I'm glad my journey is finally over."

"Liar!" said an illiterate fisherman, "you look younger than my own granddaughter."

Bartholomea rolled her eyes.

"Don't be fooled by my perky breasts and my innocent smile," she replied. "Time flows slower for people in constant motion. My body might be youthful and attractive, but my mind is old and wise."

Like most prominent historical figures, Bartholomea was instantly assigned a nickname: *The woman that came out of nowhere*. Since the end of the Age of Discovery, every Hyperborean child was taught there was nothing beyond the horizon. Now that her arrival proved everybody wrong, people tried to approach the controversy with a sense of humor, although everybody realized a meaningful explanation was urgently needed.

Arnold the Easily Convinced, Emperor of Heaven and Earth, welcomed Bartholomea to the palace with open arms and the concealed hope he was just having a bad dream.

"Your existence doesn't make sense," he said, "yet your breasts are too big to be figments of my imagination."

"Your Majesty," replied Bartholomea, "I would gladly annihilate myself, so I can conform to your world view, which I find fascinating and quite comforting, but we both know that in this Universe nothing ever disappears without a trace."

"It would be quite rude of me to demand something like this from a guest," said Arnold, "but I urge you to help me find a reasonable explanation why our instrument of observation couldn't detect the lands you are coming from."

When Bartholomea inspected the retired Scepter of Knowledge, she immediately recognized its limitations.

"I know where the problem is," she said. "When it comes to such instruments, size is of uttermost importance. An eventual enlargement would allow you to catch a glimpse of the lands that lie on the opposite side of the ocean, and if the weather conditions are favorable, even spot the mountains that lie beyond their shores. However, I must warn you that the successful completion of such a project would require a lot of resources and pose a serious economic challenge."

Arnold decided the risk was worth taking and immediately began a comprehensive upgrade, setting up to double the reach of the Scepter of Knowledge in less than five decades.

"Apart from resolving the Bartholomea paradox, this project will once and for all establish our empire as the greatest power in the Universe," announced the emperor.

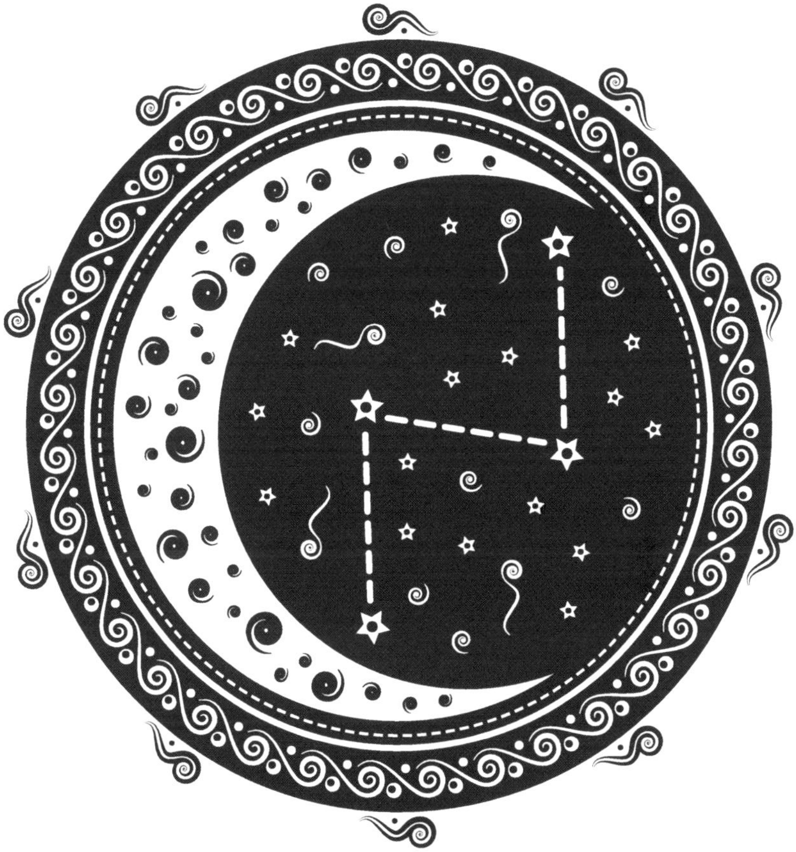

The ambitious undertaking drew the attention of the Goddess of Ice. Seeing yet another of her creations succumb to the trappings of grandeur brought her great disappointment. She knew it was just a matter of time before the Hyperboreans point their improved instrument to the skies and catch her off guard in a delicate pose, forever undermining her authority. And while she had plenty of eggs to wreak havoc on them, something seemingly insignificant might survive the next thermonuclear explosion. Inevitably, someone would dig it out of the rubble and sow the seeds of another revolt. The Goddess needed a permanent solution.

For three days and three nights she plotted her response. On the fourth morning, she took a sip of her favorite tea, gargled for a minute, and spat into the ocean. Her saliva roused the salty waters. Out of their murky depths rose a magnificent island, covered in lush forests, teaming with fantastic beasts and wondrous birds. In its center stood a magnificent palace. Its ivory walls and stained glass windows extended all the way up to the sky.

"Such marvels are unworthy of the crude Earth," said the Goddess, "yet I would rather bring the skies down than allow gravel to contaminate my sacred realms."

And thus, she put on her most beautiful dress made from the silk of heavenly arachnids—a fabric so delicate and pure, even the mildest breeze could pass through undisturbed. She took residence in the palace, along with her thousand and one servants. They brought foods and drinks that had never touched the lips of a human. Their taste was so exquisite, it could drive a mortal soul to madness. When she had her fill, the Goddess retreated to the sprawling terrace of the palace and took a nap on a hammock of golden cashmere.

Across the Arctic Ocean, King Henry the Navigator, son of Arnold the Easily Convinced, by the grace of the Goddess, forever August, Enlarger of Empires, Subjugator of Horizons, Conqueror of Worlds, and Disseminator of Wisdom, peeked through the upgraded Scepter of Knowledge in search of new dominions. As he adjusted its focus, his eyes stumbled upon the bulging breasts of the Goddess. Blinded by lust and hubris, Henry took his divine mistress for a damsel in distress.

"I just discovered a wondrous island, whose queen seems rather melancholic," he said to his minister of important announcements. "I claim her as my most precious subject and declare her realms my personal protectorate, over which I shall rule justly and perpetually."

"Inhabitants of the realm," shouted the minister through his loudspeaker, "It is my delightful duty to inform you that our most distinguished emperor just discovered a new land, ruled by a queen who doesn't seem to be in good spirits."

An hour later, Henry summoned his government.

"We live in times of constant change and they require radical decisions," he said to them. "After careful consideration, I have determined that our style of exploration is old-fashioned and needs urgent improvement. It is not sufficient to study the horizon from afar anymore. A modern ruler who takes conquest seriously cannot annex lands by mere observation. He must bravely set foot on them and plant flags in their soil. I have therefore issued immediate orders for the creation of a fleet, with which I shall depart on an expedition."

As soon as the ships were ready, Henry sailed for the island of the Goddess with a hundred of his best men. A fourth of them disappeared during a sea storm. Another fourth rebelled, demanding to go back, and were executed for mutiny. Three accidentally fell overboard while no one was looking. Twelve succumbed to food poisoning. Sixteen got drunk at a birthday party, fell asleep on the dock, and froze to death. Nineteen committed suicide because in the hassle of the initial preparations, nobody thought about bringing a counselor on board. Finally, after a long and perilous journey, in the Year of the Forlorn Geriatric Minks, Henry, the sole survivor of the first Hyperborean voyage of exploration, disembarked on the island.

"Welcome to the New World," said the Goddess.

Back home, the government, worried the emperor might have perished, authorized the minister of exploration to use the Scepter of Knowledge and search for the fleet. He followed the trail of dead bodies all the way to the island of the Goddess. There he saw his emperor, waving frantically, holding a big note in his hands. It said:

This place is awesome! You should all come over!

Part Three

BULLS, OLIVES AND HEARTS ON FIRE

"Love makes the head go round."
Caudillian proverb

The Dancing Plague

WHILE MOST DISEASES TRAVELLED on paved roads, shoulder to shoulder with merchants and soldiers, the dancing plague came through the fields, unexpected and unannounced. The first to witness its arrival in the village of Caudilla was Amalia, the widow of Alfonso the baker. She spent her afternoons under a lonesome olive tree in the middle of her family field. Rumor had it the tree grew out of a pit Amalia spat out when she was four years old. Even as a young girl, she had an insatiable taste for bitter things, and—until she discovered mourning years later—raw olives were her favorite treat.

Amalia was having a siesta, curled up in the roots of the tree, when a delicate, melodic hum spread all over the empty field. Like most old people, Amalia was easily annoyed even by the smallest surprises, and the subtle noise woke her up as if it were coming from an invading army. She looked around, desperate to scold someone, but instead of a battalion of shouting soldiers, she saw a single girl in a plain white dress, mindlessly pirouetting in the shimmering wheat. Amalia's annoyance gave way to genuine bewilderment—a feeling she had almost forgotten, for it had been a while since she witnessed something she couldn't immediately explain.

"The days of our lives are numbered—one, two, three," sang the girl while her swirling pirouettes brought her closer and closer to the tree.

Amalia knew the song. She last heard it from the lips of her husband, on that winter night when God took him away.

"And death will come for all of us—four, five, six," went on the girl, spinning faster and faster.

As her husband sang those words, they stirred such fire in Amalia that she lost her sense of self. It was not until Alfonso's hands abruptly let go of her breasts when she regained her sanity and realized something was wrong. Alfonso's soul had departed, leaving a lifeless heap of flesh, stuck between her legs.

"Let's dance before we all stumble—seven, eight, nine," continued the girl, just a stone-throw away from the tree. Amalia felt her heart bounc-

ing off her rib cage, as if it was trying to escape her body. The blinding sunlight of the early afternoon now looked unusually pale.

"It is every woman's calling to satisfy her husband's desires, for this is the way new life is begotten," said the priest at Alfonso's funeral. "But when a woman herself takes pleasure in the act of union, her loins get infested with evil spirits and she becomes a conduit of death. Such sins could only be absolved by God himself after years of contrition and remorse."

Brokenhearted, Amalia spent the rest of her life in solitude, hopelessly waiting for forgiveness. Now, old and decrepit, she didn't need it anymore, for she had gotten used to feeling guilty and cursed just like her fellow villagers had gotten used to being happy and righteous. Instead of using psalms to educate their flock about the dangers of sin, the priests just pointed to the black widow, who once let the devil in her womb. And although people prayed for her salvation every Sunday, what they secretly hoped for was for God to confine her to the seventh circle of Hell with the heaviest of chains, for if wretches like her were granted forgiveness, it would embolden others to sin without restraint.

"We'll rest when our bodies crumble—ten and done!" continued the girl before she entered the shadow of the olive tree and her body disintegrated into a cloud of lilac ash. Amalia's heart skipped a beat and she fell into a faint.

The afternoon wind spread the lilac ash to every house in the sleepy village. It settled on the tightly shut window blinds, where it stuck to the feet of geckos and insects who brought it inside through the cracks in the walls. A hour later, Caudilla woke up to life. Just like any other day, men rushed to the wells for water and women began washing pots and pans. But instead of the usual cacophony of random clicks and clacks, a steady rhythm spread from door to door. It wasn't long before people's feet, compelled by an unknown force, began to tap along. Their hands soon joined in and people came out on the streets, dancing and clapping.

"Praise the Lord," shouted the priest, "such celebration is a gift from Heaven."

"Praise the Lord," replied the merry crowd.

People realized they weren't in control of their limbs when an old woman fell down. While she was in pain, begging for someone to help her stand up, her body was tossing and turning like a wounded snake. A ring of dancing people formed around her, each trying to lend her a hand but to no avail. The power of their will was no match for the enchanting rhythm.

"Enough already," shouted a man, beating his legs with his cane.

"I can't breathe," howled a pregnant woman, drenched in sweat.

Drowned by screams and moans, the joyful parade quickly turned into a spectacle of terror. By the time the Sun went down, the only one still dancing was the priest, his hands jerking towards the sky, pleading for mercy. The endless invocations of the name of the Lord had long dried his throat, and his pain, trapped inside his lungs, had forced him to tear his robe with his bare bleeding hands. When the crescent of the Moon appeared behind the mountain ridge, his soul let go of his tortured body and Caudilla once more fell silent.

It was night time when Amalia opened her eyes. The dancing girl was gone and the filed was eerily calm under the moonlight. On her way back, she noticed her legs didn't ache like before. She understood why once she got home and looked at herself in the mirror. In front of it was the young woman she once was, before the death of her husband. It seemed that God had finally forgiven her.

The Olive Child

IT HAS BEEN ALLEGED—BUT NOT VERIFIED—that once upon a time in Caudilla a pregnant woman got such a craving for green olives, she stripped a whole tree of its unripened fruits in a single afternoon.

Apparently, the tree grew angry with her, but since plants and humans rarely talk, the woman remained unaware of its feelings until nightfall, when she fell asleep, and the abused plant paid her a visit in a terrifying dream. The woman tossed and turned under the sheets like a hen in the hands of a butcher. When her husband pinched her behind to wake her up from the nightmare, she told him a wooden snake slid through her most intimate of body openings and, while she lay paralyzed and helpless, snatched her unborn child.

The husband found the nightmare harmless, but knowing superstition adorns pregnancy like stars bedeck the night sky, he went to the dining room, took the icon of Santa Olivia that hung over the dinner table and, just in case, nailed it right over the marital bed, assuring his wife the saint won't let anyone—much less an imaginary wooden snake—to cause the slightest harm to their unborn child.

When the nightmare occurred again the following night, the woman's faith in the power of the Santa Olivia was greatly diminished and she went to see her neighbor, a widow of ninety-six years, who was once known as a gifted seer and excellent interpreter of dreams and nightmares. The old woman wiped the dust off her crystal ball and spent an hour polishing its surface. Eventually, she concluded the snake was the vengeful spirit of the very olive tree whose progeny the woman gobbled up during her gluttonous fit.

Scared out of her wits, the woman implored her husband to cut the tree but he stubbornly refused, telling her plants didn't have spirits, not to mention ones prone to vengeance. The woman went to bed unconvinced. Once her husband started to snore, she grabbed his axe and rushed to confront her tormentor. The fear of losing her precious child turned her into a berserk woodcutter and by midnight, the sturdy trunk of the olive tree gave in. Once the woman saw the terrifying plant helplessly prostrated on the ground, she spat on it, wiped the sweat off her head, pulled all the splinters out of her hands, and went to bed.

When her husband woke up in the morning, he saw his wife lying next to him, silent like a fish and dry like a raisin. Out of her belly was sprouting a tiny olive tree.

The Great Caudillian Schism

LONG TIME AGO, in a year whose number nobody cared to remember, Caudilla was split by a Great Schism that left no marriage unspoiled or friendship unblemished.

In those days, people could neither sing nor dance, and to keep them entertained, the merciful God provided every village with an idiot. And since Caudillians were, without a doubt, the most pious and devout of all, the Almighty sent them an idiot of unsurpassed talent. He could walk like a monkey, speak like a donkey, and—as if that wasn't enough to amuse even the saddest soul—he could also squeal like a pig and catch flying cabbages with his oversized mouth. The joy he brought increased people's morale so much, even the laziest peasants became hard-working and self-sufficient. Soon enough, the granaries were overflowing, and hunger became a memory more distant than the horizon.

Alas, what could be a fitting ending for a fairy tale was just the beginning of a tragedy. While peasants became happier with every passing day, the idiot grew pensive and sad and soon enough he started crying. Since no one had ever heard of an idiot with feelings, people ascribed the symptoms to inflammation, which they tried to cure with a concoction of herbs that only exacerbated the unfortunate situation. The poor idiot was driven to such despair that seven days after the beginning of his treatment, he decided to hang himself on the highest olive tree. It was early spring, the air was full of pollen, and just before he put the noose on his neck, the idiot felt a tickle in his left nostril, sneezed, lost balance, and as he fell down on the ground, hit his head on a stone and his poor spirit departed to the afterworld.

Citing scripture peppered with subjective conclusions made with the utmost regard to objectivity, the village priest refused to conduct a proper burial. Because of the intended suicide, he said, the soul of the idiot was not only deemed ineligible for the comforts of Heaven but was strictly relegated to the lowest circle of Hell, where, instead of cabbages, his head was going to be pelted by fiery balls of sticky boiling magma.

Since despite their unwavering faith, many Caudillians choose to follow their conscience, they dug a grave and buried the idiot, together with a couple of his favorite cabbage balls. When news of this reached the ears of the priest, he promptly excommunicated everyone involved, which turned out to be half of the population. Barred from their place of worship, the excommunicated peasants built their own church. It was an exact replica of the old one with one exception, barely noticeable to the naked eye but terribly irksome to a jealous mind: It was taller by two inches.

In the minds of the old believers, the extra layer of bricks brought the new church closer to God. Even though they were convinced the Almighty was on their side, they decided it was wise to regain the front row of his attention. They erected a bell tower that soared in the sky like a heavenly ladder.

As a response, a group of overzealous new believers constructed a trebuchet and slung a burning ball of manure at the bell, setting the tower ablaze. Moment after the fire reached the altar, the old church collapsed into dust and ashes. Out of it, like a phoenix from the flames, emerged a terrible fury that gripped the hearts and minds of old believers. It was the beginning of the Caudillian Civil War that, like all wars before and after, lasted until all brave soldiers met their end, and left behind timid and cowardly deserters who swiftly negotiated a ceasefire, so that peace and understanding can once again rule in Caudilla. And it was in those times immemorial when people realized that laughing at idiots should be avoided at all costs.

Juan Mequetrefe and the Bull that Laid Golden Eggs

BLESSED BE THE ALMIGHTY GOD, who gives a chance even to hopeless idiots, for he feels a certain responsibility for his own failure to make all humans perfect. One day, as the Lord was peeking through the clouds, he saw that as usual, Juan Mequetrefe was procrastinating instead of working on his field.

"Poor child of mine," said God, "everyone else's wheat is already sawn, while Juan's field is full of weeds and rabbit holes. It's too late to make anything grow in this obscene wilderness, but I shall nevertheless give Juan a chance to survive the winter."

So God snapped his finger, and a mighty bull fell down from the sky. It landed with such a thunderous roar that Juan wet his pants, thinking the Devil had finally come to get him. But when he realized the beast was a gift from Heaven, he fearlessly approached to inspect it, so he could make sure everything was in working order—back in those days of divine grace and leniency, everyone could return a blessing with no questions asked and appeal for a reasonable substitute.

The bull was well built, with bulging muscles, sharp sturdy horns, and steaming nostrils. But when Juan looked between his hind legs, he found no single testicle in sight. Before he could even open his mouth to complain about it, the beast let a huge fart and out of his ass plopped a shiny golden egg.

"The good Lord is getting old and must have messed things up again," thought Juan Mequetrefe, "but eggs are better than balls, and I can easily sell them."

Thus, Juan Mequetrefe took the bull home to his wife, Marieta Machada.

"Tete, keep this beast in the backyard and don't tell anyone about it," he said to her. "It doesn't have any balls but when it farts, it shoots golden eggs out of his ass. We'll get rich like royalty!"

The next morning a wandering healer passed by Juan's house and heard a loud fart accompanied by a thumping sound.

"These people have healthy bowel movements," he thought. "Let me see what they ate last night because it might be useful for my medicines."

The healer peeked through the fence and saw Marieta Machada pick up a golden egg.

"Such a freakish beast could only be a blessing from our demented Lord," thought the healer, "if I steal it, I will become rich like royalty and wouldn't have to wander from town to town selling potions."

And so the healer devised a cunning plan to steal the bull. He waited until Juan Mequetrefe left the house and knocked on the door.

"Good day, señora," he said when Marieta Machada opened the door, "perhaps you heard that one of the royal bulls that lays golden eggs ran away from the castle yesterday morning. There's a big reward for those who return it. Have you by any chance seen it?"

"Good day, stranger," replied Marieta, who thought of herself as a wise woman that couldn't be easily fooled. "I haven't heard anything about this. Are you sure it's true? And what kind of reward would be big enough to match a bull that lays eggs of gold every time it farts? It seems to me that whoever found the animal is set for life!"

"You are as wise as you are beautiful, señora! But what you don't know is that the royal cows lay diamonds that are worth more than golden eggs. I have it on good authority that whoever returns the king's favorite bull will be rewarded with a cow in exchange."

"If I were a king," thought Marieta, "and had lost a beast that's not only valuable but also dear to my heart, I would have offered the same reward. This man seems to be telling the truth. I better be honest with him."

So she gave the bull to the healer, who promised to take it straight to the castle and return with a diamond-laying cow the next morning.

When Juan Mequetrefe came home and found out about the whole affair, he burst into tears.

"Stupid woman," he shouted, "I worked so hard for this blessing, and all you did was squander it! I am so angry I could hatch you to pieces with my axe, as you deserve! But death is not a fitting punishment for what you did. Instead, I shall find you the stupidest man on Earth, so you can marry him instead."

Thus Juan packed a bag of food, put on his sandals, and went off to wander the world, looking for a fool to match his dear Tete. On the ninth day of his journey, he reached a village where all cows bore calves made of solid gold. When he asked why, the people told him a duck endowed with bull testicles fell from the sky and began feverishly copulating with the cattle.

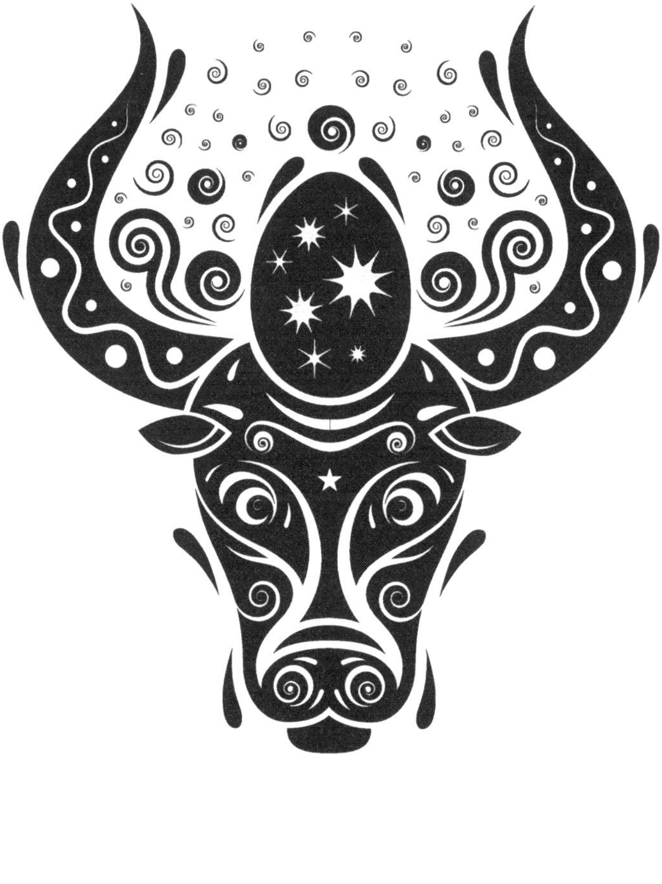

"I have it on good authority," said Juan Mequetrefe, "that this duck belongs to the king and he has promised a big reward to those who return it."

"Do you take us for fools?" replied the people. "What reward could surpass a herd of golden calves? And as loyal subjects, we have already promised to send one to the king every month as a gift anyway."

Realizing he couldn't trick anyone, Juan Mequetrefe came back home and said to Marieta Machada:

"Tete, we deserve each other!"

The Ascent of Santa Lucía

A NUN AT THE RUBICÓN MONASTERY named Lucía was so devout and pious that every Sunday, God himself paid her a visit to encourage her spiritual adventures. They would chat merrily all night long, and at sunrise The Almighty would climb back to Heaven on the first ray of light, leaving Lucía sad and lonely.

"My Lord," she said to him once, "every time you come down to see me, I am filled with delight and happiness. But I can't bear the heartache when you leave. I would give anything to always be with you."

"Dear child," replied God, "had the first people heeded my advice and not eaten from the fruits of knowledge, your wish might have been possible, but in a sinful world like this, it is only through heartache and pain that people can experience happiness."

"My Lord, I am ready to renounce this world to be forever in your presence. I wish to join you in Heaven no matter what the cost might be!"

God loved Lucía so much, he spent the entire night trying to persuade her she's better off on Earth. But the faith of the nun had grown so strong that her devotion had become boundless.

"Alright then," said God. "Tomorrow, right before the Sun goes down, walk into the river and its waters will carry you to my heavenly palace."

On Monday morning the nuns were surprised to see Lucía with a smile brighter than the rising Sun. When they asked what was going on, the pious nun revealed everything. She told them all about God's visits, how they spent their time together, and how he finally agreed to take her to Heaven.

The nuns told the cook. The cook told the guards, and by noon all the people in the monastery and the nearby villages knew about the upcoming ascension. Soon enough, the place was besieged by a crowd of curious onlookers, eager to witness the miraculous event.

Lucía bid farewell to her sisters, who, still in shock, did everything to make her reconsider. Their pleas were drowned out by the crowd, whose noisy jubilation sounded like the singing of angels. People laid wreaths of roses at Lucía's feet, trying to gain the favor of the soon-to-be saint.

"Remember me, Sister Lucía," cried a mother who held a sick baby in her arms, "and ask God to cure my only daughter."

"Ask him to restore my eyesight," said a blind beggar.

A young man noticed Lucía's feet were bleeding from the thorns of the roses and took her in his arms. "I'll carry you to the river, Sister Lucía," he said. "Please ask God to make the son of the shoemaker fall in love with me."

At the shore, Lucía blessed the crowd and wished them well. Ready for her a blissful ascension, she stepped into the water and let out a piercing cry.

"It's freezing!"

"How could that be?" said the people. "It's the middle of summer."

"God must be testing me," stuttered Lucía.

"Nonsense! Ascend already! The Sun has almost set!"

Lucía bravely stepped forward. Her eyes widened in horror. The cold invaded her insides and left her breathless. Frost spread all over her skin and as the last rays of the Sun disappeared, her body became a lifeless block of ice.

"That's not a saint," said the mother of the sick baby, "that's a witch!"

"We have been tricked," said the blind beggar.

"Destroy that demon!" shouted the young man.

The disappointment of the crowd turned into a maddening rage. People started pelting Lucia's body with stones, until there was noting left but a silvery cloud of icy dust. The night wind carried it higher and higher, all the way to the firmament of the seventh sky where, at last, Lucía was reunited with her beloved God.

The next day, the blind beggar regained his sight, but fearing Lucía's blessing was a curse, he gauged his eyes out and continued living in darkness.

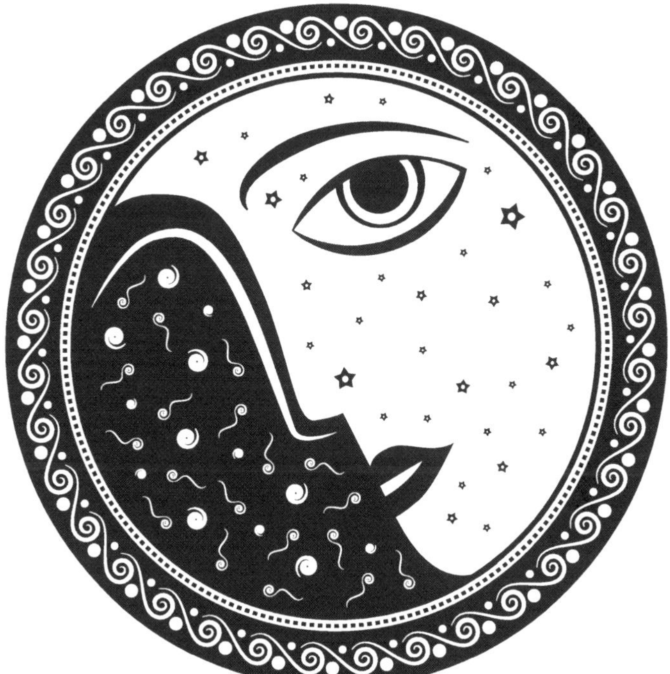

The Two Sides of Dolores Urdemalas

ONE MORNING Marieta Machada passed by the house of Dolores Urdemalas and overheard a quarrel. When she saw her again later that day, she insidiously remarked how harmonious her own marriage was:

"Juan and I never fight. My mother, blessed be her soul, once told me a marriage is not made in bed but with in the kindness of the waking hours. One should avoid arguments, especially early in the morning, for bitterness can spoil the brightest of days!"

Dolores got the sneer and swore to teach Marieta a lesson. For three sleepless nights she plotted a revenge, ignoring the pleas of her husband to come lay down beside him and perform her spousal duty:

"Shut up, Pedro, I'm busy! I won't let that righteous bitch get away with this. I'll show her where marriages come from!"

On the fourth day, right before sunset, Dolores came out wearing a mask and a long robe that was black on one side and white on the other. She smeared tar on her horse to match her attire, and when she saw Juan Mequetrefe approaching from the opposite side of the road, she let out a loud cry. When Marieta peeked through her window to see what was going on, the disguised Dolores spurred the horse, snatched one of Marieta's chicken and galloped away.

"Help! A white knight stole my chicken," shouted Marieta.

"Stupid woman," said Juan Mequetrefe, "have you gone blind? The knight was all black."

"Black is the crow that poked your eyes, you good-for-nothing!" replied Marieta.

"And white was the color of our bedsheets after our wedding night, you harlot!"

The two started fighting so loudly, their insults made the setting Sun blush.

That night Dolores and her husband ate chicken for dinner, performed their spousal duties, and peacefully fell asleep.

Frog Empress

IN A CERTAIN EMPIRE, in a certain land—no one remembers whether near or far—lived an emperor who had three sons. The older two were obedient and hardworking; the youngest—a careless good-for-nothing.

They lived carefree princely lives until one day the emperor called them and said, "There is no more place for you in my home for you've grown beards and armpit hair. Go to the open field and shoot an arrow. Wherever it falls, there you shall marry."

The princes obeyed. The oldest shot at the rising sun. The middle one aimed at a flock of swallows. The youngest drew his bow without any consideration. The arrow of the oldest prince fell on the porch of a rich merchant, whose daughter was beautiful and meek. That of the middle prince—in the backyard of an army general, whose daughter was obedient and hardworking. The arrow of the youngest prince, that careless good-for-nothing, fell into a swamp. In its middle, on a throne of lilies, sat a croaking frog with a mischievous smile. When the prince came to pick up his arrow, his feet got stuck in the mud.

"Like it or not, there is only one way you can make it back alive," spoke the frog with a human voice, "and it's with me as your bride."

"Well then, I choose to die covered in mud rather than in shame. A marriage to a frog is worse than death, for everyone will laugh at me."

"I'd laugh at you myself if I didn't pitied you so much for being so naive," replied the frog. "It is said that only cowards choose premature death when faced with difficulties. I swear on my brothers and sisters that roam this earth, a great fortune awaits you if you take me for a wife!"

The prince, whose mind was easily swayed, agreed. He came back home with his bride-to-be, and the emperor held a wedding that lasted three days and three nights during which people could neither drink nor dance because they couldn't stop laughing.

"You promised I'd be spared the ridicule," said the youngest prince to his bride.

"Have patience, husband," replied the frog, "every giggle will soon be repaid!"

After some time, the emperor called his sons and said, "Now that each of you has settled with a wife, let's see who's the worthiest to succeed me. Ask your wives to make carpets for the throne room and whoever makes the best one shall receive all my lands and titles!"

The emperor gave them precious threads of all colors and ordered them to finish in a week.

The youngest prince returned home sad and weary.

"What weighs on your mind, husband?" asked him the frog.

"Our father has finally decided to disown me," replied the prince. "We better go back to the swamp, for there is no future for us here."

"Didn't I tell you not to give up prematurely?" said the frog. "Stop whining and explain what happened."

The prince told her about the impossible task. The frog smiled and said, "Listen to me, this is just a test. Your father rules by divine will and he doesn't need an excuse to disown you if he so desires."

"I have never been good at tests," said the prince.

"And I have never been good at weaving carpets," replied the frog, "but if I lend you my wit and you lend me your hands, we might get something done together."

The prince began weaving according to his wife's instructions.

When the time was up and the emperor summoned his sons, the oldest prince revealed a marvelous carpet depicting the Sun.

"Your presence, father, always fills us with light, and therefore I asked my wife to make a carpet worthy for your crown."

The middle son presented a carpet as blue as the sky.

"Your deeds, father, are righteous and pure like those of the angels in heaven, and I asked my wife for a carpet worthy for your feet."

The emperor praised the insight of his sons and complemented the work of their wives. When the time came for the youngest prince to reveal his carpet, everyone started to giggle.

"Father," said the eldest son, "be kind to our brother, for although he is a careless good-for-nothing, he didn't luck out with a wife."

"I don't need pity," said the youngest son and rolled out a carpet twice as big as those of his brothers. Instead of the Sun and the sky, it depicted the Earth, as explored by the countless relatives of his wife. On it could be seen every village, road, forest, and meadow. In its center lay the very swamp where the arrow of the youngest prince fell.

189

"Who made this?" asked the emperor.

"I did the weaving," replied the son, "but it was my wife who guided my hand."

The emperor was filled with so much admiration, he had no choice but to give his empire to the frog. Thus she became the first and only amphibian to reign over humans. She lived happily ever after with her husband, who always followed her advice.

Head Crusher

LONG TIME AGO in the town of Bruno there lived a philosopher named Jordán, who had the pernicious habit of insulting Our Lord with his blasphemous ramblings. Soon enough, the local bishop—a learned man distinguished by his god-fearing intellect—ran out of patience and decided to shut this loudmouth for all eternity by sentencing him to death.

As Jordán's face was fastened on the head crusher, the throng of worshippers that gathered to witness the execution let out a jubilant cry, eager to see the philosopher's brain squirting through the sieve of the rusty contraption. It was a once-in-a-lifetime spectacle.

By protocol, these elaborate executions involved two headsmen. One would turn the handle of the head crusher very slowly, so the skull bones break in ascending order, starting with the lower jaw. The other headsman would hold a tiny hammer and gently bang on the metal head cap, so the vibrations could increase the agony of the offender. Needless to say, all this was done with humane considerations, for it was proven that if an already doomed soul was made to suffer extensively before its well-deserved death, its chances for leniency in hell increased exponentially.

However, Jordán was so tainted by countless transgressions and clamorous insolence, the authorities abandoned all established protocol. The place of the second headmaster was taken by the bishop, who had neither the intention nor the competence to wield any hammers, regardless of their size. His presence was deemed necessary just in case Jordán uttered yet another exotic blasphemy that could infect the crowd with its brash extravagance.

The bishop's worry was justified. Moments before Jordán's brain squirted out of his deformed ears, he blurted out his most incendiary theory, postulating the existence of multiple universes, each created by a separate deity, equal in power to Our Lord.

"Let it be known far and wide," proclaimed the bishop, "that those who imagine the impossible will follow the same gruesome fate."

Despite the stark warning, the scourge of polytheism spread across our lands like a wildfire. The bishop was put on trial for instigation of blasphemy and found guilty, for the heinous idea of the philosopher was clearly a consequence the delirious state of his mind, driven to insanity by the unspeakable torture. Since then, sinners are treated humanely and with abundance of caution, lest they lose touch with reality, and start blabbering despicable ideas that infect the minds of the innocent.

Rubicón's Daughter

LONG TIME AGO, when God was still crafting the corners of the world, and the waters of creation remained largely untamed, the first humans lived a restless life, full of anguish and disappointment. They roamed from place to place, looking for a plot of land that would welcome and sustain them, so they could multiply and subdue the yet unfinished Earth.

It so happened that one day, they reached the bank of a mighty river whose waters ran so fast that anything dropped in them would swiftly disappear downstream. On its other side they saw a lush garden, dotted with flowers of various colors that shone like precious stones. And in the middle of the garden grew a most curious tree with elegant branches, heavy with glittering lilac fruits the size of a giant's fist.

"In this garden we shall settle," said the humans in one voice, for they were hopelessly charmed by the exotic beauty of that place, just a stone throw away from where they sat down to rest after their exhausting journey. Once they recovered their strength, they devised a plan to build a mighty bridge and cross into their promised land, so they could finally escape from all the hardships of existence. Stone by stone, day by day, they were advancing towards their bright destiny until, after three months of hard work, the bridge was complete. But barely a moment after the last stone was laid, the waters of the river came rushing in and destroyed everything.

"No river has a will on its own," concluded the humans. "This must be a deity in disguise." Thus, they gathered in a circle and started dancing, so they could tempt the divine entity to reveal itself. Soon enough, it possessed the body of a young girl.

"Puny humans," echoed the voice of the deity through the girl's mouth, "How dare you strap a saddle on my body as if I were a beast! I am Rubicón, and through me flow the birth waters of the Universe. No mortal can stop me. No god can divert me. My body is a grave for the flesh and a cradle for the spirit."

The girl's hips shook fast like leaves battered by torrential rain. Four young men approached her, dancing and pounding the ground until a thick cloud of dust engulfed their calves. "Forgive us, bearer of divine water," they said with grunts and shouts, furiously beating their chest, "allow us to pass, so we can escape our misery."

The girl raised her hand and the dancing stopped abruptly. The echo of the boy's heavy breathing dissolved in the dusty air.

"No stones can bridge my body," said Rubicón through the girl's mouth. "Only flesh can resist the power of my waters. If you don't want your bridge to crumble, you must build it over the body of a fair maiden."

After she delivered her message, Rubicón left the body of the girl. When the humans made sure she was truly gone, they said to each other, "We didn't get here by betraying each other or leaving anyone behind. It is through shared strength and solidarity that we survived the challenges of this flawed world that is still under construction. We shall find a way to cross together or not at all."

And so they spent forty days, scheming how to trick the bearer of the universal waters, so they could finally reach their coveted destination. On the forty-first day, they completed a marvelous creation—a maiden made of clay and hay. She looked so lifelike, she would have driven God into a bout of jealousy, if only he paid any attention to this side of the world.

The humans embedded her body into the bridge and when they laid the final stone, the waters of the river rose up again and a deluge, twice as furious, came pouring. But after the wave subsided, the bridge was still standing.

"It is done," cheered the humans, packed all their belongings and headed to the other side. When they reached the middle of the bridge, the suddenly saw the clay maiden standing in front of them.

"My mother is very disappointed in you," she said.

Another wave rose and the river devoured everything.

The Gruesome Death of Diego Suárez

ONCE UPON A TIME IMMEMORIAL, there lived in the village of Caudilla a young man of otherworldly beauty called Diego Suárez. Even the heart of the local priest, who had willingly given up the pleasures of the Earth, raced like a wild rabbit while Diego stopped by to confess his sins.

While beauty might be a blessing for those who possess it without knowing, Diego was quite conscious of all the advantages that came with it. His favorite victims were young girls who, shielded by their loving parents, hadn't yet suffered any disappointments. A single smile would make them to rush into his arms. But once he had his way with them, he would move on to his next victim and break their hearts.

At that time in Caudilla lived a girl with blond hair and blue eyes called Clementina. Her father loved her dearly and, aware of Diego's tricks, wouldn't let his daughter anywhere near him. Alas, the father's resolve only provoked Diego's determination, and soon enough the young man managed to charm the innocent girl by promising he would marry her if she would only agree to spend a night with him. Needless to say, he didn't keep his promise.

One day a caravan of strangers arrived and set camp at the outskirts of the village.

"People of Caudilla," proclaimed the strangers through a large tube that made their voices very loud and crisp, "We are gypsies from a far away country, where instead of grains and milk, we harvest joy and amusement. We came to trade them with you."

Among the various pavilions in the gypsy camp there was one owned by an old woman called Mesmeralda. A sign over the entrance claimed she sold love potions at an unprecedented discount. It was exactly what Clementina was looking for.

"I don't have much, madam, but I will be forever grateful if you help me get back the man I desperately love."

"Young girl," replied Mesmeralda while she was still unpacking her potions, "there are two important things in life you need to learn. First, forever is a very long time. Second, nothing good has ever come from desperation. So I suggest you reconsider your pledge."

"Forgive me, madam! I meant no disrespect," said Clementina. Mesmeralda turned away from her shelf and looked at the girl with her dark piercing eyes.

"Oh, you pretty thing," said the old woman. "You are truly bewitched!"

"I am in love," said Clementina.

"I beg to differ dear! The hearts of those in love are whole. Half of yours is missing. Sit down and tell me more about that man."

Clementina's story made Mesmeralda frown.

"Dear child," said the old woman. "You're young, innocent, and as a result nobody takes you seriously. Therefore, I am going to tell you my biggest secret. All the potions you see on my shelves are nothing but colored water. They have no power on their own. You can drink them all, one after the other, and you won't feel a thing. What makes them work is people's faith in them. My real job is not to sell drinks, but to inspire people to believe their wishes can come true. Just like potions, faith comes in different flavors. There is faith born of self-esteem and there is faith born of despair. If you choose self esteem, you will take back the missing half of your heart from the claws of that good-for-nothing and give it to someone else who deserves it. If you choose despair, you might get your Diego but you will pay a terrible price."

"I am ready to pay whatever price there is just to be with him," said Clementina.

"Very well then," said Mesmeralda and handed her a potion. "Drink this at the next full moon, and he will eventually fall in love with you."

"How much do I owe you?" asked Clementina.

"It's not me you have to pay," said Mesmeralda. "Now go and may the Lord have mercy upon you!"

By the next full moon, the gypsies had already left Caudilla and Diego, chasing the beautiful girls in their caravan, followed them from town to town, beyond thrice nine lands, through deserts and mountains, queendoms and empires, until one day, after many many years, the caravan once again came full circle and stopped on the outskirts of Caudilla.

Diego was an old man, his once beautiful face wrinkled by smoke and liquor. The pleasures he used to chase had become distant memories, blurred by meaningless promises and tasteless lips. He felt tired.

When night fell and Diego once more heard the wheat fields murmuring under the caress of the nocturnal winds, he realized he was ready to settle. There's no better place than home, he thought. Everything was like he remembered it, except a subtle whisper that circled around his ears.

"Diego!" it said.

He looked around the empty camp but there was no one outside.

"Diego!" repeated the whisper.

A tiny moth landed on its chest. He tried to catch it, but it slipped through his fingers.

"Come with me," it said.

The moth flew towards the village and Diego followed it, mesmerized by its glittering wings. After all these years, Caudilla had changed too. The wooden fences from his memories were replaced by impenetrable hedges, covered with vines and ivy. The benches where people gathered to gossip were empty and silent.

The moth led Diego to a porch framed by beautiful lilac bushes in full bloom. Right under it stood Clementina.

"Welcome home, my love!" she said.

She looked exactly like he remembered her—young and radiant, as if time had passed her by.

"I knew you would come back," she said. "Glory be to God, who rewards those who wait and punishes the impatient. Neither humans nor angels could shake my faith in you, Diego Suárez, for I always believed that once you saw the world with your own eyes, you would realize our love is much bigger than all its wonders."

When morning came the gypsies went looking for Diego door to door. Nobody had seen or heard of him. Finally, they reached the ruins of an old house.

"Only a madman would enter it," an old woman told them. "It belonged to Clementina the Witch who died of sorrow. On a quiet night, you can still hear her ghost crying."

Since back in those days the gypsies weren't afraid of ghosts, they immediately went in. It was all too late. They found Diego's lifeless body embraced by a rotting corpse. There was a gaping hole in his chest.

Sugar Rush

WHEN THE FIRST HUMANS CAME TO BE, they had no care in the world, for everything they needed was provided by their maker. But deep inside their souls, in a place dark like a ripe olive, there was a grain of discontent that grew stronger and stronger until one day, all the blessings God bestowed upon them lost their value.

"We shall not rest," said the humans, "until we are able to provide for ourselves and thus become your equals."

"Fair enough," said God, who was tired of caring for his numerous creations anyway, "I shall grant you independence, but know that once done, it cannot be reversed."

"Rest assured we won't regret it," replied the humans, "for it doesn't make the slightest sense to do so."

God shrugged, the heavens shook, and lightning struck the earth. The humans were now free and after ages of taking constant care of them, God retreated to his quarters to have a well-deserved nap.

A day passed and then another. The humans got hungry and waited for the trees to bear fruit, as usual. Yet there was nothing on the branches.

"Perhaps we shall go to ask God why that is," someone suggested.

"Nonsense," replied another. "We can figure it out, now that God has granted us the ability to learn and improve on our own."

And they thought and thought while their tummies rumbled and rumbled. On the third day, they found a solution that made the trees bear twice as much fruit as before.

"I knew we could take better care of ourselves than the old man," someone said. "Not only has the harvest increased but our fruits are larger!"

"Let us celebrate," said another. "Let's light a huge fire, drink some wine and dance!"

"We could do that," said someone else, "But how about we spent that precious time thinking about how to further increase our harvest."

So instead of celebrating, the humans started thinking and thinking until on the third day, they found an even better solution that made the trees bear so much fruit, their branches were touching the ground.

"In only six days we have increased the efficiency of all trees in our garden threefold," said someone. "Imagine what we could achieve in another six."

And so it went for days and months until, after a year, the trees bore fruits as big and heavy as melons. It was around that time that God woke up from his nap and came to check how everyone was doing. To his surprise, instead of careless laughter and joyful songs, he heard anxious chatter and heated discussions. The humans were trying to figure out how to rid the trees of leaves, so there would be more space for fruits on their branches.

"What have I done!" said God. "These poor creatures have lost their joie de vivre. I must find a way to fix this, impossible as it might be."

He thought and thought, and in three days he figured out a way to restore things back to how they were.

"Dear children," he said, "I cannot bear to see you so stressed and anxious, for I created you to be happy and carefree. So rest assured that even though you're free and independent, I shall nevertheless provide you with all the food you need, so you won't have to worry about your survival."

And as he said that, God created an endless forest of trees that bore fresh fruits as soon as the ripe ones were picked.

The humans rushed to have a taste.

"These fruits are quite lovely," they said, "But they could be a bit sweeter."

Let There Be Light

ON THE SIXTH DAY OF CREATION, God looked at the magnificent Universe in all its splendor. He counted the stars and clustered them in galaxies. He made a home for each animal on Earth according to merit or convenience. The snakes he put in holes of sandy soil because their bodies were thin and slippery. The rabbits became neighbors of the snakes because they were good at digging. The birds he put on branches, since, being able to fly, they were the only animals that could survive a fall from a tree.

Just when God was about to congratulate himself on a job well done, he felt something was missing:

"I filled the Universe will all kinds of creatures, yet none of them resembles myself. If I want to be worshipped properly, I better create someone that looks exactly like I do, so all living things can behold me even when I'm absent."

And thus, God created Woman.

"You are the pinnacle of my designs," he told her. "Anyone who lays eyes on you will marvel at my own beauty!"

When all God's creatures looked at Woman, they were filled with awe. The birds stopped flying. The rabbits stood still. Even the snakes refused to crawl into their holes to hide from the afternoon heat. No one could take their eyes off her.

"This is not going as well as I thought," said God, who realized that his own beauty was too much to behold for lesser beings.

Yet he couldn't bring himself to banish Woman from the world. Instead, he spun the finest silk thread and made a dress that covered her from head to toe, except for her eyes, which were left exposed, so she wouldn't trip while she was walked.

"You shall only undress in private," commanded her God, "for your beauty is too overwhelming and could bring everything to a standstill."

But it was too late, for the Sun himself had fallen in love with Woman and wanted to possess her. Since his rays couldn't penetrate through the dress, the Sun asked his brother, the Ocean, for assistance.

"Brother Ocean," he said, "I beseech you to help me be with my beloved!"

The Ocean, afraid the burning desire of the Sun would soon deprive him of his waters, sent a gust of wind that lifted the silk dress. A ray of sunlight sneaked in, and soon after, Woman felt something growing inside her belly. When God found out about this, he got angry.

"You have been desecrated by the Sun," he told Woman, "and you shall therefore take him as your husband. You will wake up and fall asleep at his command and he will be the one who feeds you and protects you until the day you die."

Nine months later Woman gave birth to a child called Man. And this is the origin of all humanity.

The Bull's Bride

LONG TIME AGO, before people domesticated cattle, lived a widower who had a beautiful daughter named Olivia. Her hair was pitch black like a starless night. When he was done mourning his dead wife, he decided to marry a widow. She had a daughter of her own, named Blanca. Her hair had the color of ripe wheat.

Olivia was always respectful to her stepmother but in return she only got scorn and complaints. But the more the old woman insulted her, the more beautiful Olivia became. Her dark skin never got sunburnt when she worked in the field, while that of Blanca got covered in sores and lesions, as if the Sun hated her.

The stepmother got so jealous of Olivia, she decided to get rid of her. One day, when she was sowing the field, she prayed to the god of fertility for a rich harvest in exchange of the hand of her stepdaughter. That way, thought the mother, she would not only deal with Olivia once and for all, but she would also get something back.

On the next day, when Olivia was carrying water from the spring, the god of fertility appeared to her in the shape of a beautiful bull with big glittering horns. "Fair maiden," he said. "You are destined to be my wife!"

Terrified, Olivia threw her buckets and ran back home. The bull followed her and knocked on the door with his mighty horns.

"Come out, fair maiden, for you were promised to me by your mother!"

When Blanca heard this, she assumed her mother found her a beautiful husband and came out. The bull snatched her and departed to the land of the gods, from which no human had ever returned. Outwitted by destiny, her mother died of bitterness soon after.

EXTRAS

"Knowledge is suffering; ignorance is death."
Sigismund Alegrius

A Succinctly Brief Encyclopaedia of Clangorous Hearsay, Curious Factoids, and Occasional Spoilers

Geography

▶ **Abharazarhadarad** · a republican city state in the *Far West*. Located at the shore of the *Sunset Ocean*, Abharazarhadarad is a cosmopolitan trading hub and a cultural melting pot. Its citizens worship a female deity known as the *Goddess*. This monotheistic religion rejects spiritualism and focuses on practical matters like wealth acquisition. Its doctrine is outlined in the *Great Book*.

▶ **Arctic Ocean** · an icy ocean, gateway to the *Extreme North*, and birthplace of the Hyperborean civilization. It extends all the way to the *Great Abyss*. On its shores lie the kingdom of *Cynocephalia*, the queendom of *Barbaria*, and the city of *Trondheim*. Other notable places include the *Cycloptic Archipelago*, the *Island of the Blessed*, the *Island of the Goddess*, and the island of *Severia*. The ocean remains uncharted by continental civilizations and is considered extremely dangerous. Reckless explorers risk freezing to death in its icy storms or falling prey to bloodthirsty *unicorns*. According to Barbarian folklore, the ocean is home to iceberg riders that occasionally interfere in human affairs.

▶ **Barbaria** · a queendom located on a peninsula in the *Arctic Ocean*.

▶ **Barren Desert** · a vast, sandy desert, spanning all the way from the *Orient* to the *Far West*. It is largely uninhabited by humans because of its inhospitable climate. Its monotonous landscape attracts reckless explorers and suicidal spiritualists. According to a Qurtuban legend, the goddess *Ibliz* built a *Pillar to Heaven* in the middle of the desert and left her sacred animals, the *sirens,* to guard it. Various historical accounts from the *Orient* claim that centuries ago, the desert was covered by lush vegetation and its transformation into a lifeless wasteland was caused by magic, whose origin is hotly disputed. Famous explorer *Bartholomea of the Desert* comes from a nomadic tribe that lives around the northern edge of the Barren Desert.

▶ **Caudilla** · a village in the Northwest whose isolationist and self-absorbed population is completely devoid of curiosity.

▶ **Choleropolis** · a city state in the *Far West*, one of the most prominent centers of medical research. Famous for its face implant clinics, frequented by decadent royalty and wealthy criminals.

▶ **Clonfert** · the largest island in the *Sunset Ocean*. Its predominantly agrarian culture is dominated by ancient traditions, many of whom are preserved in myths and legends. Clonfertians believe their island was the first landmass to rise out of the primordial ocean and a legendary battle between a Clonfertian king and invaders from *Trondheim* reversed the spin of the Earth. There is a historical rivalry between the East Coast, dominated by shepherds, and the West Coast, dominated by goatherds, each side claiming superiority over the other. The island is the birthplace of famous explorer *Isidore of Clonfert*. Hyperborean civilization traces its origins to a ship of Clonfertian virgins, kidnapped by criminals from *Trondheim*.

▶ **Cycloptic Archipelago** · an archipelago in the *Arctic Ocean*, home to a civilization of cyclops that went extinct before the islands were rediscovered by fugitive criminals from *Trondheim*, who, along with their Clonfertian wives, founded *Storkhome*, a settlement that became the cradle of the Hyperborean civilization.

▶ **Cynocephalia** · a kingdom located on the shores of the *Arctic Ocean*, inhabited by dog-headed people. It has one of the most developed judicial systems in the world, since the rule of law and the distribution of justice are considered essential values in Cynocephalian society. Long time ago, the Cynocephalians were great explorers but they eventually recycled their maps to produce paper and write down their laws.

▶ **Epiphagia** · an egalitarian queendom located on the shores of the *Arctic Ocean*, to the east of the island of *Severia*. It is inhabited by a race of headless people whose faces are located on their chests. The mutation has been attributed to their unique system of government called *democracy*. Most political decisions, regardless of scope, importance, or urgency, are taken by nation-wide referenda. Besides geographically, the Epiphagians are also culturally isolated from the rest of the world because they speak *French*—a peculiar language no one else understands. Their capital is called *Acephalopolis*.

▶ **Extreme North** · a vaguely defined region encompassing the yet unexplored *Arctic Ocean*, the mythical *Great Abyss*, and the *Nothing but Nothingness* that supposedly lies beyond it.

▶ **Far East** · an unexplored region of the world that serves as a placeholder for people's imaginary fears and fatalistic obsessions. It is assumed that it's infested with uncivilized freaks and dangerous monsters.

▶ **Far West** · a region comprising of the westernmost part of the *Barren Desert*, its coastline on the *Sunset Ocean*, and the island of *Clonfert*. The largest cities in the Far West are *Abharazarhadarad* and *Choleropolis*.

▶ **Glacier Mountains** · an impenetrable mountain range along the northern border of the *Kingdom of the Word*.

▶ **Great Abyss** · the northern end of the world, where the waters of the *Arctic Ocean* (allegedly) disappear into the *Nothing but Nothingness*.

▶ **Hyperborea** · a reclusive civilization in the *Extreme North*, founded after criminal fugitives from *Trondheim* kidnaped a ship of Clonfertian virgins and settled on the *Cycloptic Archipelago* in the *Arctic Ocean*. Their first colony, *Storkhome*, became the capital of a powerful egalitarian state, subsequently transformed into a matriarchal monarchy with the coronation of *Helen the Gorgeous* as its queen. When her dynasty ended after the tragic death of the last matriarch, *Birgit the Assertive*, Hyperborea became a patriarchy. King *Arthur the Serendipitous* established the *Great Hyperborean Empire* after he excavated the *Scepter of Knowledge*, an instrument that allowed close observation of distant lands—an act that Hyperboreans equated with political conquest. The ephemeral expansion of the empire ceased abruptly when the limit of the optical instrument was reached during the reign of *William the Conqueror*. After a period of cultural and political stagnation, Emperor *Arnold the Easily Convinced* upgraded the *Scepter of Knowledge* with the help of explorer *Bartholomea of the Desert*. His son, *Henry the Navigator*, embarked of the first expedition of conquest, lured by the sudden appearance of an artificial island, created by the *Goddess of Eternal Ice*. Shortly thereafter, the entire civilization became extinct.

▶ **Kingdom of the Great River** · a kingdom in the *Far East*, birthplace of the dark art of telepathy.

▶ **Kingdom of the Word** · a kingdom ruled by a bureaucracy of librarians obsessed with the preservation of human knowledge. Their *Library of Superb Enlightenment* holds the greatest book collection in the world and is constantly expanding. The official religion is a monotheistic cult to *Clearchus,* an omnipotent librarian-god.

▶ **Library of Superb Enlightenment** · the biggest library in the world, located in the *Kingdom of the Word,* whose rulers have the sacred duty to preserve every book ever written.

▶ **Island of the Blessed** · an island in the *Arctic Ocean,* discovered by Hyperborean emperor *William the Conqueror.* Despite its alluring name, it has never been visited by a human being.

▶ **Island of the Goddess** · a magical island that appeared in the *Arctic Ocean* after the *Goddess of Eternal Ice* spat in its waters. It served as her residence on Earth while she was plotting the downfall of the *Great Hyperborean Empire.* The island was discovered by emperor *Henry the Navigator* after the upgrade of the *Scepter of Knowledge* and became the destination of Henry's first (and final) voyage.

▶ **Margraviate of the Windswept Hill** · a country on the outskirts of the civilized world, ruled by enlightened aristocrats with refined manners and exquisite taste. Its inhabitants follow the teachings of a prophet called *Vulnicurus* who preached that love was the most powerful force in the Universe. Because the margraviate is located next to the eastern end of the *Talas Corridor,* it is frequently exposed to barbarian invasions that are always unsuccessful despite the fact that the margraviate doesn't have a military of its own.

▶ **Nothing but Nothingness** · a geographical non sequitur, describing a pseudo-imaginary region that supposedly extends beyond the end of the world. Most philosophers question the validity and usefulness of the term. Explorer *Isidore of Clonfert* states that although nonsensical, the term shouldn't be dismissed as a logical fallacy because human imagination is not able to cope with actual limits. The *Nothing but Nothingness* is often confused with the *Great Abyss,* which is the place where the waters of the *Arctic Ocean* fall off the edge of the world. In reality, or rather in the imaginary reality of common people, the *Great Abyss* precedes the *Nothing but Nothingness.*

▶ **Ooh'ah** · a country located in the exact center of the world, but completely isolated from it due due to the thick forests of poisonous cacti *(Acrifolium gigantea)* that surround it from all sides. The Ooh'ahians worship the Point of Emergence, a bottomless pit that, according to their scripture, gave birth to everything.

▶ **Orient** · a vast region east of the *Barren Desert,* home to matriarchal (and often misandrist) cultures, organized in various competing queendoms. Known as the birthplace of alchemy.

▶ **Patasarriba** · a land where everything is upside down: days begin with sunsets, and people put their carts before their horses.

▶ **Pillar to Heaven** · a pillar built by the goddess *Ibliz* in the *Barren Desert* as a gateway to her heavenly palace. It is guarded by *sirens.*

▶ **Point of Emergence** · a bottomless pit the middle of *Ooh'ah*. According to the *Scroll of Ooh,* it is the place from which everything was born in four consecutive eruptions and where everything will disappear during the final days of the Universe. The *Point of Emergence* is revered as the holiest site on Earth by all Ooh'ahians.

▶ **Pythagorea** · a city in the *Orient,* known for it mathematical schools.

▶ **Rubicón** · a mythical river containing the birth waters of the Universe. It can neither be crossed nor bridged.

▶ **Queendom of the Briny Lake** · a matriarchal queendom in the *Orient.* Its inhabitants are grotesquely ugly because of its harsh climate.

▶ **Qurtubah** · the largest city in the *Talas Corridor* and main economic rival to the merchant city of *Abharazarhadarad.*

▶ **Saint Brendan's Hole** · a giant whirlpool in the southernmost part of the *Sunset Ocean* and a gateway to the *Underworld.* Discovered by explorer *Saint Brendan of Compostela.*

▶ **Severia** · an island queendom located in the *Arctic Ocean.*

▶ **Schmetterdorf** · a village in the North, famous for the discovery of *The Schmetterschwanz Manuscript.*

▶ **Sunset Ocean** · the second largest ocean, known for its calm climate. Many important trading posts are located on its coast, the most prominent being the city of *Abharazarhadarad*. The largest island is *Clonfert*. In the southernmost part of the *Sunset Ocean,* there is a giant whirlpool known as *Saint Brendan's Hole.*

▶ **Storkhome** · the first human settlement on the *Cycloptic Archipelago* and consequent capital of the *Great Hyperborean Empire.*

▶ **Talas Corridor** · a strip of land between the *Barren Desert* and the *Glacier Mountains.* To its western side lies the *Kingdom of the Word*, and to its eastern—the *Margraviate of the Windswept Hill.* The Talas Corridor is a strategic trading route and a neutral zone, governed by the *Libertarian Council.* Its de facto capital is the city of *Qurtubah.*

▶ **Trondheim** · a city located on the shore of the *Arctic Ocean.* A legend from *Clonfert* associates it with a legendary monster, defeated in a cataclysmic war that reversed the spin of the Earth. A more trivial version of the same legend replaces the monster with an invading *Trondheim Armada.* The Hyperborean civilization traces its origin to a group of criminals fleeing a prison near *Trondheim.*

▶ **Underworld** · a dark and inhospitable part of the world, discovered by *Saint Brendan of Compostela* who survived a fall trough a whirlpool in the *Sunset Ocean* that was later named after him.

Herbiary

▶ **Acrifolium gigantea** · a species of gigantic poisonous cacti that grow in forests surrounding the region of *Ooh'ah*, completely isolating it from the rest of the world.

▶ **Lilac poppy** · *(Meconopsis violacea)* · a plant native to the *Talas Corridor*. Above ground, its appearance mimics that of of the common poppy *(Papaver rhoeas)*, while the actual plant resides in a bulb, wrapped in its extensive root system. The bulb is protected from predators by a hard shell. The plant generates electricity that is instantly discharged when the bulb cracks and can easily kill a human. World renown barista *Juan of Qurtubah* developed a safe method to open the bulb with a machete. The seeds and petals of the lilac puppy contain an extremely potent hallucinogen that can alter both people's perception of reality and the actual reality itself.

▶ **Shepherd tree** · *(Pyrus pastoris)* · a tree that grows near *Cynocephalia*. Its blossoms give birth to lambs. The resin is used to make *lapis vitae*. Its leaves contain an oil used for hair curling and air purification.

▶ **Tree of the bound will** · *(Acer insciens)* · a tree from Ooh'ahian mythology that flowers irregularly. Its fruits restore innocence, reversing the effect of the fruits of the *tree of the knowledge of good and evil*.

▶ **Tree of contrarian trickery** · *(Persea contraria)* · a tree from Ooh'ahian mythology that has flowers instead of leaves and leaves instead of flowers. Since it cannot procreate, it is practically immortal.

▶ **Tree of eternal life** · *(Musa eterna)* · a tree from Ooh'ahian mythology that perished due to senseless vandalism.

▶ **Tree of the exalted departure** · *(Vulnicura venerosa)* · a mythical tree upon which the prophet *Vulnicurus* preached until he was abducted by a *rukh* and allegedly ascended to Heaven.

▶ **Tree of fatal attraction** · *(Mangifera exitiosa)* · a tree from Ooh'ahian mythology whose nectar is toxic to bees. The tree propagates by injecting seeds in the dead insects trapped in its flowers.

▶ **Tree of the knowledge of good and evil** · *(Malus scientifica)* · a tree from Ooh'ahian mythology, whose fruits ferment before they ripen and excrete a sugary alcoholic juice that can trigger self-awareness in innocent human beings.

▶ **Tree of misplaced affection** · *(Bertholletia inamata)* · a tree from Ooh'ahian mythology, whose pollen is too heavy to become airborne and accumulates around its roots, attracting pests and parasites.

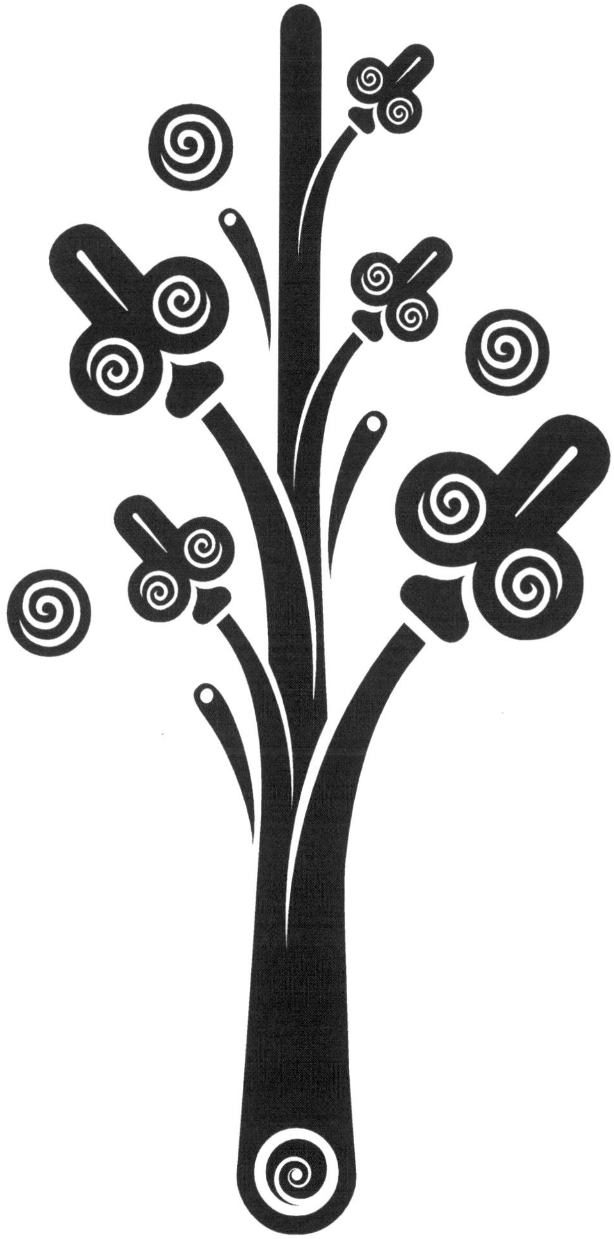

▶ **Tree of missed opportunities** · *(Prunus praeterita)* · a tree from Ooh'ahian mythology, whose blossoms fade before they can be pollinated. The tree can only be propagated by grafting onto rootstocks.
▶ **Tree of submissive arousal** · *(Prunus algophila)* · a tree from Ooh'ahian mythology that flowers only when it's repeatedly insulted and humiliated.
▶ **Tree of unnecessary drama** · *(Morus histrionica)* · a tree from Ooh'ahian mythology whose leaves produce a noise that resembles human whining.

Bestiary

▶ **Aphrodontus** · a winged horse that pulls the chariot of the *Goddess of Love*. Known for its tendency to veer off course.
▶ **Arctic wasp** · *(Vespula arctica)* · a tiny insect of the wasp family whose wings produce a staggering amount of noise. It procreates by injecting its eggs into the bloodstream of a *mermaid*. The hatched larvae attach to the mermaid's heart and feed on red blood cells. The blood of an infected mermaid has a distinctive lilac color and is used in the production of the powerful opiate *burundanga*.
▶ **Caudillian fly** · *(Lytta caudilliana)* · a blistering beetle that secretes the psychotropic substance *catharsidin*—the most popular drug among sailors. Its hallucinatory effect, often causing complete detachment from reality, is partially responsible for various exaggerations in the accounts of sea travelers.
▶ **Dogfish** · *(Latimeria canina)* · an animal native to the *Arctic Ocean* that has the head of a dog and the body of a fish. Not to be confused with the *fishdog*.
▶ **Fishdog** · *(Canis latimeris)* · an animal native to the *Cycloptic Archipelago* that has the head of a fish and the body of a dog. Not to be confused with the *dogfish*.
▶ **Mermaid** · a sea mammal, native to the *Arctic Ocean*. It shares a common ancestor with humans.
▶ **Polar bat** · *(Chalinolobus polaris)* · a flying mammal native to the *Cycloptic Archipelago*. It has neither eyes nor legs. Its wings are completely transparent and the fur on its body is highly reflective. The polar bat spends its life in perpetual flight, feeding on *arctic wasps* and small birds. It gives birth to its young mid-flight.

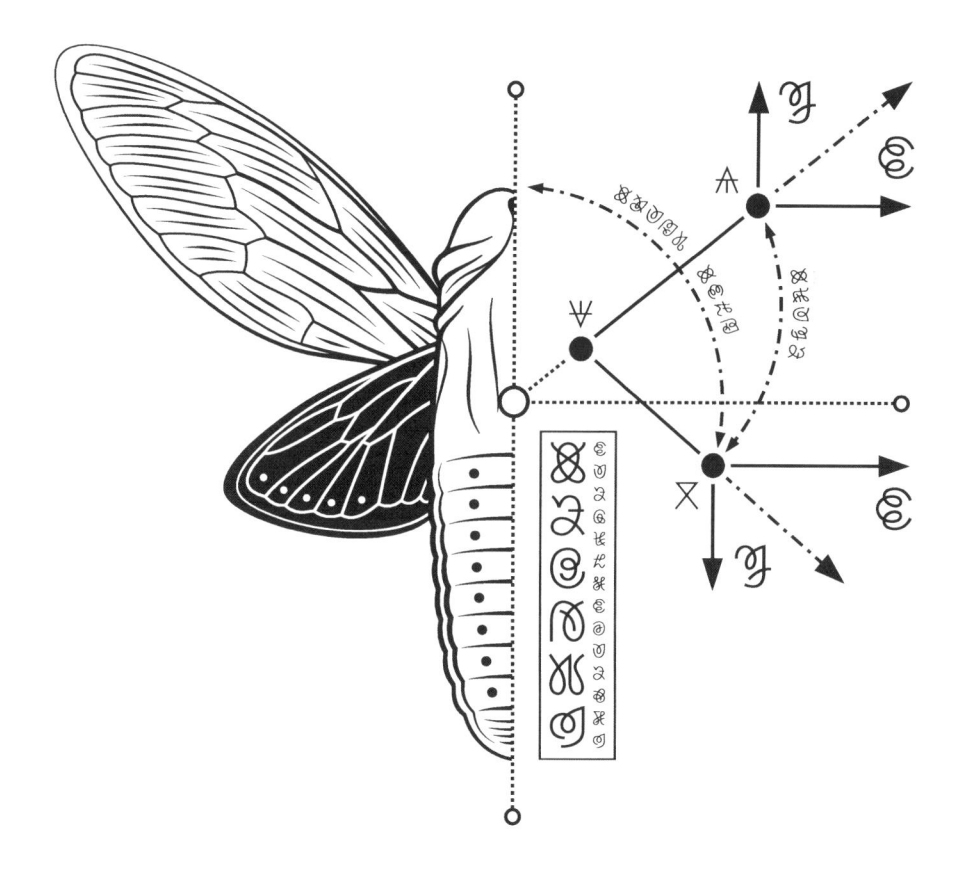

An illustration from the restored version of *The Schmetterschwanz Manuscript* allegedly depicting the flight mechanics of a Caudillian fly *(Lytta caudilliana)*.

▶ **Polar elephant** · *(Loxodonta polaris)* · a large mammal native to the *Cycloptic Archipelago*. Although omnivorous, the polar elephant feeds mainly on *mermaids* and *polar squirrels*.

▶ **Polar hydra** · *(Hydra acuatica subsp. polaris)* · a two-headed animal native to the *Cycloptic Archipelago*, known for its unique diet. Its left head is vegetarian, while its right—carnivorous. If left hungry for a long period, the carnivorous head will eat the vegetarian one.

▶ **Polar minks** · *(Mustela polaris)* · an semiaquatic animal native to the *Arctic Ocean*. Farmed by the Hyperboreans for its fur. Its intensely blue eyes are often preserved in resin and used for decoration of clothes and jewelry.

▶ **Polar rhino** · *(Rhinoceros polaris)* · a small mammal native to the *Cycloptic Archipelago*. Areas hosting large populations of polar rhinos can be dangerous for humans because the animals use their horns to dig holes in the ice, where they deposit food. These holes weaken the ice and make it easier to crack.

▶ **Polar sloth** · *(Bradypus lentus polaris)* · a sea mammal native to the *Arctic Ocean*, known for its phlegmatic nature. Polar sloths spend most of their long and uneventful lives floating on the surface, waiting for seagulls to accidentally drop food into their mouths.

▶ **Polar squirrel** · *(Otospermophilus polaris)* · a small mammal native to the *Cycloptic Archipelago*. The *polar squirrel* is a scavenger feeding on the food reserves of *polar rhinos*.

▶ **Polar unicorn** · *(Unicornis carnivorae)* · a sea mammal native to the *Arctic Ocean*. Its head resembles a horse, while its body—that of a whale. The forehead of the polar unicorn is equipped with a long horn, which it uses as a spear to impale and kill its prey. The animal is extremely dangerous to humans who, captivated by its beauty, often approach it without consideration only to be maimed and slaughtered. Unicorns are the only animals known to kill for entertainment.

▶ **Rukh** · *(Megagallus fabulosum)* · an extinct bird native to region of the *Talas Corridor* and the *Margraviate of the Windswept Hill*. Adult *rukhs* feed on insects but hatchlings are exclusively carnivorous.

▶ **Siren** · *(Hottentotta canorus)* · a giant scorpion that lives in the *Barren Desert* and guards the *Pillar to Heaven*. It procreates by laying eggs in the hearts of humans lured by its irresistible singing.

▶ **Terror bird** · *(Phorusrhacos terribilis fabulosum)* · an extinct bird of prey with an insatiable appetite. Some terror birds could shape-shift, taking the form of their victims.

Science and Scripture

▶ **Age of Discovery** · a historical period that marked the progressive expansion of the *Great Hyperborean Empire* through the means of *armchair conquest*. Emperors used the *Scepter of Knowledge* to remotely discover new lands which they nominally claimed. Since all these new territories were uninhabited icy deserts, there was no need to conquer them militarily or administer them politically. The *Age of Discovery* ended in the *Year of the Delighted Geriatric Minks,* during the reign of *William the Conqueror,* when the *Scepter of Knowledge* reached the limit of its observational range.

▶ **Age of Certainty** · a period in Hyperborean history that began in the *Year of the Delighted Geriatric Minks,* when Emperor *William the Conqueror* made the last discovery with the *Scepter of Knowledge,* and ended in the *Year of the Smiling Settled Minks* with the arrival of explorer *Bartholomea of the Desert.*

▶ **Aphrodisiology** · a science that studies love and its effects on the human mind. *Aphrodisiology* was the main field of research of Oriental scientist *Ana Loveless,* whose experiments with blood magnetism led to her discovery of the *platonic fluids.*

▶ **Bartholomea paradox** · a controversial event in Hyperborean history when *Bartholomea of the Desert* appeared out of nowhere and singlehandedly brought the end of the *Age of Certainty* by informing everyone that the world extended much farther than their eyes could see.

▶ **Blood magic** · a metascientific branch of *aphrodisiology,* dedicated to the study and practice of mind control through rebalancing of the platonic fluids with the use of *lilac dust.*

▶ **Burundanga** · a powerful psychotropic drug distilled from the blood of a *mermaid* that has been infected with the eggs of an *arctic wasp*.

▶ **Chronic dissatisfaction** · a fundamental force that spontaneously arose from the quantum vacuum in order to prevent the collapse of the Universe after the *God of Serendipity* sacrificed himself to alter the total amount of cumulative happiness.

▶ **Discovery fatigue** · a disorder that affected some Hyperborean emperors who found the duty to perpetually expand their empire too stressful and believed in a prophecy stating that one day there will be nothing new left to discover. The prophecy was fulfilled when the *Scepter of Knowledge* reached the limit of its observational range in the *Year of the Delighted Geriatric Minks,* during the reign of *William the Conqueror*.

▶ **Doubletruth** · a logical paradox in Ooh'ahian religion, stemming from the acceptance of mutually contradicting claims in the *synoptic gospels* as equally true.

▶ **Frittata paradox** · a natural phenomenon whereby food materializes out of thin air when more than a hundred people gather to witness an event of public shaming. It is both a physical and a logical paradox, since on one hand it contradicts the first law of thermodynamics, and on the other—human logic. The logical contradiction arises because, no matter how hungry the crowd might be, all the food is spontaneously hurled at those subjected to the shaming and therefore completely wasted. According to sociologist *Saint Simon de Rouvroy,* both aspects of the paradox ultimately cancel each other out, so in the end, it is neither a violation of the laws of physics nor of those of logic.

▶ **Great Book** · a compendium of financial advice that governs the cult of the *Goddess* in the merchant city of *Abharazarhadarad*. The book is often quoted in both formal and informal contexts.

▶ **Gregorian calendar** · a state-sanctioned system for time organization, derived the concept of *historical objectivity*, and introduced by King *Gregor the Pedantic* of *Hyperborea*. It measures time in centuries, subdivided in decades, years, weeks and days. Centuries are defined by an emotional modifier, reflecting the successive spiritual states of an aging human being: *happy, cheerful, delighted, smiling, indifferent, serious, frustrated, resentful, vengeful,* and *forlorn*. Decades are defined by modifiers reflecting the evolving physical state of an aging human being: *newborn, walking, talking, pubescent, adult, promiscuous, settled, mature, aging,* and *geriatric*. The years of the *Gregorian calendar* are named after the ten most common arctic animals: *mermaid, sloth, squirrel, elephant, dogfish, fishdog, hydra, rhino, bat,* and *minks*. The calendar begins with the *Year of the Happy Newborn Mermaid*.

▶ **Historical objectivity** · a Hyperborean concept, pioneered by King *Gregor the Pedantic,* who introduced a calendar that standardized the passage of time and eliminated human subjectivity regarding the recollection and commemoration of important historical events. The concept promoted consensus rather than conflict in the study of history and put an end to the widespread harassment of historians by people who didn't agree with their assessments.

▶ **Knot of Reason** · the highest civil decoration in the *Kingdom of the Word*, awarded to exceptional individuals who have successfully recovered from a romantic infatuation.

GREGORIAN CALENDAR CHART
Four hundred and twenty years of Hyperborean history

Age of Discovery years *Age of Certainty years* *Main event*

1. Death of *Gregor the Pedantic* and coronation of *Arthur the Serendipitous*
2. *Scepter of Knowledge* discovered (Beginning of the *Age of Discovery*)
3. Death of *Arthur the Serendipitous*
4. Birth of *William the Conqueror*
5. Death of *William the Conqueror* (End of the *Age of Discovery*)
6. Coronation of *Brandon the Flaccid*
7. End of *Age of Patriarchy*
8. Arrival of *Bartholomea of the Desert* (End of the *Age of Certainty*)
9. Coronation of *Henry the Navigator*
10. Arrival on the *Island of the Goddess*

▶ **Knowledge singularity** · a hypothetical event in the future when the physical weight of the vast catalog of the *Library of Superb Enlightenment* in the *Kingdom of the Word* would increase so much it would render it practically unusable.

▶ **Lapis vitae** · petrified raisin from the *shepherd tree*, used as a laxative.

▶ **Lilac dust** · a powerful aphrodisiac, naturally present in human blood, discovered by Oriental scientist *Ana Loveless*. Its magnetism enables physical attraction between people whose blood has a matching *platonic fluids* composition. When ingested in pure form lilac dust can cause lightheadedness, sexual excitement, romantic infatuations, delirium tremens, romantic melancholy. An overdose in people suffering from narcissistic disorder can trigger a permanent state of transcendental meditative self-adoration.

▶ **Plane of Existence** · a sheet of paper used by the librarian god *Clearchus* to create the world by scribbling with his quill.

▶ **Platonic fluids** · the four major components of blood, whose proportions define human character. The platonic fluids were first discovered by Oriental scientist *Ana Loveless,* who pioneered the treatment of emotionally unstable people through character calibration. They were named after Ana's cat, *Plato*.

▶ **Scepter of Knowledge** · a sophisticated instrument, engineered by an extinct cycloptic civilization that has the ability to collapse space and allow people to observe objects from a great distance. The instrument was found by Hyperborean king *Arthur the Serendipitous* in a pile of petrified cycloptic remains. With its help Arthur amassed great amounts of knowledge and, laying claims on everything he could observe with it, he vastly extended the Hyperborean domain, transforming his kingdom into an empire. The expansion continued under his successors. During the reign of *William the Conqueror* the *Scepter of Knowledge* reached the limit of its observational range, causing a political and cultural crisis that ended the Hyperborean *Age of Discovery*.

▶ **Schmetterschwanz Manuscript, The** · a cryptic manuscript whose meaning has remained a mystery since its discovery by *Jörg Holzhacker* in the village of *Schmetterdorf*. The manuscript is one of the most prized possessions of the *Library of Superb Enlightenment*.

▶ **Scroll of Ooh, The** · the holy book of the Ooh'ahians. Its original version, dictated by the deity *Ooh* itself, was accidentally damaged by *Saint Benedict the Distracted*. The inevitable divergence of the subsequent copies eventually caused a schism in the *Most Holy Church of Ooh*.

Pantheon

▶ **Almighty Evolution** · an amorphous deity put in charge of the world by a demiurge who was too busy to take care of it. Like all managers with an inferiority complex, the *Almighty Evolution* is capricious and takes random, often emotional decisions that benefit no one.

▶ **Clearchus** · a demiurgic librarian worshipped in the *Kingdom of the Word* who created the world while he was writing his own biography on a sheet of paper called *Plane of Existence*. His teachings encourage the constant acquisition of knowledge, since the only thing that brings meaning to the world is people's awareness of its existence.

▶ **Goddess (Abharazarhadarad)** · a demiurgic deity worshipped in the merchant city state of *Abharazarhadarad*. Her cult encourages trade and wealth acquisition. She is never referred to by name or depicted in any way. Her teachings are preserved in the *Great Book*.

▶ **Goddess of Eternal Ice** · the supreme deity of the *Arctic Ocean*, extremely jealous and vindictive, known for causing mass extinctions whenever she feels her authority is threatened by the people who inhabit her realms. It has been alleged her volatile temper is the main reason why there are no long-lasting civilizations in the *Extreme North*.

▶ **Goddess of Despair** · a deity worshipped in the *Queendom of the Briny Lake*. She is perpetually gloomy and doesn't appreciate irony.

▶ **Goddess of Hope** · a deity worshipped in the *Queendom of the Briny Lake*. She is constantly chirpy and hopeful, even in situations that are objectively bad. She is in an open relationship with the *God of Denial*.

▶ **Goddess of Infidelity** · a deity worshipped in the *Queendom of the Briny Lake*. She possesses an insatiable sexual drive that influences every decision she makes.

▶ **Goddess of Love** · a deity worshipped in the *Queendom of the Briny Lake*. She is a hopeless romantic and often exaggerates the importance of feelings. She travels on a chariot pulled by *aphrodonti*.

▶ **Goddess of Missed Opportunities** · a deity from the land of *Patasarriba*, protector of all bubble-bursters and unadventurous skeptics. Unhappily married to the *God of Serendipity*.

▶ **God of Serendipity** · a deity from the land of *Patasarriba*, who sacrificed himself in order to increase the total amount of cumulative happiness in the Universe, triggering the emergence of a mysterious force called *chronic dissatisfaction*. He is happily married to the *Goddess of Missed Opportunities*.

▶ **Ibliz** · a demiurgic deity whose origins are shrouded in mystery. She is worshipped by some as a goddess of the *Barren Desert*, implying a possible link to the Abharazarhadaradian *Goddess*. Other cults attribute her a dual personality, split between the human and the divine realms.

▶ **Ooh** · an Ooh'ahian deity born out of the *Point of Emergence*. A hermaphrodite, *Ooh* impregnated itself and gave birth to the first humans: a man called *Ah* and a woman called *Meh*. Since *Ooh* didn't understand the concept of male and female, it assumed its children were disabled.

▶ **Saint Benedict the Distracted** · an Ooh'ahian scribe who accidentally damaged the original version of the *Scroll of Ooh*, triggering a chain of events that will lead to a schism between the neoörthodox and post-reformist factions in *Most Holy Church of Ooh*. After the schism was resolved, he was canonized as a saint.

▶ **Saint Brendan of Compostela** · an explorer who accidentally discovered the *Underworld* when he fell into a whirlpool in the *Sunset Ocean*. Canonized as a saint after he was devoured by a whale that subsequently expelled him through its blowhole with such force that Brendan, still alive, effortlessly ascended to Heaven.

▶ **Saint Simon de Rouvroy** · a sociologist and a polymath from *Severia*, the only explorer who traveled extensively motivated not by wanderlust but by his thirst for knowledge. His seminal work, *Studies on Bread and Circuses,* was published just a minute before his death because Simon wanted to include in it everything he learned throughout his long fruitful life. After a woman got pregnant just from sitting on his tombstone, he was canonized as a saint.

▶ **Siobhan of Slutsend** · a female leprechaun known for her beauty. Died from a bladder infection after her pot was stolen by an elderly gentleman who refused to return it unless she agreed to marry him.

Notable Characters

▶ **Ah** · the first man in Ooh'ahian religion.

▶ **Alan Loveless** · husband of Oriental scientist *Ana Loveless*. Alan suffered from emotional inertness, a rare disorder that prevented people from experiencing romantic love. Ana eventually discovered the disorder was caused by *lilac dust* deficiency. When she secretly started adding the substance to Alan's drinks, he developed feelings for her and they soon married. Their relationship ended after Alan had an affair.

▶ **Albert the Diffident** · son of the Hyperborean Queen *Birgit the Assertive* and last male member of the royal dynasty founded by *Helen the Gorgeous*. He was allegedly born by parthenogenesis and committed suicide after the accidental death of his mother on his fiftieth birthday. His death inspired a movement for male emancipation that brought the matriarchal system to an end and heralded the advent of patriarchy.

▶ **Ana Loveless** · an Oriental multidisciplinary scientist, whose experiments in *aphrodisiology* led to the discovery of the *platonic fluids* and *lilac dust*. After her husband, *Alan Loveless,* had an extramarital affair, Ana suffered a nervous breakdown, destroyed all her research and retreated to the desert, where she allegedly began practicing *blood magic*. It is suspected that Ana might have achieved immortality and is in fact the mysterious *Queen of the Orient*.

▶ **Anubis II** · king of *Cynocephalia*.

▶ **Arnold the Easily Convinced** · a Hyperborean emperor who initiated the upgrade of the *Scepter of Knowledge,* following the advice of explorer *Bartholomea of the Desert*. The upgrade was finished during the reign of his son, *Henry the Navigator*.

▶ **Arthur the Serendipitous** · son of *Gregor the Pedantic*, Arthur became the longest ruling Hyperborean monarch (62 years), and was granted the title *eternal emperor* after he discovered the *Scepter of Knowledge*.

▶ **Athelstan the Fecund** · the first Hyperborean king consort, husband of Queen *Helen the Gorgeous*.

▶ **Bartholomea of the Desert** · an explorer from a nomadic tribe in the *Barren Desert*. After leaving home at an early age, Bartholomea became the first woman to travel the world from end to end. She and her crew were the only foreigners who visited the *Great Hyperborean Empire*. Because the Hyperboreans believed the world ended at their observable horizon, her visit became known as the *Bartholomea paradox*. In order to resolve it, she instructed Emperor *Arnold the Easily Convinced* to upgrade the *Scepter of Knowledge* and extend its observational range. This marked the end of the Hyperborean *Age of Certainty*.

▶ **Birgit the Assertive** · a Hyperborean queen, the last female member of the incestuous dynasty founded by the matriarch *Helen the Gorgeous*. Since tradition dictated that royals could marry only members of their own family, she married herself. Birgit gave birth to a son (allegedly by parthenogenesis), *Albert the Diffident,* whom she breastfed until the age of twenty. She died while sleepwalking into a giant birthday cake, made for Albert's fiftieth birthday.

▶ **Brandon the Flaccid** · a Hyperborean emperor, son of *Edgar the Meek*. He was a womanizer and anarchist, constantly at odds with the bureaucrats in his government. Eager to break links with the past, he ordered the decommission of the *Scepter of Knowledge*. He openly challenged the institutionalized mysogyny of Hyperborean society and the idea that women are responsible for the sexual urges of men.

▶ **Calculania of Pythagorea** · a genius mathematician who discovered the first algorithm for factoring rational polynomials, right at the moment when her favorite dog, Actaeon, was attacked by a pack of homeless cats. Afraid she was going to forget her idea if she didn't write it down on the spot, she immediately reached for her notebook. By the time she finished, Actaeon was already dead. Acknowledging her sacrifice, the government of *Pythagorea* deified her after her death.

▶ **Dolores of Barbaria** · a fiercely conservative queen of *Barbaria*, so dedicated to royal protocol that she referred to herself in third person even in casual private conversations. After she found out that her daughter, princess *Esmeralda*, started an affair with a miller named *Joy*, she banished him in the *Arctic Ocean*. Her decision sparked a popular uprising that coincided with an invasion of an Hyperborean army. Dolores was deposed and succeeded by her daughter.

▶ **Dolores Urdemalas** · a character from Caudillian folklore, married to *Pedro Urdemalas*.

▶ **Edgar the Meek** · a Hyperborean emperor, son of *Harold the Disconsolate*. Disappointed that he was unable to make everyone happy, Edgar abdicated only twenty days after his coronation. He was succeeded by his son, *Brandon the Flaccid*.

▶ **Edmund the Disappointed** · a Hyperborean king consort, father of Queen *Birgit the Assertive*. When his grandson, *Albert the Diffident*, who had yet to be weaned off his mother's milk, turned twenty years old, Edmund gave him a candy bar. When Albert got severely sick, Birgit accused Edmund of a poisoning attempt and executed him.

▶ **Epidemius of Choleropolis** · a scientific genius from *Choleropolis* who discovered the cure for influenza while he was running after a thief who stole his wallet. Caught up in the pursuit, he postponed writing down his discovery. Unfortunately, once he recovered his wallet, he found out that he couldn't recall the exact recipe for the cure. He became known as a petty man who put his own needs before the needs of the many.

▶ **Esperanza of Barbaria** · the first queen of *Barbaria* who married a commoner. Daughter of *Dolores of Barbaria*.

▶ **Esther** · the most talented executioner in *Severia*, officially awarded the honorific title *Harbinger of Justice* by King *Anubis II* of *Cynocephalia*.

▶ **Godwin the Emphatic** · a Hyperborean emperor who invaded the queendom of *Barbaria* to depose the unpopular Queen *Dolores* in favor of her daughter, *Esperanza* and her lover, *Joy*.

▶ **Gregor the Pedantic** · a Hyperborean king and mathematical genius, who invented the *Gregorian calendar,* advocated *historical objectivity,* and introduced a social reform that forced women to cover their bodies in public. He dismissed the importance of independent knowledge derived from personal experience, and created a compulsory educational system that disseminated only state-sanctioned information. His ideas were embraced by the newly emancipated patriarchal establishment and continued to influence Hyperborean culture for centuries.

▶ **Harold the Disconsolate** · a Hyperborean emperor, son of *William the Conqueror*. Harold was raised to be passionately curious, so he could continue the long tradition of discovering new lands with the *Scepter of Knowledge*. When his father died and brought the end of the *Age of Discovery*, Harold ascended to the throne unprepared to deal with the challenges of the coming *Age of Certainty*. He eventually went mad and started murdering senior politicians until he was poisoned by his health minister. Harold was succeeded by his son, *Edgar the Meek*.

▶ **Hatshepsut IV** · a queen of *Cynocephalia*. She was accused of committing the crime of matrimonial assassination by sexual witchcraft against her husband, *Thutmose XVII*, who died from the bite of a snake that was inexplicably coiled inside his anus. *Hatshepsut IV* was tried, found guilty, and executed by *breaking on the wheel*.

▶ **Helen the Gorgeous** · a priestess who became the first queen and matriarch of Hyperborea. Her reign marked a transition from egalitarianism to a divided class system. She introduced the institution of marriage as a means to ensure the preservation of wealth among the aristocracy. She married *Athelstan the Fecund*.

▶ **Henry the Navigator** · the last Hyperborean emperor, son of *Arnold the Easily Convinced*. Henry was seduced by the *Goddess of Eternal Ice*, who built an enchanted island in the *Arctic Ocean* as a trap, luring the emperor to go on an expedition and conquer it.

▶ **Isidore of Clonfert** · a cosmopolitan explorer and philosopher from the island of *Clonfert* who left his homeland at an early age with the goal to become the first human to travel the world from end to end. Unfortunately he was beat to it by *Bartholomea of the Desert*.

▶ **Joy** · a miller who fell in love with Princess *Esperanza of Barbaria* and was banished into the *Arctic Ocean* by her mother, *Queen Dolores*. His sentence inspired a popular uprising that led to a civil war. After *Queen Dolores* was defeated with the help of Hyperborean invaders, Esperanza ascended to the throne, and *Joy* became king consort.

▶ **Jörg Holzhacker** · a lumberjack from *Schmetterdorf* who accidentally discovered *The Schmetterschwanz Manuscript* and, unaware of its value, sold it to fortune teller *Mesmeralda Yagishna*.

▶ **Juan Mequetrefe** · a character from Caudillian folklore, the personification of laziness, married to *Marieta Machada*.

▶ **Juan of Qurtubah** · a barista from *Qurtubah* who invented a safe method of cracking *thunder nuts* (*lilac poppy* bulbs) with a machete. Died in a tragic accident caused by a measurement error.

▶ **Lucius** · an Ooh'ahian librarian and botanist, author of one of the synoptic gospels—an interpretation of the *Scroll of Ooh* that became fundamental for the neoörthodox faction of the *Most Holy Church of Ooh*.

▶ **Marieta Machada** · a character from Caudillian folklore, married to *Juan Mequetrefe*.

▶ **Maurucius** · an Ooh'ahian librarian, author of one of the synoptic gospels—an interpretation of the *Scroll of Ooh* that became fundamental for the post-reformist faction of the *Most Holy Church of Ooh*.

▶ **Meh** · the first woman in Ooh'ahian religion.

▶ **Mesmeralda Yagishna** · one of the most prominent fortune tellers and magicians in the world. Her origin is shrouded in mystery. She purchased *The Schmetterschwanz Manuscript* from *Jörg Holzhacker*, and after she allegedly deciphered its content, she sold it to philosopher *Morpheus Baudrillard* from *Abharazarhadarad*.

▶ **Morpheus Baudrillard** · a natural philosopher and cryptanalyst from *Abharazarhadarad*, who purchased *The Schmetterschwanz Manuscript* from fortune teller *Mesmeralda Yagishna*, hoping to decipher its meaning. Due to the unreasonable price he paid for it, he was sacked from the *Council of Commercial Strategists*.

▶ **Nuncaguapa II** · a warrior queen from the *Orient*, notorious for her insatiable sexual appetite. Since she had the habit of shouting state secrets while she had sex, her countless lovers had to be confined into a harem with impenetrable walls, from which they could never escape. Towards the end of her reign, the harem became so populous, it was officially assigned the status of a city. She was succeeded by her daughter, *Casibella II,* who freed all of her mother's lovers.

▶ **Occam the Barbarian** · a savage warlord, the epitome of toxic masculinity, who invaded the *Margraviate of the Windswept Hill* with the sole purpose to eradicate its sophisticated culture. He ended up trapped in a permanent state of *transcendental meditative self-adoration*.

▶ **Odissius** · a deaf merchant from *Qurtubah*, who had an affair with the goddess *Ibliz* and climbed the *Pillar to Heaven* to help her reconcile her split personalities. As a reward, the goddess made him *Supreme Master of Trade*.

▶ **Pedro Urdemalas** · a character from Caudillian folklore, married to *Dolores Urdemalas*.

▶ **Pensius** · an ancient philosopher and misanthrope who spent his life living and conversing with his dogs. The dogs didn't necessarily endorse his views but stuck around because her fed them every day.

▶ **Plato** · the favorite cat of Oriental scientist *Ana Loveless*. He died during an accident in Ana's lab that led to the discovery of *lilac dust*. The *platonic fluids* were named after him.

▶ **Queen of the Orient** · a mysterious queen who traveled through the *Barren Desert*, selling exotic goods that made men hopelessly fall in love with her. While she presented herself as a queen, most people referred to her as a goddess that enjoyed manipulating people, especially rich, confident men.

▶ **Queen of Severia** · a queen that ruled the island of *Severia* and relentlessly terrorized her subjects. After she sentenced her devout vizierienne to death, her subjects revolted and murdered her.

▶ **Shrink of the East** · an Oriental psychoanalyst, founder of the school of *progressive subjectivism*. Her teachings emphasized the precedence of personal freedom over cultural tradition and social hierarchy.

▶ **Shrink of the West** · an Oriental psychoanalyst, founder of the school of *conservative structuralism*. Her teachings rejected the concept of free will in human society, arguing that human behavior was predicated on social status and institutional hierarchy.

▶ **Sigismund Alegrius** · an esteemed professor and chief examiner of the *Library of Superb Enlightenment*.

▶ **Sklud** · the first imperial concubine during the reign of Hyperborean emperor *Brandon the Flaccid*, known as the temptress of saints.

▶ **Sons of Occam, The** · a horde of savages that pillaged and destroyed *Schmetterdorf*.

▶ **Sophisticus the Wise** · margrave of *Windswept Hill* during the invasion of *Occam the Barbarian*, whom he defeated by sheer accident.

▶ **Sultan of the Dry Sea** · a ruler of a country with an unspecified location. According to court etiquette, it is impolite to face him with a full stomach, so anyone asking for audience is required to fast for three days.

▶ **Trondheim Armada** · a mythical force from *Trondheim* that invaded *Clonfert* in prehistoric times. It is described either as a military expedition or as a giant monster.

▶ **Vizierienne of Severia** · the first minister of the *Queen of Severia,* with whom she was hopelessly in love. She was executed by the queen after she failed to persuade her that ruling by love is better than ruling by fear.

▶ **Vulnicurus** · a prophet who founded the official religion of the *Margraviate of the Windswept Hill*. He preached that violence should always be answered with love. His cult gained popularity after people misinterpreted his abduction by a *rukh* for an actual ascension to Heaven.

▶ **William the Conqueror** · a Hyperborean emperor, who, in the words of his minister of royal funerals, "scraped all mystery off the horizon." His reign marked the end of the *Age of Discovery*. He was succeeded by his son, *Harold the Disconsolate*.

Story Notes

The Merchant from Abharazarhadarad

I don't believe in miracles, but this story wrote itself from start to finish. The only thing I did was hang around in various cafes, typing with one hand and eating donuts with the other.

I witnessed two robberies. The first time, a man armed with a taser took all the money from the cashier. The second time, a woman pretending to be a beggar stole my iPhone right under my nose. Who said writing books was boring?

Original Bliss

Like most atheists, I have cultivated a condescending habit to ridicule creation myths. The blatant certainty, with which they attest how everything came into being has always fascinated me. Here's the darkness. Here's the void. Alexa, turn on the lights! Voila—world!

I guess the simpler the Universe you live in, the less you suffer. People find comfort in easily digestible ideas. If only everyone turned to science, you think. And then you look at what scientists have to offer—a Big Fucking Bang. You rub your eyes in disbelief. Could they have picked a more ridiculous name? For starters (no pun intended), bangs happen when there's air around. The primordial *nothing,* in which the early Universe supposedly "big-banged," had no air. In fact, space itself didn't exist. Even nothing wasn't yet invented. It's a human concept and reflects the limitations of our own senses.

Simplicity is sexy. It saves us a lot of thinking. Many mathematicians swear it's directly related to beauty. An equation that can fit on single line is better than one that takes a whole page, they say. Some physicists go even further. They equate simplicity with truth. Einstein's $E=mc^2$ is like a divine revelation to them. Architects like Mies van der Rohe adopted the slogan *Less is more,* emphasizing function over form.

But there's always something rumbling below the uniform facade of simplicity. Einstein was horrified by the uncertainty of quantum mechanics. Mies van der Rohe and Le Corbusier unintentionally inspired a lot of horrible architecture, devoid of character, inhabited by people who traded their personality for the lowest common denominator of comfort.

With this in mind, let's be more forgiving when we read creation myths from the past. They might be fundamentally flawed, but we should take them for what they are—a sincere attempt to explain the world with whatever means the human race had available at the moment. And unlike the Big Bang, they're quite poetic. Just open the Old Testament:

> *In the beginning God created the heaven and the earth. And the earth was without form, and void; and darkness was upon the face of the deep. And the Spirit of God moved upon the face of the waters...*

There's the difference between a textbook and a novel. If your life resembles the former, perhaps you missed out on something.

The Book of Love

Isidore of Clonfert is an amalgam of two of my favorite historical characters: Isidore of Seville and Saint Brendan of Clonfert. The first one was an archbishop, most famous for his *Etymologiae,* an encyclopedic set of studies hoarded from all available sources during the Late Antiquity. It became the fundamental textbook of the Middle Ages. While Isidore could be described as an armchair researcher, Saint Brendan was a restless explorer. He had a penchant for sea travel in the company of monks. If most accounts of his life are to be trusted, he was especially fond of visiting mythical places like the *Island of the Blessed* and meeting mythical characters, like Judas, who he encountered on a rock in the middle of the ocean. In my eyes, both men symbolize insatiable curiosity, which is the essence of being human.

This story juxtaposes curiosity and love—an all-too common conflict in human relationships. Its most popular depiction is infidelity, but I looked at it from a different angle—that of predestination. There must be a million ruined romances because someone—either the main characters or a third party—thought they weren't "meant to be."

The story grew naturally from a verse I wrote: *hope is spread thin/on a world that has no meaning whatsoever/without you.* I'm not a poet. Occasionally verses just crystallize in my mind, but I rarely write them down. This time it was different. I was in love—a classic case of *boy meets boy,*

boy falls in love with boy, the other one doesn't give a fuck. When I was a teenager, I took things like these personally. Now I'm wise enough to know people don't owe me their feelings. I've learned to respect their choices. Yet despite all that sober reasoning, my mind simply couldn't let go. I was trapped in an infinite loop of unrequited hope—which is different than unrequited love, but just as... hopeless. Why couldn't I stop caring? Why couldn't I just move on, enthusiastic about the next encounter?

The lines came to me as I was walking. I stopped to write them down on my phone. Look at me, I thought, writing poetry on the street. I badly needed a sociopathic bureaucrat to slap me across the face. And some milk and cookies.

Sophisticus the Wise and Occam the Barbarian

All You Need Is Love is a terrible song, just like *Make love, not war* is a terrible slogan. The first suggests you don't need chocolate; the second implies love and war are opposites. I know people who love chocolate so much, they'd go to war to get it. The Ancient Greeks got it right—their goddess of love, Aphrodite, was married to their god of war, Ares. The Greeks knew that passion could easily turn from benevolent to toxic. Today this idea survives only in cheap action movies, when a careless villain murders the wife of the main protagonist, who happens to be a former marine and has unlimited access to ammunition.

Blame Christianity. It turned love into a political cause. Now we're stuck with it, blindfolded by unrealistic expectations.

The Masks of Beauty

Of all the stories, this one is probably the most autobiographical. I grew up thinking I was a monster. My body was extremely hairy from a very young age. I lost count how many times I've been called a gorilla or advised to "take off my sweater." I know people who like gorillas when they see them in the zoo. I have never gone to a zoo, but I've watched a bunch of TV documentaries, and I'm pretty sure I don't like those animals. They lack elegance. You can imagine the psychological damage when people compared me to them. Why couldn't I be a gazelle, I asked myself? If only I could choose the insults of my bullies like salads at a restaurant, the world would have been an amazing place.

I wasted a lot of time. From my early twenties up until my late thirties, I never set foot on a beach. I never undressed in front of a mirror. Then I met some people who told me I was beautiful. What a bunch of perverts, I thought. How dare they like gorillas? Or perhaps they were lying? Here's some advice for do-gooders—don't get in the way of people's self-loathing unless you have balls of steel. Be careful with the possessed if you don't want projectiles of green vomit in your face. Use compliments subversively. Most of all, be patient. With a little bit of luck, one day you might break the curse and make them look at themselves through your eyes.

Genesis

This story was written in one take. I wondered what would life feel like if people lived forever. I wasn't interested in the biological aspect. What fascinated me was the mind of an immortal being. Does infinite life come with infinite memory?

Imagine you've lived for a thousand years. Would you remember everything that ever happened to you? And if you wouldn't, how far back could your memories go without becoming completely fragmented? And here's the kicker—would it really matter how long you've lived if you can't recall a single event beyond a certain point in your past?

The Seed of Love

I can't remember how many times I've heard the line *I know exactly what I want from love.* I used to believe the people who uttered it. They were my heroes. Not anymore. Take a closer look at anyone who basks in such imposing certainty and you will see a crack. Get even closer and the crack will expand into a hole.

We don't know what we want from love because we don't understand it. We have no idea whether it is a dangerous delusion or an expression of divinity. Perhaps it's an invention of the mind, redefining our animalistic instincts to something less embarrassing. Clearly, if there was a simple answer, we would have found it so far. So we're stuck with ambiguity, which sometimes could be tiresome for a writer.

But what if I imagined a world where love was a drug like opium? The simplicity of this premise felt liberating—no more endless musings, just plain old chemistry. That's how I came up with the lilac poppy in *The Merchant from Abharazarhadarad*. In the last story, I wanted to expand on its origins. When I started writing, I imagined and ordinary plant, a fusion between poppies and coffee. Its roasted beans contained a special chemical that induced love in those who consumed it. As the story developed, the plant's complexity increased. Mimicry and electricity crept in. Finally, its heavenly origin completely obliterated the simplicity I was aiming for. Perhaps the goddess of love wanted to teach me a lesson.

Terror Birds and Wanton Hearts

Some people unwittingly become abusers because they don't know how to handle the love that's been given to them. Few of them know this better than I do.

Growing up as a gay man in an ultraconservative society was profoundly traumatising. The often mentioned bullying was the easy part. It didn't harm me all that much. What fucked me up was the relentless message that homosexuality was wrong. That I was unworthy of love and I could only experience it in a way that was morally degrading. This messaged was so pernicious that I eventually internalized it all the way down to my bone marrow.

There were a couple of girls that fell in love with me and made the mistake of telling me. And, unsurprisingly, what I felt in return was embarrassment, disgust and anger towards them.

On its surface, *Terror Birds and Wanton Hearts* is a story cycle about a servant hopelessly in love with her mistress. For her, love is more than a feeling; it's a philosophy. And she would rather die than give it up.

But there's a deeper layer to it. That of the sovereign who can't handle being adored and uses fear to isolate herself emotionally. It's a person who, at some point in her life, has been robbed of the opportunity to confide in anybody else. For her, love *equals* terror. It's a feeling that threatens to undermine her power, and therefore—her dignity. Ultimately, her refusal to accept the boundless love she's being offered literally tears her apart.

The Ebbs and Flows of the Great Hyperborean Empire

I think I read my first fiction book when I was eighteen years old. Before that, the only books I enjoyed were history textbooks. I honestly don't know why most people don't enjoy reading them. I can talk for hours about the history of states I've never visited and would probably never visit (Hi, Russia!).

The life of a state is very similar to that of a human being, which is hardly surprising because states are made by and of humans. We think of them as political and bureaucratic entities but before everything else, they are stories that help us label ourselves. No matter what your history teacher says, states don't consist of institutions, but of human emotions and aspirations—dreams, fears, hopes, anxieties.

Of course for a state to truly function, it has to detach itself from its makers. It has to look bigger than life in the eyes of its creators. But that's just an illusion that most people willingly participate in.

The second story cycle from *Codex Hyperboreanus* is about an empire whose rise and fall are not much different than its real equivalents.

The Dancing Plague

I spent a large part of my childhood playing on the street of my grandparents. My hometown was so small, we didn't have streetlights because there were barely any cars passing by. So the streets were practically playgrounds.

The most popular game was called *ръбче* (which is the Bulgarian diminutive of the word *edge*). Each player would pick a sidewalk and throw a ball at the opposite one, aiming at its edge. Ideally the ball would bounce back and the player would score points once he caught it. Because the sidewalks were uneven, it was hard to predict the ball's trajectory. Instead of the hands of the player, the ball would sometimes land in somebody's yard. In those times people didn't lock their homes, so retrieving it was rather easy. We would get an occasional scolding if the ball squashed a few flowers but not much else. But there was one yard we had to steer clear of. If our ball landed there, we would usually call and adult to negotiate its return. That yard belonged to an old widow, who was known as *vrachka*, which is the Easter European version of a *witch*.

Although on paper Orthodox Slavic cultures frowned upon all forms of witchcraft, people who engaged in it were never persecuted, much less burned at the stake. In fact, the vrachka (or her male equivalent, the vrach) performed the role of councilors and healers. They could relieve you from a traumatic memory, find a missing person, cure terminal illnesses, and even communicate with the dead. People admired them as much as they feared them because they had a constant hotline to the spirit world. You never knew which side they were on. If you piss them off, they could as go back home with an extra curse rather than a solution to your problem.

The main character in *The Dancing Plague* was inspired by the vrachka that lived on the street of my grandparents. Her name was Milka. In the eyes of a child she looked menacing but the grown up in me can't help but wonder how she really felt about the world. People like her were both feared and needed and being a widow, her life must have been lonely. Did she feel rejected or misunderstood as a human being? Or was she an introvert who turned her social anxiety into a profession?

The Olive Child

I adore olives. They're quite popular in Bulgaria but our climate doesn't allow us to grow them domestically. So the first time I saw an actual olive tree was in Rome. It was love at first sight.

My fascination with olives grew even stronger when I moved to a small Spanish village called Torrijos. It was surrounded by dry fields that could only grow wheat and olives.

Have you ever seen an apple orchard? Apple trees all look the same, like soldiers on parade. Olive trees are their exact opposite. Each has a personality. Their branches twist like copulating snakes in all directions. Frankly I'm surprised there aren't any major horror movies starring olive trees.

The Great Caudillian Schism

Like every other rural place, my hometown had its own village idiot. His name was Kiro but people called him *Crazy Kiro,* as if the adjective was an inseparable part of his name. I don't think he was particularly crazy. He was just a harmless drunkard who was turned into a caricature in order to fulfil a very important social function—providing a safe target for ridicule.

It's often said that the anonymity of the big city makes people less empathetic that those living in rural areas. The truth is everybody has a potential to be an asshole, whenever it's considered socially acceptable. Every village has its idiot and every court—its jester. As above, so below.

Juan Mequetrefe and the Bull that Laid Golden Eggs

This story was inspired by an African folktale about a lazy man and his favorite calf. It diverged from the original the moment I started writing and by the time I was done, the calf had turned into a bull that laid golden eggs. Go figure!

The Ascent of Santa Lucía

This story was inspired by a Japanese tale about a monk who was stoned by a crowd after it became obvious that his planned ascension to paradise was just a publicity stunt. I decided to up the ante a little bit. In my version, there's a devout nun named Lucía whose attempt at ascension is honest. And while the Japanese monk survived, albeit with a bleeding head, Lucía was turned into ice and shattered to smithereens that eventually reached Heaven, carried by the wind. So in a way she did what she was promised, just not the way she imagined it.

The Two Sides of Dolores Urdemalas

The character of Dolores Urdemalas was inspired by a Latin American folk hero *Pedro Urdemales*. But the premise of the story was borrowed from an African folktale called *Two Friends and Their Childhood*. In it, a trickster made two good friends quarrel by putting on a costume with a different color on each side. In the end, the trickster was punished and everything went back to normal. But I wanted to add a more sinister edge and settled on gossip as the main driver of discontent.

Frog Empress

This is my own take on the Russian version of *Frog Princess*. I love Russian folklore just like I love the *Arabian Nights* but I can't really stomach the rampant misogyny. So every time I stories like this, I get so pissed, the only way to simmer down is to rewrite it. So in my version, the frog doesn't just end as a princess. She's reigns supreme because of her superior intellect. Long live meritocracy!

Head Crusher

I'm both outraged and fascinated by medieval practise of public executions. It's really hard for me to accept that such a spectacle was even remotely justifiable, much less enjoyable for the masses. And I'm just wondering which of our current habits would appear barbaric to future generations.

Rubicón's Daughter

Most of my stories come to me like God intended—in black letters on a white computer screen. This one, however, popped in my mind like an already completed movie. The dancing part gave me goosebumps.

The Gruesome Death of Diego Suárez

It might seem irresponsible to give away the ending in the title of the story. But it can also be an advantage because it once you know what's going to happen, you start wondering about how it's going to happen. Ain't that a nice trick?

Sugar Rush

Our obsession with unlimited growth is often blamed on capitalism, as if we live in a ideological simulation directed by a superhuman overlord. The truth is human nature is insatiable by design.

Stephen Sondheim put it brilliantly in his song *More* from the *Dick Tracy* soundtrack: *I'm no mathematician / All I know is addition!*

Satisfaction is not about quantity. It's an ever moving target. The desire to add more to what we already have is what drives us since times immemorial. Do you think that when he reached Mesopotamia, Emperor Trajan looked around and said, *I'm done conquering!* What made him stop from moving even further east were his overstretched supply lines and the might of the Persian military. So no, enough is never enough, with or without capitalism.

Let There Be Light

Soon after I finished *Codex Hyperboreanus,* I started studying folklore and fairytales. The more I examined the various traditions from all over the world, the more similar they seemed. Eventually everything fused together in a common, organic narrative. Mashups like *Let There Be Light* which combines Judaeo Christian and Native American genesis myths might come across as contrived. But actually, they happened spontaneously.

The Bull's Bride

No story collection is complete without a tale about an evil stepmother. So I wrote one, abiding by all the rules and conventions of the genre. Because deep in my heart, I'm a hopeless conformist.

About the Author

Yanko Tsvetkov is a Bulgarian-born interdisciplinary artist who lives in Spain, writes in English, and publishes books in France, Germany, Russia, Italy, Turkey, China, and Korea. He has visited several continents, traversed thick jungles, picnicked in scorching deserts, and booked a few taxis in busy metropolises. When night falls, he turns into a beautiful princess who fights prejudice with her giant laser.

Alphadesigner is a creative alter-ego of interdisciplinary artist Yanko Tsvetkov, specialized in visual forms of expression like book design, typography, photography, illustration, and cartography. Among his most notable projects is Mapping Stereotypes—a vast collection of satirical maps that became an instant Internet sensation in 2010 and continues to inspire cartographic memes to this day. Alphadesigner has received worldwide acclaim for his typographic reinvention of medieval Cyrillic and Glagolitic scripts. Since 2011, he is the cover designer of the German literary magazine Krachkultur. He has designed, typeset, and illustrated all books by Yanko Tsvetkov.

Printed in Great Britain
by Amazon

efde2cfc-f13b-4524-b6ef-11ba9ee80be6R01